FAIR DECEPTION

Fate seems to intervene when Kit Kydd rescues Susanna Fair from abduction. Kit must appear settled to be made his great-aunt's heir, and Susanna is an actress. By pretending to be engaged during a visit to Lady Penfold, Kit can protect Susanna from further danger. But Lady Penfold lives in the horse-racing town of Newmarket, which holds the secret of Susanna's scandalous past. And the dishonourable Rafe Warwick has wagered two thousand guineas on making Susanna his mistress. Now how will she cope with her theatre company's request to make a final public performance . . . and falling in love with Kit?

JAN JONES

FAIR DECEPTION

Complete and Unabridged

ULVERSCROFT
Leicester

First published in Great Britain in 2008 by
Robert Hale Limited
London

First Large Print Edition
published 2009
by arrangement with
Robert Hale Limited
London

British Library CIP Data

Jones, Jan, *1955 –*
Fair deception.
1. Great Britain- -History- -George III, *1760 – 1820*
- -Fiction. 2. Love stories. 3. Large type books.
I. Title
823.9′2–dc22

ISBN 978–1–84782–894–1

To Barbara, with love
and, as always, to the RNA

1

London. February 1816

Susanna was halfway through the Indian hunters' opening dance when she became aware of the flaxen-haired gentleman in the second tier of boxes. A moon-bright flash caught her eye as she pirouetted across the Sans Pareil stage and she glanced up to see one of the lanterns shining on his head. She would have looked away, *should* have looked away, but for two things. First, the young man was quite extraordinarily comely and secondly, he was smiling directly at her.

Susanna was so startled she nearly missed a step. There was nothing new in being ogled, the Indian hunters' gauze tunics, like the majority of the chorus costumes, left shamefully little to the imagination. But this gentleman was smiling warmly, not leering, and furthermore his eyes were on her face not her body.

Susanna traversed the front of the stage in a series of leaping stretches, whirled around, laid her hand on her costume dagger and glanced up again. This time there could be no doubt. He was smiling in admiration. Directly into her eyes. A most peculiar sensation fluttered in Susanna's breast. Just for a moment the shell of detachment she had learnt to cultivate in the thirteen weeks since the season opened cracked a little. She smiled back.

On stage, the Indian chiefs were setting the scene. Susanna sank respectfully to one knee as if to listen. Out of the corner of her eye she could see the flaxen-haired gentleman's profile. His countenance had an attractive openness. He wore a blue coat and only moderate shirt points so he was certainly no dandy. His lively expression showed that he was following the dialogue between the chiefs and their wives. Another crack zig-zagged down Susanna's shell. In her experience a London theatregoer who payed attention to the play was quite a rarity. Most were more anxious to be seen themselves than to be entertained by the actors.

It was time to spring up for the spear dance. In the front row of the pit, a group of drunken Cits cheered and ogled lasciviously. Susanna masked a shudder of distaste. The brief glow engendered by the fair-haired gentleman's admiration died, swamped by the desolate reality of her situation. Why had she ever thought coming to London would prove the answer? All it had done was to swap one set of problems for another.

★ ★ ★

' . . . and so, Miss Fair, I would appreciate it if you did *not* use my melodrama as a vehicle for attracting a beau.'

'I beg your pardon, Miss Scott. It won't happen again.' It irked Susanna to apologize for merely smiling at a young man in the audience when some of her fellow actresses went to far greater lengths to advertise themselves, but she needed this job too badly to antagonize the Sans Pareil's star and *raison d'être*.

'I am glad to hear it. I should have thought you of all people would have learnt the danger of encouraging advances from admirers.'

Susanna gritted her teeth. 'I collect you are referring to the Honourable Rafe Warwick. I assure you, his pursuit of me is none of my doing.'

'Dishonourable, surely? No *honourable* gentleman would lay a wager on your virtue as he has done.' Miss Scott smiled at her own wit, her good humour restored. 'Well, well, go and change. You are singing tonight, are you not?'

Susanna inclined her head and went into the chorus-room to put on her blue muslin dress. The neckline was lower than she liked, but one of the first lessons she had assimilated at the Sans Pareil was that one did not earn repeat performances at a variety theatre on the purity of one's voice alone — and a song on the bill was worth three shillings in her purse at the end of the week.

She had chosen a favourite ballad this evening, that of an innocent country lass led astray by a fine gentleman. It was better being on stage by herself. Calmer. More like it had been with the Chartwell Players. She took a deep breath, felt the persona of the wronged maiden settle around her and started to sing. When she looked up at the close of the final refrain, still in the grip of the girl's emotion, it gave her a piercing thrill to see the flaxen-haired young man on his feet applauding. His warmth was quite dazzling and Susanna found herself unable to resist it. For a full five seconds their eyes met and held. Ridiculous, said a sane corner of her mind. Ridiculous to read anything extraordinary into a smile and a pair of vivid eyes. But for that moment, it did not seem so absurd. The feeling filled her, clothed her in stardust . . .

An irritated hiss from the wings recalled her. Flushing, she left the stage to make way for the spectacle of a man climbing a pole with no visible means of support.

The interval passed uneventfully. Susanna told herself she hadn't expected the young man to brave the crush of the green-room to meet her. He was a lively swell out for an enjoyable evening. There was no more to it than that. She changed into her Young Witch of the Woods costume for the pantomime and brushed out her hair in order to appear wild and untamed. She winced as she crossed in front of the glass. Her red-gold curls went almost indecently well with the bronze gauze. As had become her custom, she left her day clothes ready for a swift exit. She might deal in fantasies on stage, but her reality was rooted in common sense. It had been borne in on her that just because the unpleasant Mr Warwick was not in the audience, it didn't mean he would not be waiting outside as soon as the curtain fell.

★ ★ ★

The show was done. Susanna pulled the hood of her cloak closer and inched out of the alley. A dozen steps would take her past the portals of the Sans Pareil. Another dozen and she would be safely in the midst of the departing crowd. She scanned the faces for Rafe

Warwick — and stopped, her feet stuck fast to the cobbles. Directly in her path, moon-bright head shining in the glow from a lantern, stood the flaxen-haired gentleman. He was tall, she hadn't realized that, and more finely dressed than he'd appeared in the box. An ache like an impossible dream swept through her as she took in his bright hair, vivid blue eyes and loose-limbed form. Even though every instinct was screaming that she must get away in case Warwick appeared, she found herself unable to move.

The gentleman was half-laughing, half-arguing with a dark-haired lady and another man into whose arm her hand was tucked. 'Why should I not?' he was saying. 'Deuce take it, Nell, it's devilish off-putting having you and Hugo smelling of April and May all day long. Why should I not find a little comfort for myself?'

'Because you have no money with which to buy it, brother of mine. Or do actresses now give away their favours as freely as their smiles? Come away, Kit, do. We are trying to *solve* your pecuniary problems, not compound them.'

They were talking about *her*! Susanna's cheeks burned with mortification. She made to withdraw into the shadows but her movement must have alerted him. Over his sister's head his eyes met hers. They widened with recognition and she felt her heart beat faster. Then, with the tiniest quirk of his lips, he returned some laughing answer and gestured to his companions to proceed along the Strand.

Susanna leant against the wall, weak with relief. For a devastating moment, she'd thought him another in the endless line of men who thought they had only to admire her hair and toss her a couple of guineas for her to be in their bed. He had transcended them though, and shown himself to be a true gentleman. It mattered not a whit that she would in all likelihood never see him again. Her feeling on stage had been vindicated. As she moved, her hood caught on the rough brickwork. Without any sense of danger, she fumbled to free it. And felt a vice-like grip on her shoulder.

'Well, well,' said a smooth voice. 'If it isn't my little songbird. And there I was thinking you were avoiding me. Has nobody taught you it is impolite to spy upon your betters, wench? Or are you imagining that a pretty face is like to be looser in the pocket than an experienced man of the world such as myself?'

'Let go of me!' All thoughts of the flaxen-haired gentleman vanished. Susanna twisted out of her captor's grasp, cursing under her breath for letting herself be distracted.

'Let go of me, *sir*,' corrected the Honourable Rafe Warwick. His half-lidded eyes glinted. 'It is going to be such a pleasure to teach you manners, my dear.'

Susanna suppressed the nausea which rose in her throat. From the moment Rafe Warwick and his friends had strolled into the greenroom just after Christmas and his calculating gaze had rested on her unusual hair and gauze-clad figure, she had hated and feared him. She loathed his cold eyes, his dissipated countenance and his small, cruel smile. She detested the way his long fingers closed on her arm as if judging just how much pressure was needed to bruise the delicate skin. It hadn't needed company gossip to tell her he was rich and merciless and not accustomed to being crossed. She had known it from that first flesh-crawling inspection through his quizzing glass. Susanna swallowed. For over a month now she had managed to avoid him by hastening home as soon as she came offstage or else staying close to her fellow players on her way to and from her lodgings. Tonight it seemed her luck had run out.

A malicious smile played on Warwick's lips

as he relished her dilemma. Susanna's eyes flicked desperately down the alley but there was no one in sight and he was cutting off the route back to the stage door. With a quick movement she gathered up her skirts in order to sprint along the open street.

'No you don't, jade.' Warwick's cane whipped out to strike hard at her ankle. Her thin shoes offered no protection at all. As she screamed and stumbled, he grabbed a handful of her cloak and dragged her towards him. 'I have been patient long enough. Tonight I'll have my reward.'

'Never!' Susanna struggled in his nightmare hold. He laughed, overpowering her easily, enjoying her fear. She smelt spirits on his breath as his mouth came closer to hers. 'Help!' she shouted, really terrified now. 'Help me!'

His eyes were distorted with lust. 'You delude yourself, my pretty. No one is like to interfere between a gentleman and his lightskirt.'

Susanna wrenched her face aside, the stabbing pain in her ankle hampering her efforts to escape. 'I am not a lightskirt. Nor will I ever be *yours*!'

An icy voice spoke from behind her. 'Which appears to make you wrong on three counts, sir. Four if you include the fact that you are assuredly no gentleman either. Be good enough to unhand the lady at once.'

In the instant of incredulity when Warwick's muscles stilled, Susanna broke from his grasp, falling against the opposite wall of the alley with a cry of agony as her injured ankle gave way. Looking up, her heart thumped with disbelief. The flaxen-haired young man from the audience stood there, breathing hard. Inside his well-cut evening clothes he was alert and tense. He flicked a quick glance at her, then trained his implacable gaze on Rafe Warwick.

'Lightskirt, actress, whore. Three words with but a single meaning,' drawled Warwick. 'Take your misplaced zeal elsewhere, puppy. The wench is mine.' He stretched out his gloved hand to seize Susanna's wrist in a grip of iron.

'The lady does not appear to think so.'

'The *lady*,' Warwick made the word an insult, 'is well aware of the strength of my feelings for her.' He twisted her wrist upwards without compunction, forcing a whimper from her lips. 'You see? She pants for me.'

Still the gentleman kept his steady, blue-eyed gaze on Warwick's face. 'I have not heard her say so.'

'Nor will you,' ground out Susanna. 'I would rather die!' The pain in her ankle and wrist was near making her faint; she had to bite her lip in an effort to remain upright.

The gentleman's friends had arrived by this time. His sister whispered something in her companion's ear. He nodded and disappeared.

'This really is too foolish,' said Warwick in a dangerous tone. His free hand caressed the top of his cane. 'Go home, boy, you are becoming tiresome.'

Susanna's champion smiled widely. 'My besetting fault,' he agreed, and cut upwards without warning to land a powerful blow on Rafe Warwick's chin, following it with a solid left-hand drive to the midriff.

Warwick collapsed onto the greasy cobbles of the alley. Susanna gaped at his insensible form, unable to take in her miraculous escape. She barely heard a horse clatter to a halt.

'It is well for you that Hugo has a talent for finding hackney drivers, Kit,' said the dark-haired lady with some asperity. She turned briskly to Susanna. 'You had best make haste and tell the jarvey your direction. I doubt your admirer will be incapacitated for long. My brother has always had more enthusiasm than science.'

Reaction was beginning to set in. Susanna felt her whole body start to shake. Her bruises throbbed. 'I thank you, ma'am,' she said in a thread of a voice, 'but I fear I am unable to — ' And indeed, as she moved away from the support of the alley wall, the white-hot pain in her ankle pitched her forward.

Strong arms were instantly around her, taking the weight off her crippled foot with a gentleness that almost made her weep after the violence which had been buffeting her. She received a confused impression of dancing blue eyes and gleaming hair that feathered her face as her rescuer bent to hoist her up. 'Truly a maiden in distress,' he said, a laugh in his voice to match the irrepressible devilry in his gaze. 'The evening gets better and better. She had best come to Half Moon Street, Nell. So talented as Hugo is, I feel sure you will soon catch us up.'

Before Susanna could gather sufficient words to protest the impropriety of any such action, she was lifted into the hackney carriage and the driver given the off. The sudden lurching motion, coupled with the pain in her ankle, made her feel very sick indeed. She closed her eyes until the sensation receded, and upon opening them found herself being regarded with wry sympathy.

'I am afraid I do not commonly carry a

bowl around with me, but if you wish I can ask the driver to pull over for a few minutes.'

Oh, good heavens, she hadn't imagined it. She was in a hackney carriage with a gentleman she had seen for the first time tonight! 'I . . . certainly not!' Susanna might be momentarily disoriented, but nothing would induce her to vomit in the street. 'I may be only an actress, sir, but I do have standards.'

'There is no 'only an actress' about it,' he said. 'I have never heard that song performed so well. Why did you not have any speaking roles?'

Susanna blinked at the unlikely question. 'By the time I joined the Sans Pareil they only had chorus parts to offer.' And after walking the streets for a week, she had been glad enough to accept.

'But you are a proper actress.' It was less a question than a statement of fact.

'I . . . yes, I was formerly with a touring company in the west country.' The hackney lurched, knocking Susanna's foot against the side panel and bringing on a recurrence of her nausea. 'Sir, I am most grateful for your intervention, but I beg you will take me to my lodgings now.'

He frowned. 'Oh, I don't think so.'

Susanna's heart thumped in alarm. Had

13

she jumped, or more correctly fallen, from the frying pan into the fire? To be sure, this gentleman was a thousand times more comely than Mr Warwick, but even so . . .

That overheard snippet of conversation about *finding a little comfort* drummed in her ears. She swallowed hard and looked at him directly, colouring to the roots of her hair. 'Sir, I must tell you that you may have mistaken my . . . that is, I am not in the habit of — '

'Lord, I could tell that,' he said, thrusting his long legs out as best he could in the cramped space. 'It is the Dishonourable Rafe's habits which concern me more. He doesn't have the reputation of letting sleeping dogs lie.'

The carriage jolted again, jarring Susanna's foot so badly that she could not suppress a gasp of pain.

'You really are in no condition to fight him off should he pursue you, you know.' Her companion inclined his head in a mock-formal bow. 'Christopher Kydd, at your service. My friends call me Kit.'

Reluctantly, Susanna shook his hand. Even though she could not see his face properly in the shadows, his presence filled the space between them with a terrifying potency. She was right to be wary. The mere touch of his fingers was enough to set a tingle of heat rushing through her veins. 'Miss Fair,' she said, jerking her hand away. 'And I assure you that my landlady is quite capable of — '

But the hackney had already stopped and a young footman was opening the door. His eyes widened as he took in Susanna's tumbled hair and dishevelled attire.

'It's not what you think, Tom, so stop catching flies and pay the driver,' said Mr Kydd, alighting from the other side. 'Miss Fair twisted her ankle outside the theatre. I'll need cold water and a bandage of some sort to make a compress.' He reached in at Susanna's door and lifted her in his arms without so much as a by your leave. 'As soon as you can manage,' he added.

'Mr Kydd!' said Susanna in outrage. 'Put me down at once. I am well able to walk.'

'Tosh, your foot is considerably swelled and will be worse if you rest any weight on it.' He carried her masterfully into the narrow hall, negotiated the staircase and shouldered open the door to a comfortable drawing room. 'There,' he said, depositing her on a sofa next to the fire. 'Let's take a look at the damage. This may be a trifle painful.'

Painful was an understatement. By the time he had eased away her shoe, Susanna had given up remonstrating. She felt so wrung out that she could have played any number of ghosts without recourse to the chalk box at all.

'Good girl,' he said. 'As well you were not wearing a boot. I should have had to cut it off. There is a worse ordeal to come, however.'

She looked at him in alarm. Surely her foot was not broken! Whatever would she do?

He gazed back, straight-faced. 'Your stocking. Either you must contrive to take it off yourself, or I shall have to do it for you.'

He was even more handsome at close quarters, with a disquieting imp at the back of his eyes. Susanna gathered up the shreds of her dignity. 'If you will turn your back, sir?'

Mr Kydd grinned. 'You're game to a fault. I'll give you that.' He moved to a side table. 'Would you care for a glass of Madeira?'

Instinct told Susanna to refuse but the manoeuvring she was obliged to do in order to roll her stocking down, and the ensuing sight of an angry weal running crosswise over a stretched, puffy prominence which this morning had been a perfectly sound ankle, tested her fortitude so highly that she said, 'I have never tried it before. It is a type of sherry-wine, is it not?'

'It is, and a very good one.' Mr Kydd brought two glasses across and handed one to her. 'To your recovery,' he said. His eyes really were quite remarkably blue.

Susanna gulped down a mouthful of the amber wine and nearly choked on the unexpectedly rich taste. It *was* good, much better than the thin stuff they drank in the greenroom, and a hundred times more flavourful than the small-ale which had been her travelling company's staple beverage. Mr Kydd was still watching her. She looked away hurriedly.

'Here you are, Mr Kit,' said the footman, entering with a tub of water. He deposited it by Susanna's foot and produced a roll of linen from his pocket. 'Nasty,' he said, inspecting the injury with cheerful interest. 'That'll need resting up, that will.'

'I am inclined to agree with you, Tom,' said Mr Kydd. He knelt next to the tub and before Susanna could divine his intent, lifted her leg and lowered her foot into the cold water.

Her gasp was less for the icy temperature than for the fact that his grasp on her calf had been disturbingly sensuous.

'I beg your pardon, did I jar you?'

'No, I — '

But he was frowning and gently stroking the red weal. 'The ankle I saw you twist, but how did this happen?'

'Mr Warwick has a cane,' said Susanna, twitching at his touch and thanking God that her foot was already becoming numb. 'And an uncertain temper.'

Mr Kydd sat back on his heels. 'As well you did not provoke it further. I have heard that cane doubles as a swordstick.'

Susanna stared at him in horror. 'And you hit him with your bare fists? He might have drawn on both of us!'

'That's Mr Kit for you,' said the footman. 'Acts first and thinks later. Always has done.'

'Thank you, Tom. Don't let us keep you from your duties, will you?'

The footman grinned and withdrew. Mr Kydd divested himself of his coat and began to roll up his sleeves. He glanced at her, a little shamefaced. 'Think nothing of it. It is only what anyone would have done. Drink up now, this may hurt a bit.'

As he started to wind the wet linen around her ankle, Susanna did drink. Not to dull the pain, but as a distraction from the way his gently efficient hands were placing each turn of the bandage against her far too responsive skin. It was a relief when he at last lifted her foot clear of the tub and placed it on a low stool.

'All done,' he said, finishing his own drink just as footsteps were heard on the stairs and his sister's brisk tones sounded outside the door.

Susanna hastily scraped her hair back from her face in an attempt to appear more seemly, ruing that in her haste to leave the Sans Pareil she had not stopped to pin it up.

Mr Kydd grinned. 'Nell, allow me to present Miss Fair to you. Miss Fair, my sister and her husband, Captain and Mrs Derringer.'

'How do you do? No, pray don't get up. Oh, Kit, you have not bandaged Miss Fair's foot yourself? How terribly improper. I dread to think how you will get on by yourself when Hugo and I leave for Vienna next week.' Mrs Derringer turned to Susanna. 'I am surprised you are not half-dead from embarrassment.'

To her astonishment, Susanna found herself defending him. 'I am much too grateful to be embarrassed, ma'am.' The sight of her bare toes emerging from the folds of linen, however, did cause her some unease. 'If I could just have my shoe back on . . . '

'I hardly think it will fit.' Mrs Derringer took off a green velvet evening cloak that made Susanna's black wool look shabbier than ever. She handed it to the footman saying, 'Tom, ask Annie for my loose cream slippers, would you? Will you be able to walk?'

'I think she must stay here tonight,' said Mr Kydd. 'After overturning the Dishonourable Rafe's plans for this evening, the least I can do is ensure Miss Fair is protected from the consequences.'

To be safe, even for a day! Susanna felt light-headed with relief until reason reasserted itself. What was she thinking? These people were Quality — and wasn't she living proof that the gentry were not to be trusted?

'Who is this Rafe Warwick?' said Mrs Derringer, accepting a Madeira from her husband, who then went on to refill the other glasses. 'I have not heard of him.'

'I should hope not,' said her brother severely. 'Drinker, gambler, proud as the devil, more money than principles and more vices than either. The sort of man who whips his servants and rides a horse into the ground to win a bet simply because he can. Not a pleasant character. Miss Fair, was this an isolated incident? Do you have no one but your landlady to protect you?'

'I . . . ' Susanna took refuge in her drink, at a loss as to how to answer. Telling gentry she had barely met that Rafe Warwick had wagered two thousand pounds on her being his mistress by the end of February was not to be thought of.

'Hush, Kit. Can you not see she is suffering from shock?'

Susanna was starting to feel scarily detached. Mrs Derringer must be correct; she was tired from the evening's performance, and it was the after-effect of Mr Warwick's brutal assault which had induced the unnerving lassitude in her body. Certainly this eccentric family who joked with their servants, knocked down strangers in the street and treated variety actresses as equals didn't help her confusion. Perhaps if she just sat here quietly until her head was clear she could decide what she ought to do. She moved her foot tentatively. Would it be better by tomorrow?

'Devilish nuisance that it's only Friday, not Saturday,' said Mr Kydd.

Surprised to find her own thoughts echoed, Susanna looked up. For some reason, the rest of the room took a while to follow. A crease was marring Mr Kydd's countenance as he absently regarded Susanna's foot.

'Why so?' said Mrs Derringer.

'Because there are no performances on a Sunday. As it is, Miss Fair will be forced to miss tomorrow's show.'

There was such a frown on his face that Susanna hastened to reassure him. 'It is of no consequence,' she said. The words jammed in her mouth. Puzzled, she took another sip of Madeira and enunciated more carefully. 'The Sans Pareil has a large cast. They will put another song on instead of mine and play with one fewer Indian hunter and one less witch for the night.' She prayed that it *would* only be for one night. If she was forced to miss more, the management might replace her — and then where would she be? She had some money saved against emergencies, but her landlady would never let her keep the room once performance fees dried up.

She bit her lip and drank again. She knew a moment's fluttering alarm when Mr Kydd joined her on the sofa, but all he did was to poke up the fire and engage his brother-in-law in conversation. It seemed rude to interrupt them by asking whether a hackney carriage could be called. Her eyelids began to droop as she listened to the jumble of talk. Phrases like 'spring sowing', 'crop-rotation', and 'six-mile acre' washed across her consciousness. It took her back to earlier days when Mr Masterson would discuss farm matters with his bailiff whilst she pulled the drapes or brought in refreshments. Susanna jerked suddenly. Heavens, she was falling asleep! She took another mouthful of Madeira in an effort to seem alert, reflecting that she now understood why her erstwhile employer had kept this wine strictly for his own consumption and marked his bottles into the bargain. What a long time ago that seemed, a lifetime almost, yet it was only four years since she had left Cheltenham. She hummed a few notes of 'The Miser of Maidenhead' to herself.

Mrs Derringer stood, in a rustle of silk. 'Tom,' Susanna heard her say, 'lay a fire in the back bedchamber, if you please, and ask Annie for a spare nightgown. You may bring in the tea tray as soon as it is convenient.'

A whole tea tray. Not a single screw of leaves, saved up for and then used over and over until the taste was long departed. Susanna tried to remember how long her current twist had lasted. Was it a week yet? Her hair was drifting around her face again. She put up strangely leaden hands to tidy it before remembering that her hairpins were still in the Sans Pareil chorus-room.

'I beg your pardon,' said Mr Kydd's voice. 'I hope we have not been boring you. Won't you have some tea before retiring?'

Susanna blinked in confusion. She hadn't heard the footman enter. She took the cup and saucer Mr Kydd was handing her. 'Oh, the Sèvres star design!' she cried without thinking. 'How beautiful! I never thought to see it outside a catalogue.'

There was an odd pause. 'It is striking, isn't it?' said Mr Kydd. 'Grandmama was a great frequenter of china warehouses. The pride of our collection are a few pieces of Kakeimon.'

'The Japanese porcelain? I should love to see that!' Susanna sipped her tea reverently, half-closing her eyes and making every fragrant mouthful last. She was only peripherally aware of a whispered conversation between the others.

'Did you hear that? She could be the answer!'

'Kit, she is an *actress*.'

'No ordinary actress. And you know it would aid my case considerably if — '

'It is a preposterous idea! Are you finished, Miss Fair? I will call Tom Olivant to give you a hand up the stairs.'

'The devil you will,' said Mr Kydd. Before Susanna could anticipate his intention, he had scooped her up in his arms. Again! She felt the warmth of his body through his coat and waistcoat, smelt the faint masculine scent coming off him. Even as her treacherous senses registered how pleasant it was to be held by someone this comely and this strong, the overheard conversation outside the theatre came rushing back again with a vengeance.

'No!' The protest was as instinctive as her struggle to get free. Through the worn muslin of her gown, she was aware of his arm muscles bunching under her thighs in order not to drop her. Abruptly she stopped moving. 'Sir, I beg you, please do not — '

He smiled, just a flicker of wickedness at the back of those devastating eyes. 'Be easy, I am delivering you to my sister's maid. We have had this conversation, if you remember. Not *all* men are cut from the same cloth as Mr Warwick.'

Oh, now she had offended him when he was simply being considerate. What would he think of her? 'I beg your pardon. I didn't mean to imply that your morals were . . . That is, you are so very good looking, you see, that any lady might . . . It is simply that I was not brought up to . . . ' She floundered to a halt, hearing her tongue tie itself up in knots.

His eyes danced. 'No apologies necessary, Miss Fair. It is my pleasure. After all, playing St George must warrant *some* reward . . . '

2

Susanna awoke to a strange bed in a strange room. For a moment panic engulfed her, then a painful stiffness in her right foot as well as the bruising down her arms brought memory slamming into place. Rafe Warwick had tried to abduct her outside the Sans Pareil! She felt sick with the fear of what might have happened had Mr Kydd not heard her cries, and thanked God fervently for his intervention. Without it, she doubted very much that she would have woken this morning with only a sprained ankle and a muzzy head to worry about.

She groaned as she remembered the effect of the Madeira wine. Never again would she let the sweetness of a drink mislead her as to its strength. The *shame* of having to be carried upstairs! Susanna blushed over and over. Although . . . The disturbing thought flitted through her head that Mr Kydd was a different kettle of fish entirely from Rafe Warwick. Last night's mortifying ascent (during which at one point she surely couldn't *really* have nestled against his chest, could she?) had been shot though with a

26

distinctly unmaidenly excitement . . .

'You see?' she said aloud, trying to dispel the memory with mockery. 'You see where fraternizing with the gentry gets you? One more ill-considered glass, one more flight of stairs, and you'd have been as lost as Mama.'

She sat up in bed. Weak sunlight showed around the edge of the window drapes. There was a fire in the grate. On the washstand, curls of steam were rising from a decorated ewer. Astonishment made her stare. She must have slept right through a maid entering her room! For a yearning, nonsensical second, she considered pretending her injury was no better just for the comfort of staying another night and waking to this luxury again. But that would mean spending a whole day with Mr Kydd. Susanna's sense of the very real dangers to be found in that bewitching gentleman's company had her sliding from the covers and hobbling across the floor before the thought had even finished.

Washing in the warm water was bliss. She couldn't remember ever having done such a thing without having to lay the fire, draw the water and set it on to boil herself. She wedged a chair under the door handle, stripped off her borrowed nightgown and took full advantage. Patting herself dry in front of the glass she allowed her imagination a tiny fantasy in which she was as famous as Mrs Siddons and could afford to command these amenities every day.

She made a humorous face at her reflection. As if the *ton* would ever flock to see her with her flyaway red-gold hair, unremarkable grey eyes, gamin appearance and light soprano when they still remembered the divine Sarah's throbbing, tragic heroines.

There was a hairbrush and hairpins on the stand. Susanna piled her curls up in an attempt to banish last night's wanton image. A cream wool shawl had been laid next to her blue muslin. She wondered with a flush of embarrassment whether it was a reflection on the muslin's neckline or merely a comment on February's temperature? For both reasons she tucked the soft wool around her shoulders. Then, supporting herself with everything in her path, she made her way gingerly downstairs.

'Miss Fair! Should you be walking around?'

Susanna jumped at Mr Kydd's unexpected emergence from the room they had sat in last night. He must have ears like a cat to have heard her careful descent. 'An actress must needs heal fast,' she said, keeping her voice light. 'Giving in to injuries whilst on the road is most severely frowned upon.' Lord, even in the sober light of day this man had a terrible effect on her pulse rate.

He proffered his arm. 'Nevertheless, I should hate a further accident to occur to you under my roof.'

There was a wonderful aroma of coffee and hot food coming from the open doorway. Susanna hesitated, then laid her hand on Mr Kydd's sleeve.

He gave her a smile which did nothing to alleviate her sense of danger. 'That is better. Now, will you take ham and eggs for breakfast or do you make do with toast or rolls?'

'I eat whatever my landlady has to offer,' Susanna said frankly.

Mr Kydd waved a generous hand. 'Then help yourself. One of the best things about Hugo marrying Nell is that I no longer have any qualms about his contributing the lion's share of the household expenses.'

Captain Derringer grinned. 'I trust your foot is easier this morning, Miss Fair?'

'Yes, I thank you. I do not believe I need trespass any further on your hospitality.' She sipped the perfect coffee which the footman poured out for her and closed her eyes for a moment in silent homage.

'I would have described it as more an abduction than a trespass,' murmured Mrs

Derringer, lavishly spreading a damson preserve on her toast.

Susanna ducked her head. 'Either way, ma'am, I am most truly grateful.'

'Grateful enough for conversation?' said Mr Kydd. 'I confess I am curious to know how you came by your knowledge of the rarer forms of Sèvres porcelain?'

Susanna flushed and moistened her lips. Why oh why hadn't she kept her tongue locked last night? Now she would have to tell them that she used to be a maid, and then they would feel uncomfortable sharing a table with her. 'My mother was housekeeper to an elderly gentleman who had an interest in such things. I was brought up in his house and worked there from an early age. It fell to me to wash and dust his collection. He liked to lecture about the various designs while I worked.' Also he hadn't trusted her not to break his pieces or run off with them.

'And now you are an actress,' said Mr Kydd, the faintest of interrogatives in his tone.

Susanna supposed his hospitality was deserving of more explanation. She gave it as frugally as possible. 'When Mr Masterson died, we were turned off. The only lodgings we could afford whilst we looked for work

were damp.' She swallowed. 'Mama succumbed to an ague. I nursed her until the
end and then found it . . . difficult . . . to get
another position.' She coloured. 'My hair, you
see, and being so young and quite alone. I
came to acting by chance.'

'I am sorry for your loss,' said Mrs
Derringer in a gentle voice. 'Our father died
not eighteen months ago. Bereavement is a
terrible grief.'

'Lord, Nell, marriage really *has* changed
you,' said Mr Kydd. 'You were never wont to
be so sensitive to the feelings of others.'

'That is because you have all the finer
emotions of an ox,' retorted his sister.
'Sympathy with *your* exploits would have
been wasted.'

A rubicon had apparently been crossed.
Not quite believing that she was still at the
table with them, Susanna ate a sliver of ham
and gave a tremulous smile, glad of the
raillery and the change in subject. 'I take it
your wedding was at no great date since,
ma'am. My felicitations.'

'November,' said Mrs Derringer. 'But we
have put off our wedding journey to Hugo's
sister in Vienna until now because Kit needed
us at Kydd.'

Susanna's brow wrinkled. Had she missed
a sentence of explanation?

Mr Kydd met her eyes with a gleam of disquieting understanding. 'Kydd Court is my estate in Northamptonshire. I was in India when my father died. My uncle availed himself of the opportunity to well-nigh bankrupt us, so it has been all hands to the plough, so to speak, to turn ourselves around. Sadly, we have not yet managed it.'

'Can the courts not call for reparation?'

'My uncle is also now dead.'

'And, unfortunately, neither of his odious sons will join with Kit to break the entail, so he cannot sell any land to raise capital. Really, Kit, I cannot *think* why you did not have the foresight to marry and beget yourself an heir before you went out to Bombay. None of this would then have happened.'

Mr Kydd gave a short laugh. 'Perhaps I was a little tired of being chased from one side of the county to the other by every marriageable female and matchmaking mama within fifty miles, purely for the sake of my inheritance! No, my uncle's revenge is complete indeed. Any spare blunt must go towards Kydd's amelioration, and by the time I am in a position to offer marriage I shall likely be too old to do anything about providing myself with a son to pass the estate to.'

Susanna felt herself turn scarlet. He may have said it as a joke, but that comment *had* to have been aimed at her. He was telling her that although he was not averse to carrying her upstairs, he was unable to keep her as a mistress. She couldn't blame his assumption. She had snuggled up to him on the stairs last night, hadn't she? And there had been those smiles between them at the theatre, not to mention that it was what Mr Warwick wanted her for, and it was how plenty of her fellow actresses supplemented their wages. Mr Kydd wasn't to know that when her mind was unclouded by shock and strong drink it was the very last step *she* would ever consider taking.

'Kit, you are embarrassing Miss Fair! I don't know why men must be so disgracefully earthy!'

Susanna produced a dutiful smile. 'I don't regard it, ma'am, I assure you. I have heard far worse below stairs, and my present profession is hardly free from such allusions. I have frequently found it serves to be a trifle deaf.'

'You would appear to be admirably adaptable,' said Mr Kydd.

Now she was really confused. He couldn't afford a mistress, but that last remark had been laced with speculation. It was more than time she was out of this unsettling house and back in her own milieu. 'My thanks for the breakfast and for your hospitality,' she said. 'I had best take my leave before I grow quite spoiled.'

Concern crossed his face. 'Before your ankle is fully recovered? But what if Warwick should come to exact revenge?'

Susanna's insides clenched. For one glorious half-hour she had forgotten last night's ugly scene. 'Once at my lodgings I shall be protected well enough. My landlady is something of a dragon where unsavoury gentlemen are concerned.'

'I wish I shared your confidence.' Mr Kydd laid his hand on hers. 'There is one way in which I could guarantee your safety, at least for a while.'

Mrs Derringer stiffened. Her husband looked up, his gaze watchful. Susanna felt a thrill of unease and tried to turn the tension off with a jest. 'That is very noble, but I really cannot think risking your life in some dawn assignation sensible, merely on the off chance of being able to put a bullet through Mr Warwick.'

Mr Kydd gave a shout of delighted laughter. 'Adaptable *and* witty! Miss Fair, would you consider taking a short sojourn in the country — as my betrothed?'

It was as well Susanna was sitting down. For a moment the whole world spun in dizzying colours around her head. Her hand moved blindly under his. He hardly knew her! And she was an *actress*! He might admire her dancing but he could *surely* not be suggesting that —

Mrs Derringer brought her sharply back to earth. 'Kit, it is an appalling idea! I told you so last night. You cannot possibly ask such a thing!'

'Madness,' agreed Captain Derringer. 'Even by your standards.'

Susanna realized that the conclusion she had leapt to was the wrong one. 'I . . . I'm afraid I don't understand,' she said. She drew her hand away carefully, thankful that if her voice was not quite normal, they didn't know her well enough to realize it.

Mr Kydd turned his chair to face her. 'My estate is in dire need of funds. I can sell some family effects to tide us over, but that will only relieve matters in the short term. It will not pay the mortgages or provide income for my tenants if this year's harvest fails. However, I might command sufficient credit to accomplish a more permanent recovery if . . . ' He extracted a letter from his pocketbook. 'This is from my great-aunt Emma, a redoubtable lady who fifty years ago eloped with the heir of a candle manufacturer, much to the fury of Great-grandpapa. Read it.'

Bewildered, Susanna unfolded the paper. It was written in a formal style with many loops and curlicues. '*Having now no immediate family, and after giving thought to the eventual disposal of her assets, Lady Penfold invites Mr Christopher Kydd to visit her in order that all parties might become better acquainted.*'

'Great-aunt Emma married for love,' said Mr Kydd, his vivid blue eyes fixed on Susanna as if willing her to understand. 'She braved scandal, family ostracism and social condemnation for it. She believes to a quite extraordinary degree in the power of domestic happiness. Having lost her husband to gout, her son to a fever and her grandson in combat, and being reared in the belief that, however disagreeable one's relatives, money should always follow blood, she is looking at her nephews' families to see which amongst them follows her tenets enough to be deserving of her fortune.'

'Which means either us or our hateful cousins,' put in Nell Derringer.

'All of whom were browbeaten by our uncle into marrying and breeding early and thus appear to the uninitiated to be models of felicity.'

Susanna moistened her lips. 'What has this to do with me?'

He smiled ruefully. 'You must see that I am at somewhat of a disadvantage having *not* chosen to become leg-shackled whilst I was still wet behind the ears. I am offering you the role of my betrothed for the duration of a short visit. I believe I can say with all due modesty that I am enough of an actor to carry my part through.'

Hugo Derringer entered the conversation. 'No one who had the doubtful privilege of sharing your formative years could argue with you on that, Kit, but you dwell too much on being as yet unattached. Lady Penfold cannot believe that *all* young men of five-and-twenty are rakes. Unless she is a fool, she will see quite well the state of affairs existing in your cousins' families.'

'But we don't know that for sure. And as they had last year's profits from Kydd and the majority of the reserves in the bank to boot, I am disinclined to let them also have Great-aunt Emma's money without making a push towards securing it for the Court! By visiting her with my affections seen to be engaged, I give us a fighting chance.'

Susanna's brain was in turmoil. It was a deception straight out of a stage farce. Such things simply did not happen in real life. One part of her mind whispered that it would indeed remove her from Mr Warwick's orbit.

Another demanded to know how she thought she would get her job at the Sans Pareil back if she left with so little ceremony now. A third felt overwhelmingly let down and disappointed in Mr Kydd. He was not unconditionally chivalrous after all. And considering that she had always prided herself on her practicality, it was ridiculous that this hurt sensation dictated her reply. 'It is flattering that you think me proficient enough to help,' she said in a low voice, unable to meet his eyes, 'but I believe I must decline.'

'Well, naturally you must,' said Mrs Derringer. 'I cannot imagine by what right Kit thinks he may disrupt your life like this!'

'I am sorry,' said Susanna, twisting her hands together.

Mr Kydd stilled them. His touch felt like hot coals. 'Don't be. I would not have you feel guilty because I made an unacceptable suggestion.'

She swallowed with difficulty. 'I had best go.'

He stood up abruptly and strode over to the fireplace. 'I shall see you to your lodgings. Call it a sop to my conscience.' Susanna was shocked to see very real concern in his eyes.

'Do not judge Kit too harshly,' said Nell Derringer when the men had left the room. 'Kydd Court means a lot to him. I hope we meet again when I return from Vienna. I should like to know you better.'

'Thank you.' Susanna was unexpectedly touched. She had to remind herself that the gentry were renowned for saying things they did not mean. It was in the highest degree unlikely that their paths would cross again, so Mrs Derringer was quite safe in expressing such pretty sentiments.

She was taken aback to find that Mr Kydd intended driving to her lodgings in his curricle. She knew perfectly well the conclusion her landlady would draw at the sight, but then returning in a hackney carriage at eleven in the morning would not be so very much better. At least this way she would save the fare, and it *was* undeniably smart to be perched so high above the street.

As if to impress upon her that she should forget his proposition, Mr Kydd adopted a buoyant air which Susanna was glad to play along with. He handled the traces lightly, did not brush against her leg any more than might be construed as accidental, and tossed remarks over his shoulder to his groom that showed it was not just with his footman that he disregarded the employer-servant barrier. Indeed, by the time they drew to a halt outside the Sans Pareil and he asked her to tool the bays up the street and back whilst he dropped off a note of her indisposition, she was sufficiently at ease to inform him that handling horses had not been considered part of a housemaid's duties in Mr Masterson's establishment.

His vivid grin made her unguarded senses swim. 'No matter, Johnny will hold their heads. I shall not be many minutes.'

Susanna allowed herself the liberty of admiring the shine on his Hessians and the elegant way his caped driving coat swung as he disappeared inside the theatre. 'Have you been with Mr Kydd long?' she asked the groom curiously.

John Farley's thin, rather serious face lit up. 'Oh yes, miss. I was born on the Home Farm. Me and Tom Olivant and Mr Kit and Miss Nell used to run all over the estate together. I went into the army after the *old* master, that's Mr Kit's father, died, but I didn't really suit soldiering so as soon as I got the chance I came home.'

A haunted look appeared in his eyes. Susanna had seen the same expression on the faces of other soldiers returned to normal life since the hostilities with France had ended. She noticed how he started at a noise further up the street and the way his hand went to the bays' heads. She felt cross on his behalf. It was most unfair to have brought a nervous groom to the hustle and bustle of London. 'I daresay you will be glad to get back to the country, will you not?'

'We all will, miss. Horses can't gallop properly here. Nor Mr Kit can't get the fidgets out of hisself neither. He needs to be adoing.'

That did surprise Susanna. Kit (when had she started to think of him thus?) seemed to her the embodiment of a man about town. She would have questioned the groom further, but the object of their conversation reappeared and swung up to the curricle seat. 'They don't expect you until Monday. Look lively, Johnny.'

Susanna glanced at him. He seemed less insouciant than before. 'What is it?' she asked, her heart sinking. 'Was Mr Scott very angry?'

He shifted as if slightly uncomfortable. 'No. I fancy they were surprised to see me is all. They seemed to expect someone else.'

Rafe Warwick. The entire theatre knew of the hateful man's bet. Susanna felt hot colour flood her face. 'I assure you there is no reason for them to,' she said in a constricted voice. She could not, simply *could not* tell him about the wager.

They turned off the Strand and all Kit's attention was then on the narrow streets.

Susanna got the impression he was glad to have the distraction of avoiding gutter refuse and lounging pedestrians. He did not speak again until he handed her down outside her lodgings. His hand steadied her waist for just a second. Under his curly-brimmed hat, his eyes had regained something of their mischief. 'I suppose I had best not carry you this time?'

She couldn't repress a smile. 'Not if I want to keep what reputation I have left.'

'Would it survive you resting on my arm?'

'Thank you, I think I might risk that. Good morning, Mrs Brown.' Her landlady had materialized in the narrow hallway. 'Mr Kydd and his sister were kind enough to come to my aid when I sprained my ankle leaving the theatre yesterday.'

Mrs Brown appraised Kit with a thoroughness which made Susanna blush.

'Did I pass muster?' he whispered as they trod the uncarpeted stairs to her room.

'Can you doubt it?' Susanna's response was drier than normal because of the twin hazards of not resting too much weight upon her foot and consequently leaning far more than convention decreed on his arm. She needed all the willpower she possessed not to let his nearness affect her. His chuckle of appreciation at her riposte didn't help.

When they reached her room, Kit glanced at the empty grate then strolled over to the shelf which held her books. '*The Task*,' he said, taking the well-worn volume down and flicking idly through the pages. 'Cowper has always been a favourite of mine. '*Knowledge is proud that he has learned so much . . . .*''

Susanna smiled. ' . . . '*Wisdom is humble that he knows no more.*' '

'Too easy. '*The Nurse sleeps soundly, hired to watch the sick . . . .*''

' ' . . . *whom, snoring, she disturbs.*' You have found out my weakness. I spend vast tracts of time reading and am unable to pass by even the shabbiest table of books in the hopes of finding a bargain.'

'It is hardly a vice,' he said with a laugh. 'Tools of the trade, surely? Come now, which is your favourite Shakespeare play?'

Susanna pulled her shawl tighter. 'You will despise me.'

His eyes sparkled. 'What? Not a tragedy? Can you admit it?'

'*Twelfth Night*,' she said mournfully.

'No wonder you are not at Drury Lane. But you must apply, should they think of reviving *A Midsummer Night's Dream*. You would make a splendid Titania with that hair.'

A chill shivered Susanna's skin. Her hair was the source of all her troubles. 'I would as lief be dark like your sister.' She realized she was still wearing Nell Derringer's shawl and crossed to the trunk to replace it with her own.

'What the devil!' Kit dropped the book on the bed. His hand shot out to catch her wrist, his eyes riveted on her arms.

Looking down, Susanna saw the livid contusions left yesterday by Rafe Warwick's fingers. 'I bruise easily,' she said, embarrassed. She hurriedly wrapped her own shawl around her. 'A piece of scenery fell on me one time when I was with the Chartwell Players and you would have thought I had been in the worst kind of tavern brawl.'

'It seems an odd change — from maid to actress. How did it come about?'

'By the veriest chance. Before she was a housekeeper, my mother was a governess. She had an especial fondness for poetry and plays, and I reaped the benefit of being her only pupil. The Chartwell Players were staying at an inn where I had found temporary work. Their principal actress had developed a putrid sore throat and I knew the *Comedy Of Errors* by heart.'

'A lucky accident, then.'

'Indeed it was most fortunate. Mama's illness had taken all the money we had. It seemed to me a miracle to get a whole guinea

44

merely from acting out in public what I had often read aloud for pleasure.'

Kit glanced out of the window. 'I had best go. Your landlady will be imagining all manner of dark things.'

Susanna smiled. 'Thank you again. I am more grateful than I can say for your timely intervention last night.'

'It was little enough.' His eyes went from her concealed bruises to the key which stood ready to turn in the lock of the door. 'Goodbye.'

He raised Susanna's hand before she was aware of his intent and kissed it. Through her worn glove, she felt the warmth and gentleness of his lips invade the very fabric of her skin. 'Goodbye,' she whispered.

He hesitated, still holding her hand. 'Promise you will send to Half Moon Street if you are in need? The offer I made you remains open.'

Blood pounded in Susanna's ears. She pulled away from him. 'Mr Kydd, you can have nothing to do with me. You saw the street outside, the dingy buildings, the filth in the alleyways, the card game taking place outside the alehouse. How can you even suggest such a thing? The world I live in is not yours.'

'We breathe the same air, do we not? We

stand and fall by our own acts? At least promise you will not leave this house until you have to go to the theatre on Monday.'

She bit her lip. 'If you wish it, yes.'

After he had gone, she sat with her head in her hands. What had she been about in turning him down? Her one chance to escape this drab existence and she had let it go. It wouldn't be honest, said her conscience. He does not know the whole truth.

The gentry choose their own truth, replied her worse self. She shivered and got a second shawl out of her trunk.

A row had broken out in the card game. The raised voices caused doors to open and women to bawl at their menfolk. Susanna turned away from the window, sickened. Was this to be her fate? Old before she was thirty, shrilling at her husband in the street?

A rattle at the door made her start in alarm. She had barely time to say 'Tilly!' in a voice of strong surprise, before Mrs Brown's diminutive maid-of-all-work was backing into the room with a box of kindling in one skinny arm and a scuttle in the other.

'The gennleman said as how you couldn't do your own fire for a day or two on account of your foot being hurt. I told him as how fires was tuppence a time and you was saving against the vagueness of fate, but he gives

46

Mrs Brown a shillun and telled me to do them as long as it lasts.' Tilly dropped her voice impressively. 'And he slips me thruppence for meself! I should stick to him if I was you, miss.'

'Mr Kydd gave Mrs Brown a shilling for my fires?' repeated Susanna in astonishment.

Tilly beamed at her. 'And thruppence for me. He's bang-up, he is.'

Tears rose to Susanna's eyes. How kind of him. And after she had refused to help him too.

★   ★   ★

Arriving home, Kit headed straight for his room and rummaged in a chest, the contents of which had come in useful on several occasions.

'Kit, about your mortgages — '

'Not now, Hugo. I have to go out.'

His friend watched as he pulled on a deplorable jacket and a pair of ancient seaman's trousers, finally cramming a shapeless hat low over his bright hair. 'You put no faith in the landlady then?'

Kit felt a quick impatience. 'Devil take it, you know what Warwick is. When did he ever stay his hand for a boarding-house proprietor? And after the hints I got at the theatre,

I'll swear there's more to this business than his simply taking a fancy to Miss Fair last night. Her name is Susanna, by the way.'

Hugo frowned. 'She made you free of it?'

'Not she! She told me in no uncertain terms that we were worlds apart. I saw it on the flyleaf of one of her books. She reads Cowper.'

'Which of course puts her beyond reproach!'

'Well, do you know, I think it might. How do I look?'

'Disreputable. Would you like me to trawl the clubs for information?'

Kit gripped his friend's shoulder. 'Do you have time? Then thank you. You don't think I'm making a mountain out of a molehill?'

'Much it would matter if I did. It's easier to dam a stream in full flood than it is to stop you once you've got the bit between your teeth.'

Kit gave a wry grin. 'I may not have started whatever this is, but I certainly exacerbated it. I owe it to her to see it through.'

'And being bored with waiting on bankers and her being an actress with deuced pretty hair even when it isn't tumbled around her shoulders doesn't come into it, I suppose?'

'I refuse to answer that. Tell Nell not to wait dinner for me.'

'If your sister has not already badgered

Tom Olivant into making you up a packet of bread and cheese, I shall be amazed. Don't get yourself killed, will you? She looks shocking in black.'

Kit was still smiling when he left the house. But by the time he got to the alehouse opposite Susanna's lodgings his amusement had been replaced by a cold determination. He bought himself a tankard of ale and hunkered down next to the card game to wait.

★ ★ ★

The hours ticked by. Susanna composed a letter of thanks to Mrs Derringer, darned a rent in her cloak, read some Cowper, and tried to put Mr Kydd out of her mind. Outside her window more men had joined the card game. One was a seaman to judge by the hat pulled low over his brow, his rolling stance and the wide cut of his trousers — discharged now that Napoleon was finally exiled, and left to roam the streets like so many others. As the daylight faded, the spectre of Mr Warwick arose and Susanna's courage fell accordingly. Soon he would discover her absence from the Sans Pareil. She pictured him in the greenroom interro-gating the cast, his cold eyes merciless, his

49

cane swinging by his side.

Life had been so simple with the Chartwell Players, rehearsing lines in the jolting cart, playing in fitted-up barns or grand houses, tucking away her share of the takings, adjusting with gratitude to a new life on the road. She'd been able to forget the awful period since Mama's death, forget all the men who had seen her as an easy conquest. But that had been before she'd fallen in love with Adam, the Players' actor-manager and had done the honourable thing by his family and left. Before she had come to London in the gullible belief that all you needed to act was talent. Before Mr Warwick had shown irrevocably that wherever she went, someone would find her.

Tilly came in, bringing bread and broth and a mug of smallale. She gossiped as she made up the fire. 'Lively at the Pelican tonight,' she said with a jerk of her head towards the window. 'Some flat laying his blunt about. Mr Brown's slipping over for a piece of the action after he's ate.'

Susanna's spoon fell into the bowl with a clatter. Even though her landlady's husband was largely a cipher in the house, his presence was some sort of deterrent. She wondered uneasily if the 'flat' could possibly have been paid to provide a distraction. It seemed fanciful, but she knew how seriously men of fashion took their bets. Two thousand pounds was a great deal of money even in the circles Rafe Warwick frequented. As soon as Tilly left, Susanna locked her door. The latch turned with an impressive click, but the door itself was flimsy. How much of a barrier would it be to a determined noble?

Light spilt from the tavern doorway, illuminating the drinkers and card players outside. Women whose calling Susanna did not doubt for a second were systematically working the knots of men. Scanty dresses cut low over their bosoms were as good as a placard, even if the dimness mercifully hid the dirt on their shawls and smoothed the raggedness of their hems. The sailor, she noticed with faint amusement, brushed them away.

It was an hour or so later that she was jerked out of an uncomfortable doze by a prickling sense of danger. A tall figure in a gentleman's hat and cloak was striding down the street with an arrogant swagger. Susanna could just make out the cane by his side. As she shrank back she saw him assess the Pelican with a curl of his lips, and then cross the street to her lodgings. Dear God, it was him. The Honourable Rafe Warwick come to make good his wager. And the door

51

downstairs unlocked against its master's return, and herself easy prey in her room.

She was so caught up in her fear that she didn't hear the surge of noise. It was only when a snarl of 'Get back, rabble! Who do you think you are dealing with!' penetrated her consciousness, that she looked into the street again. What she saw made her clutch at her heart in relief. There was fighting everywhere, an out-and-out brawl! Lanterns were jerking, fists were flying, cards had been scattered. A mill was in progress over the pool of money, doors and windows were opening all along the street, householders were adding their shouts to the general confusion. How it had started she didn't know, but Susanna wept tears of thankfulness as she saw the tall figure lash out at the sailor with his cane and stride away very fast from her building. Others melted from the street equally quickly as a shout of 'Look out! The Watch!' rang out.

Downstairs a door slammed. Mrs Brown's voice was heard ringing a peel over her errant husband. Shaking, Susanna pulled the drapes and made ready for bed. In her mind's eye, she saw Kit's gleaming head bend over her hand. She felt him kiss her glove. His words beat in her veins. *The offer I made you remains open . . .*

3

'Don't say it,' warned Kit, seeing his sister's eyes widen at his appearance next day. 'I was right. Warwick tried to get into Susanna's lodging house last night. If I had not scared her away with my offer, she would likely still have been safe here.'

'Susanna, is it?' said Nell. 'Kit, I liked her well enough myself, but have you asked yourself why you are championing her so hard?'

He felt himself colour. 'I aggravated Warwick. I owe it to her to keep watch. I do not believe one setback will stop him.'

Nell looked sceptical. 'So it is not that you are tired of trying to raise money for Kydd and this gives you an excuse to dress up and act the knight-errant?'

He set his jaw and glanced at Hugo. 'Did you find out anything?'

'In the betting book at White's. *Tuesday 2 January 1816: the Honourable Rafe Warwick wagers Lord Frederick Vere the sum of £2000 that before two months have passed, the new red-headed actress at the Sans Pareil will be his mistress.*'

Hugo's words hit Kit like a blow to the gut. Swearing long and hard, he left the house at a run.

★   ★   ★

On any other Sunday Susanna would have attended church, it having been ingrained in her since childhood that to miss was akin to admitting that the world was about to end. But as she dressed in a sober grey check and tucked a decent lawn fichu around her neck, the promise she had made to Mr Kydd stayed her steps. She tried to tell herself that since it was highly unlikely she would ever see him again, breaking her word would not matter. But he had looked so grave, so serious. His proposal slid into her mind. Had it really been such a terrible thing he had asked? It was not as if he wanted to cheat the old lady. He merely wished for the promise of future security in order to persuade his bankers to give him enough leeway to bring his estate about now.

You made the right decision, said her sensible side. You know nothing about him bar that he appreciates the theatre and has an impressive right uppercut. And that he likes literature. And that he treats his servants as friends. Susanna looked at the fire in her grate. And that he is kind.

A church bell tolled. Mrs Brown and her husband sailed into the street. A shabby man who had been lounging at the corner of the alley checked his pocket watch. Susanna gazed at the scene with unseeing eyes. If she *was* to perform tomorrow, perhaps it would be as well to remain quietly in her room today. She reached for her bible. It fell open at the Gospel of St Matthew. '*The light of the body is in the eye: if therefore thine eye be single, thy whole body shall be full of light.*' Mr Kydd had beautiful eyes.

★　★　★

By Monday, Susanna's swollen ankle looked normal again, but fading bruises and a residual stiffness remained as a warning to be constantly on her guard. She girded up her courage and left early for the Sans Pareil; a new melodrama from the ready pen of Miss Scott was to be rehearsed and she intended to be safe with the cast for as long as she possibly could. She kept a nervous watch on the passers-by, but was not approached nor, so far as she could tell, followed. Indeed she herself seemed to be the one doing the following: a clerk of some sort with greying hair, cracked shoes and a round-shouldered gait was only a few paces ahead of her the whole way. She turned in at the theatre with a sigh of thankfulness, wondering for how much longer she could continue to live on a knife-edge.

The oldest member of the chorus was more direct. 'You need to find a protector, dearie. The Dishonourable Rafe was here on Saturday swearing revenge. Stands to reason, the amount of money he's got riding on you.'

'I wish to God he had not,' said Susanna in a low voice.

'From the bruise on his chin, we thought you might have a candidate already,' said another girl with a yawn.

Susanna forced a smile. 'A young blade with a noble streak and too much drink on board to be cautious. He took Mr Warwick by surprise and I got away.'

'Pity.' The second girl surveyed Susanna with sly, half-closed eyes. 'Do you suppose if I had hair to match yours, I'd have men fighting duels over me?'

'You don't want them, dearie. Not if they're Rafe Warwick. He's killed his man before. Family hushed it up.'

Susanna was glad when Miss Scott swept into the room and rapped on the table for silence. She was trembling with the effort of keeping the contents of her breakfast in her stomach as it was.

'May I borrow your old uniform, Hugo?' said Kit.

His friend looked up from packing documents into a strong-box. He blinked at Kit's unlovely shoes and straggling wig. 'It's yours. Why?'

'Because the wretched girl is at the theatre and presumably intends acting tonight. I can't decide whether to applaud her bravery or throttle her for being so stupid. Does she seriously think Warwick is going to give up?'

'She has a living to earn.'

'But — '

'Kit, this may be a quixotic adventure on your part, but it is her *life*. She doesn't have the luxury of calling for her curricle and riding away if it palls.'

Kit felt a surge of frustration. Why did neither Nell nor Hugo understand? Yes, taking on the mantle of Susanna's guardian angel was more to his taste than kicking his heels in dusty offices and cold anterooms, but she *was* in very real danger. 'Dammit, Hugo, I am not treating this as a game!'

'Nor is she, Kit. She needs to eat, she needs to pay the rent. What choice does she have?'

★　★　★

It was when Susanna came off after the melodrama that she found Rafe Warwick waiting in the greenroom. 'Very nice,' he drawled, raising his quizzing glass to inspect the new costume. 'You must wear it for me later.'

With a hasty jerk, Susanna snatched up her cloak to cover herself.

'And not crippled after all. I rejoice. One does so detest marked merchandise.'

A spark of anger came to her. 'Merchandise? I am neither for sale nor for hire.'

'You are a commodity, my dear, like all your kind.' He strolled forward, company members retreating from his path like the Red Sea flowing away from Moses.

Susanna forced herself to stand her ground. 'Everyone has rights. I have never sought your attentions and wish you would leave me alone.'

'Rights?' said Mr Warwick in amusement. 'Wishes?' He put out his hand and gripped her chin so hard she could feel the seams of his glove biting into her skin. 'Once I declared an interest, you lost any say in the matter. I have a mind to see the rest of the show, so I leave you Stebbings as a token of my intent. I would advise against any independent action on your part. He has not wit enough to understand democracy.' He traced her lips

58

with the head of his cane and then ran it, quite deliberately, down between her breasts. 'Until later, my dear.' He turned, his silk-lined cape snapping into folds behind him.

Swallowing hard, Susanna watched him say a few words to the bruiser in the doorway. One look at the man's heavy fists and coarse, leering face was enough to convince her that Mr Warwick did not intend letting her get away this time. And he had enjoyed telling her so. The true reason he hadn't abducted her right now was to give her another hour in which to dread what was coming. She schooled her face to a mask, while behind it thoughts scurried frantically like rats in a trap.

By the end of the evening, she had a single, desperate plan. To further it, she took care always to come offstage straight into the greenroom. Stebbings would already know he was guarding the only exit to the alley. What she didn't want was for him to discover the existence of the narrow passage between stage and dressing rooms.

Mr Warwick was in one of the overhanging tiered boxes on the left-hand side. At the close of the pantomime, with all the tangles unsnarled and Harlequin united with Columbine, Susanna bowed with the rest of the cast,

59

raced down the passage to the chorus-room, bundled herself into her cloak even as the curtain was closing, then sped back to the stage. Masked by the heavy drapes, she lowered herself off the left-hand side where she would be invisible from Mr Warwick's box and joined the press of people making for the exit.

Noisy as the crowd was, she could scarce hear them for the terrified thumping of her heart. Surely she would be spotted, scurrying along in her shabby black wool amongst the cits in their best clothes, the demi-monde with their outrageous headgear and bared shoulders, and the soldiers in their flaunting regimentals? So intent was she on escape that she didn't feel her cloak catch on a pillar, revealing her costume. It was only when the soldier who had been keeping pace with her swirled his cape to make a magnificent leg to a lady in diaphanous lavender that she noticed her strips of witch's gauze were visible. Fortunately, the gallantry of the soldier's action had masked her, so she was able to pull her cloak tight once again and push past without a single detaining shout.

She made it to her lodgings, locked her door and sank with sobbing breath and trembling legs onto her bed. What was it that made the worst kind of men desire her?

Would she never be free of their sick lust? This was the ostler from the Ram Inn all over again. And Mrs Lascalle's brother during her three-week duration as a governess. And the actor who had falsely promised her a part at Drury Lane.

Unbidden, Mr Kydd's laughing image rose before her eyes. His offer would remove her from the neighbourhood. She could perhaps find a new travelling company once the visit was over. But how could she ask him now? He was gentry. Likely he'd put her out of his mind as soon as he'd left on Saturday. Half Moon Street had been an interlude, a dream. This was real life.

★   ★   ★

Kit stood at the boarding-house door, unable to believe his ears. 'Miss Fair has left already?'

The little maid shifted from foot to foot. 'Yes sir, an hour since. She said she had business with the manager of the theatre.'

Kit cursed under his breath and vaulted to the curricle seat. Devil take it, he'd had a sleepless night, what with Hugo and Nell's home truths squatting in his head together with all the lascivious comments from the people around him in the pit last evening. It

61

had turned his stomach to listen to the crude suggestions as to how the dancers would perform in other areas. He was no longer under any illusion that an actress's life was one to envy, and had come to persuade Susanna to either reconsider his offer or look for different employment. And now he found she'd already left! He'd known she was full of pluck since seeing her scramble down from behind the stage curtain yesterday, but why the deuce hadn't she come to *him*? Surely he couldn't be *that* distasteful? 'Damned if I don't kidnap her myself,' he muttered to John Farley.

'You'll have nothing to kidnap her in if you don't slow down,' pointed out the groom as they surged round a corner. 'Makes a change, mind, chasing *after* a young lady instead of running away from them all the time . . . '

★   ★   ★

Susanna sat in the Sans Pareil manager's office and finished the recital of her problems. Mr Scott steepled his fingers. 'I am glad you came, Miss Fair, for I sustained a most unpleasant encounter yesterday. When you failed to appear in the greenroom, Mr Warwick concluded you'd had help and became very ugly. He made threats which,

62

given his unsavoury reputation, I am unable to dismiss as mere bluster.'

Susanna tensed. 'Threats?' she whispered.

'To my business, to my theatre and to my daughter. Loath as I am to give in to coercion, I cannot take the risk that anything might befall Miss Scott.'

Susanna stared at him, aghast. 'But I came to you for help! At Drury Lane, the management provided a guard for an actress in a similar position!'

Mr Scott smiled slightly. 'The actress in question was a leading player, not a member of the chorus, and the story was nosed abroad as much for the theatre's gain as anything. I suggest the simplest solution is for you to gather your possessions and leave before anyone knows of your being here. I will of course provide you with a full week's wages and extra money for your immediate needs along with an open letter of recommendation which you may take to any other theatre company. I am only sorry that your association with the Sans Pareil has to end under such distressing circumstances.'

His words seemed to be coming from an immense distance. Susanna took the purse he handed her and found herself at the door without any sensation of having moved. 'So am I, sir,' she said in a choked voice. 'So am I.'

She went through to the theatre in a daze, returned last night's Witch of the Woods gauze to the rail, packed her basket haphazardly, and emerged to a street overcast with incipient rain. The basket dragged at her arm. Her head felt leaden and stupid. She would have to find new lodgings and make the rounds of the theatres again. The Lyceum might take her on. Or Astley's. She was so devastated by this unforeseen change in her fortunes that she failed to notice a pair of bay horses drawing to a halt beside her.

'Miss Fair,' called a voice with a hint of relief. 'How delightful!'

The words penetrated the fog in her brain. As she slowly raised her head, the clouds parted for the one and only time that day. She blinked, dazzled. Mr Kydd's vigorous, sunlit presence was the last thing she had expected to see. She crumpled in a dead faint at his horses' feet.

Within seconds she felt him lift her. 'This is becoming quite a habit. Might I repeat history by conveying you to Half Moon Street? I am sure my sister would be pleased to renew her acquaintance with you.'

Shock and distress between them had robbed Susanna of independent thought in the same way that Kit's miraculous presence had melted her bones. She made no demur as he helped her up to the curricle seat, finding an exquisite comfort in his capable arm around her waist.

Nell Derringer was discovered surrounded by packing trunks. 'Miss Fair!' she cried, dropping the shimmering amber silk gown she had been folding. 'My dear, whatever is wrong? I can see you are in some sort of trouble. Is it Mr Warwick?'

Overset by the unexpected kindness, tears came to Susanna's eyes. Before she could stop herself, the whole sorry tale came tumbling out. 'I beg your pardon,' she finished with a sob. 'I do not know why I should be telling you all this.'

'Because I asked and because we are of an age and because you do not appear to have anyone else to seek advice from. But we leave tomorrow, so what use I can be I can't imagine.'

Kit re-entered the room and crossed to the decanter. 'I have told Tom to fetch some food. I had no breakfast myself this morning, and Miss Fair should also eat. She is by far too thin and pale.'

'How unhandsome, Kit! It is hard to believe that society hostesses allow you anywhere near their salons.'

Susanna gave a strained smile as she accepted a glass of wine, but her bruised confidence shrivelled still further. *Too thin and too pale.* How could she ever have imagined she might attract him?

'Poor Miss Fair,' continued Nell. 'After Mr Warwick has caused her to lose her place with the Sans Pareil company too.'

Kit's eyes sparkled. 'Splendid! Will you take up my offer, then? You can come to Newmarket with a clear conscience and find some other occupation when we get back.'

Susanna's hand jerked so hard the wine spilt. Had he said *Newmarket*?

'Oh, you are not still set on that plan, Kit? What of the damage to Miss Fair's character were her part to become known? And if you succeed, how will you dissolve the engagement? Great-aunt Emma will not settle the money on you if she believes you have jilted Miss Fair, no matter that you have never played fast and loose with a lady's affections in your life before!'

Mr Kydd stared at his sister for several moments. 'Damn and blast!' His eyes slid ruefully to Susanna. 'Though I do believe you could have carried it off.'

Newmarket? Susanna moistened her lips, hardly knowing what she was saying. 'Even though I do not move in your circles or know your friends or your history?'

'You know about life in a well-ordered gentleman's house. You are educated and intelligent. I daresay my great-aunt lives quite retired, so an intimacy with the social world would not be required. But Nell is right. I had not given a thought as to what would happen afterwards.'

Newmarket. Dare she? Dare she do it? In Susanna's breast her heart was beating at twice its usual rate.

'As to that,' she heard herself say, 'I could give *you* the congé. Go back to my childhood sweetheart whom I had thought lost at sea. Your great-aunt might feel so sorry for you that she couldn't possibly promise the money elsewhere.'

'You are saying you *would* do it?'

Was she? Susanna panicked. 'I . . . I don't know.'

'But you do agree you must leave your lodgings, I hope? We can take the barouche and pack up your belongings. You may at least stay here for tonight.'

'Thank you,' she whispered. But her gaze did not immediately leave his. She could see the question still repeated in them. *You would do it?*

God forgive her, she had nearly said yes.

★   ★   ★

Susanna had her story all ready. She had met an old friend who had invited her to share her house, and she was moving in immediately. The words were on her lips ready to be uttered when the opening of the front door disclosed not Mrs Brown but a pale, shrinking Tilly.

'Oh, miss,' wailed the maid-of-all-work. 'Oh, miss, I couldn't stop him! All your bits and pieces! I couldn't stop him!'

Susanna felt a blast of fear hit her. 'Who, Tilly? Who are you talking about?'

Tilly's hands twisted her apron. 'He's not been gone above ten minutes. Didn't believe me when I told him Mrs Brown was out and I didn't know where you was.'

'Susanna, stay here!'

But there was a ringing in Susanna's ears and she didn't hear Kit's admonition. She ran up the stairs with Kit hard behind her. And stopped in horror. The lock was splintered and the door to her room hung on its hinges, but that was nothing to the devastation inside. She clung to the jamb and had to clamp her hand over her mouth to prevent herself retching.

It was a scene she would never forget. Pages from the book she had been reading had been ripped out and were strewn on the boards. The rest of her books had been flung against the walls. Her mirror was broken, her comb snapped in half and her hairbrush dented. A small vase had been smashed to pieces on the hearth. Her trunk was in open disarray. Clothes had been wrenched from closet and drawers. Her second-best shawl and one good dress lay in savage tatters on the bed, petticoats and underclothes had been likewise shredded. Even her pillow had been stabbed and ripped so that drifting clumps of feathers added to the shocking air of destruction.

'By God, he's a madman!' Breathing hard, Kit spun Susanna against him and pressed his hand forcefully against the back of her head to prevent her viewing the carnage.

His heartbeat was strong and steady. Susanna buried her face in his greatcoat, a silent scream of agony in her mind.

'Tilly,' she heard him call in a surprisingly gentle voice. 'Tilly, the man who did this — did he leave a message? Did he say whether he would be back?'

Susanna heard the girl gulp. 'He said as she'd be sorry, that's all. And that it weren't the end of February yet.'

'And are *you* all right, Tilly? Did he hurt you?'

'No sir. I hid in the broom closet.'

Susanna felt him laugh. 'Very wise. Here,

buy yourself a pretty ribbon as a reward for good sense. Miss Fair is leaving today. If I were you, I would go back to the kitchen and forget you ever opened the door to us.'

'I will, sir. Thank you, sir. Good luck, miss.'

Tilly's footsteps clattered down the stairs, then Mr Kydd's voice came again, still gentle: 'I will take you outside to wait with John Farley whilst I deal with this.'

She took a shuddering breath and pulled herself free of his greatcoat. 'No, it was . . . it was just the shock. I will manage.'

He studied her gravely. 'Sure? Then let us hurry. I do not think it wise to linger.'

Susanna picked up the violated remnant of her green silk dress and had to bite down on a bubble of hysteria. 'Why would I linger? It is not as if I need be careful about creasing things!'

His eyes applauded her bravery even as his hands rapidly swept items off the bed and into the trunk. 'Good girl. Quick, then.'

When they were finished, Susanna subsided, trembling, into a corner of the barouche. Her trunk containing broken toiletries, tattered books and ravaged clothes went on the opposite seat. In her mind's eye she saw again the desecration of her room and could not control the shiver which ran through her.

Mr Kydd swore, took off his greatcoat and wrapped it around her. 'You are ill. I should have made you come out straight away.'

He was blaming himself? Susanna roused herself to stop him doing anything so unjust. 'No, it is only that I am so very cold,' she said. She leant against him with the vague thought that it would make him feel valued. His comprehensive curses were as comforting as the presence of his arm around her shoulders. He was so kind. Thank God he had been with her.

Back in Half Moon Street, Nell Derringer at once called for tea and cake, a hot brick and extra shawls. She insisted Susanna sit next to her by the fire and chafed her hands. 'What a vile man. Were all your things destroyed?'

'Some of the books survived,' said Susanna in a voice which did not seem to belong to her. 'And Mama's writing desk was wrapped in a blanket at the bottom of the trunk. He had not found that.' She shivered again. If only she were not so *cold*.

Mrs Derringer squeezed her hands compassionately. 'Tea is what you need, and here is Tom with it now, so drink up. Our old cook swears there is nothing like it for assuaging the effects of shock. We must have got through a whole crate when Papa died. She and our butler are Tom's parents, you know, and reside now with Mama at Hadleigh. That is not far from London, so whenever we are in town, she sends over great quantities of pies and cakes. This is her plum cake. I promise you it is famous in Northampton-shire. Will you not try a slice?'

Susanna drank the tea thirstily and let Mrs Derringer's comforting flow of words wash over her. At intervals, she could hear Mr Kydd on the other side of the room in angry conversation with Captain Derringer.

' . . . never more turned up in my life! I tell you, Hugo, you could see Warwick's vitriol as clear as if he had written it on the walls!'

' . . . what I have been saying! He is *dangerous*, Kit. If he should get wind of your involvement . . . '

'Damn that! I have not finally got Susanna to safety just to abandon her! We will go to Kydd. He will never trace us if we disappear now.'

'But you are summoned to Lady Penfold! How the deuce do you propose . . . ?'

' . . . go hang! I would not leave a rabid dog to such a sadist!'

The teacup was empty. Mrs Derringer pressed a piece of cake into her hand instead. Almost without knowing what she did, Susanna bit into it.

'Hugo! Kit! Stop arguing and have some tea before it gets quite cold. Should we put off our passage and *all* go to Kydd?'

So kind. They were all so kind. Not like gentry at all. If she hadn't been frozen inside, Susanna would have been overset by their generosity and unconditional helpfulness. She took another bite of the plum cake. It was rich and moist. To her raw nerves and flayed sensibilities, it spoke of recipes handed down through generations, of family retainers, of stability and continuity in an increasingly barren world. A tiny flame of warmth began to lick at the terrible coldness inside her. She ate again and focused on the plate. The Sèvres star design. What had Kit said? *Grandmama was a great frequenter of china warehouses.* Susanna suddenly, passionately, wanted to help these people as much as they were helping her. She took a deep breath and said in a shaky voice, 'I will go with you to your great-aunt if you still wish it.'

She sensed his head turning towards her, felt the concerned scrutiny of his gaze. 'You do not have to. I can find you somewhere safe.'

She raised her eyes. 'Just at the moment, I do not feel I will ever be safe on my own again. I want to do this.'

Nell Derringer reached across to clasp her

hand. 'You will need clothes. I will put you up the necessities for tonight and write a note to Lizzie Olivant who is Tom's sister and the housekeeper at the Court to show you the spare bolts of material and help you make over anything of mine that you need. And I will also write to my friend Emily Belmont that I have had an acquaintance staying with me whom Kit is escorting home, but think it very likely they will break the journey at Kydd so he can see how things go on. Emily will tell her mama-in-law, and old Mrs Belmont will tell the rest of the neighbourhood. So there will be no scandal about a young lady appearing to be staying alone with Kit and you will have time to fashion yourself a wardrobe before you go to Great-aunt Emma.'

In the bustle and confusion of making ready to depart, Susanna had no time to change her mind. All three of her hosts were so rapid and efficient and needed her aid so little that she felt as if she was encased in some sort of icy bubble, able to see and hear and be shunted between them, but without the power to touch or understand any of what was passing.

As they were about to leave, Nell hugged her. 'God speed, Susanna. Kit is dangerous when bored and devil-may-care at the best of times, but you may trust him with your life, I promise you.'

It was only later, sleepless and still emotionally numb in the jolting coach, that Susanna remembered where they were going after Kydd Court. Newmarket. The shock of it slammed into her anew and she bit her lip so hard in the darkness that she tasted blood.

Newmarket. The town her father's family came from. The place he and Mama had met and where Mama had been forbidden ever to return. Newmarket, where the only clue to Susanna's parents' scandalous past might lie.

She had promised, given her word to act this part. It was too late to renege now. All she had wanted to do was help. What if it all turned into a dreadful mistake . . . ?

4

If Susanna had thought things could get no worse, she was proved wrong the moment she stepped out of the travelling carriage onto the sweep of Kydd Court and stared in horrified disbelief at the house.

Kit made an elaborate leg. 'Welcome to Kydd Court. This is what you will be helping us to preserve.'

His bow set up an echo in Susanna's mind, but she was too agitated to pursue it. Gazing across the rolling lawns she said carefully, 'It is very . . . imposing. Are the gardens also as large as this behind the house?'

'Lord, no, this is just for show. At the back they only extend as far as the wood.' Kit waved a hand at a small forest situated halfway to the horizon. 'The Home Farm and most of the estate lies to the south. Don't you like it? The house is generally held to be rather fine.'

Susanna eyed the vast expanse of weathered stonework projecting outwards in at least two wings from the grand porticoed entrance and very probably more. She moistened dry lips. 'Just how big is your estate?'

Kit shrugged. 'Couldn't tell you to the exact acre. I suppose it might be a couple of hundred over three thousand.'

'Three thousand acres!' repeated Susanna, appalled. 'I cannot possibly pretend to be engaged to a man with *three thousand acres*!'

'Might be nearer four.'

Panic was creeping through Susanna's veins. 'This house has been in your family for generations! Lady Penfold grew up here! She will know me at once for a fraud!'

She had taken her bonnet off in the carriage and could feel the pins in her hair slipping. Kit put out a hand to tuck a fly-away strand into place. 'Nonsense,' he said bracingly. 'Just imagine it as Mr Masterson's house on a slightly larger scale.'

'*Slightly* larger?' said Susanna, her voice rising. 'Apart from his dairy farm, Mr Masterson's grounds comprised a neat lawn, a flower walk, a small shrubbery and a kitchen garden!'

Kit's eyes danced. 'Yes, but we almost certainly use less rooms than he did.'

'Your house in Half Moon Street is *modest*,' wailed Susanna, disregarding him. 'It has no right to be lived in by someone who owns three thousand acres of Northampton-shire! Kit, I cannot do this!'

'Of course you can. You are an actress. I

warn you, if you are expecting luxury inside, you are far and away out.' He turned towards the entrance with unimpaired good humour. 'Come, for this week you are simply a friend of my sister's whom I am escorting home. There is no need to pretend anything.'

Susanna followed him, horribly conscious that she was going to fail. The impression wasn't relieved when she stepped through the front door and surveyed the beautiful oak-panelled, immensely large area which awaited her. 'I just know this is called the Great Hall,' she said, cricking her neck to look up the sweeping staircase.

'Only when we want to impress,' Kit assured her. 'Come through to the saloon. I daresay Lizzie Olivant bespoke tea the moment she heard the carriage.' He shot her another mischievous glance. 'Although it will, of course, be quite cold by the time it gets here from the kitchen.'

Susanna felt a little better as they entered the saloon. It might not seem luxurious to Kit, being furnished in the style of some sixty or more years before, but to her it breathed happiness and loving use. A gentleman and a lady beamed down from twin portraits on the near wall as if welcoming her into their home.

'Papa and Mama,' said Kit, seeing the

direction of her gaze. He went to warm his hands at the fire.

Susanna studied the portraits. Kit had inherited his mother's colouring. There was nothing of him in his father's face except perhaps for the directness of his regard and a certain humorous mobility about the mouth. 'He looks to have been a very amiable gentleman,' she said.

'He was the best of men,' replied Kit soberly. 'He brought Nell and me up to be as fearless in our quest for knowledge as in our love of adventure. We were never confined to the nursery or banished from adult company or forced into what the world perceives as conventional behaviour. It was a great sadness that he was taken from us so untimely.'

'At least you knew him,' said Susanna. 'My father died when I was only a few months old. He was with the Militia in Ireland.'

'Which is why your mama became a housekeeper. Yes, I see. Board, a wage and a roof over her infant's head. A very practical solution.'

It was on the tip of Susanna's tongue to correct this favourable construction of the facts, but what he didn't know wouldn't pain him. At least, that was what Mama had always told *her*.

'If you have never known a father, you had

79

best be the niece of one of Papa's correspondents for Great-aunt Emma. Can you turn your employer into an uncle, do you think?'

Susanna gave a bitter laugh. 'Yes, provided I do not have to counterfeit an affection for him. Mr Masterson was not a warm man in any sense. Sixteen years, Mama worked for him, and he left her not a penny in his will.' Her sense of remembered injustice burned. 'His heir was as bad. Shut up the house directly and turned us all out into the street. I believe it was shock as much as the damp which lowered Mama's resilience to the fever.' She glanced up and saw the disgust on Kit's face. 'I beg your pardon. I did not mean to make you uncomfortable.'

'Tosh!' said Kit forcefully. 'You cannot believe your feelings are less to be taken into account than mine!'

Susanna looked at him in surprise. 'It is the way of the world. Gentry do not wish their evening's entertainment ruined due to ill humours amongst the cast. Masters do not like their comfort disturbed by disagreements below stairs.'

Kit's eyes flashed. 'Not in this house! What, should an accident of birth prevent my riding for the surgeon if my footman breaks his leg? Should I insist on a hot dinner with two full courses when my cook is laid up with influenza? God in Heaven, I am not such a monster! How can you think it?'

Susanna stared at this fire-breathing champion of the lower orders that she had inadvertently unleashed. 'I dare not beg your pardon again,' she said. 'I can only say that such sentiments are quite beyond my experience.'

A woman who had to be Tom Olivant's older sister came into the room carrying a tray. 'Nothing enrages Mr Kit near so much as to be accused of being one of the privileged classes,' she observed. 'Welcome to Kydd, miss.'

Then why was he so intent on saving the estate? Susanna was baffled. She glanced up again at his father's portrait, as if to find some clue in that gentleman's face to his son's bewildering thought processes.

'The rest of our forebears are in the Long Gallery,' said Kit gruffly. 'You can view them on the grand tour. And then tomorrow we'll ride over the estate to give you the feel of it.'

Susanna looked at him in dismay. 'But I do not know how to ride. I thought you realized.'

For a moment he seemed genuinely taken aback. 'Oh! Well, likely you'll be wanting to bury yourself in sewing anyway, the quantities of fabric Nell crammed into the carriage.'

Nell. With all her heart, Susanna wished Kit's sister was here now, not en route to Dover and points south.

★　★　★

Candlelight flickered over the panelled walls of the Long Gallery, making wavering shadows. Susanna pulled her shawl closer around her. 'Not the cosiest of apartments,' she murmured.

'You don't mind, do you?' said Kit, moving along the portraits. 'I want to find Lady Penfold's likeness as soon as possible. *Know your mark*, as the sharps say.'

A plain dinner served with the minimum of fuss had done much to restore Susanna's composure. She raised her eyebrows at his knowledge of thieves' cant. 'I never realized the gentry led such interesting lives,' she commented drily, and felt a wriggle of pleasure when Kit grinned.

'Here we are,' he said, holding his branching candlestick closer to one particular canvas. 'A family group. Great-grandpapa, Grandpapa and Augustus behind, and Emma with Great-grandmama in front. Lord, look at that chin. Just like my sister's. Do you think it will serve if I treat Lady Penfold as an older version of Nell?'

Susanna considered the painting. On the surface, a demure brunette in a hooped, rose-pink ball gown sat next to her mother on a gilded seat. It was only when you looked closer that you saw an obstinately lifted chin and eyes which had plainly never been subservient in their life. 'You can try,' she said.

★　★　★

Susanna hadn't liked to make free with Nell's material, but Lizzie Olivant showed her the note which positively exhorted their guest to use up as many remnants as she could find, especially blue ones, for the colour had never become Nell and it was all left over from Mama's wardrobe, so would be wasted else. Accordingly, they fashioned underthings, made over a couple of nightgowns and were deep in the construction of a walking dress in pale blue sarsenet when Tom opened the door to announce, 'Mrs Belmont and the Dowager Mrs Belmont.'

Susanna sprang to her feet, her heart hammering in her chest. She cast a petrified glance at Tom, who jerked his head in the direction of the fields. She hoped that meant he had sent for Kit. Lizzie slipped out in his wake. Susanna watched the housekeeper go as if she was the last boat leaving a deserted island.

The younger of the visitors proffered her hand directly. 'Good morning, Miss Fair. May I introduce myself? I'm Emily Belmont, one of Nell's oldest friends. She wrote saying you might be stopping here on your way home, and as Cook heard from the butcher's boy this morning that Kit was back, nothing would do for Mama-in-law but that we should call. I hope you do not mind.'

'No. No indeed. I am glad to meet any friend of Mrs Derringer.' *Help! What did the gentry talk about between themselves?* 'Do you live at any great distance from here?'

The older woman answered, black button eyes inquisitive. 'Our East Wood borders Kit's spinney. Kydds and Belmonts have been neighbours these half-dozen generations. Now, my dear, it's a poor lookout for you with only that scapegrace Kit in the house and you not knowing anyone in the district, so you must both dine at Belmont House tonight. It will only be a small gathering. Emily's parents, the Graingers, all the normal people. Emily thought it short notice but I said, depend on it, my dear, they will be very well pleased to have some company and we never have stood upon ceremony hereabouts.'

To her huge relief, Susanna heard booted

feet pounding along the passage. Thank goodness — Kit would know how to decline the invitation without offence.

'Mrs Belmont,' said Kit. 'And Emily. Both of you as handsome as ever. How very kind of you to call. You will not mind me in all my dirt?'

'No indeed, so long as you both dine with us tonight. Daresay half the county will know you're home again by now and will be looking for you.'

Kit bowed. 'That sounds splendid. I only regret that I am unable to return your hospitality. I am bidden to Newmarket in a few days to visit Grandpapa's sister, Lady Penfold.'

The dowager's eyes popped pleasurably. The family estrangement was evidently well known. 'You don't go with him, I hope, Miss Fair? Newmarket is not a town for ladies.'

'Mr Kydd is to escort me home first,' said Susanna.

'And where is home, my dear?'

Susanna froze. They had forgotten to invent this detail. 'Norfolk,' she said, rather wildly.

Mrs Belmont's eyebrows rose. 'That is a roundabout journey to be sure.'

'Indeed, it is very good of Mr Kydd to go so far out of his way.'

Tom's entry with refreshments gave Kit a chance to turn the conversation. The ladies departed soon afterwards.

'Off to tell the rest of their acquaintance, no doubt. You do not mind dining out, Susanna? Only I have known them all my life and could not refuse without it looking strange.'

'Mind dining out? With no evening dresses to my name and with families who have been acquainted with you from the cradle and who will of course not dream of catechizing me to see where I fit into your life? Oh, dear me no.'

Kit grinned. 'No matter — you find something of Nell's to wear and I'll look up Norfolk in the almanac. Norfolk, though! Whatever possessed you? I've never even been to Norfolk and I daresay you haven't either.'

'I beg your pardon, I was panicking. It was somewhere distant. And pray how I am to wear something of your sister's that her closest friend will not know instantly to be borrowed?'

'I don't know. Put a fresh ribbon on it or something.' He disappeared, leaving her to go upstairs with a sympathetic Lizzie Olivant.

'The pale green silk is new,' said Lizzie, opening the door to the closet.

Green? Instantly the dress that Rafe Warwick had slashed to tatters leapt to

Susanna's mind. 'No!' she said, rather louder than she intended. She swallowed and added apologetically, 'I beg your pardon, I have no great liking for green.'

'Oh, well, there is a white figured muslin that Miss Nell never liked above half. I doubt she ever wore it in company. Will we try that one?'

Kit, when they assembled for the short drive to Belmont House, was inclined to be indignant. 'Isn't that the gown Nell stigmatized as ugly?'

His housekeeper bristled. 'We did think of the peridot silk first, Mr Kit.'

Kit's eyes met Susanna's. 'No,' he said after an infinitesimal pause. 'Green would never do.'

He had remembered! Susanna felt a tiny shock go through her. 'I preferred something unremarkable,' she said, 'which, you have to admit, this is.'

Kit considered her so judiciously that she began to feel embarrassed. 'I suppose it is exactly the sort of thing a recluse's niece from Norfolk would wear. It becomes you more than it did Nell, that's for sure.'

'Thank you — I think.'

Kit proffered his arm, a gleam in his eye. 'To the lion's den, then?'

Susanna, laying her hand on the sleeve of

his greatcoat, thought he had summed it up very well.

The moment of walking into the saloon and seeing far too many heads turn towards her was quite as dreadful as she'd anticipated. But Emily Belmont took her in tow and, just as she had always done on stage, Susanna found herself sinking into the fabric of her costume to give a reasonable picture of a shy young lady with faintly bluestocking tendencies. After a while the only thing to cut up her peace was the sight of all the young ladies of the district making a dead set at Kit. One in particular, a beautiful girl with a cascade of corn-gold ringlets, was particularly assiduous in seeking his attention.

'It isn't fair,' muttered a sprig of fashion standing near Susanna, resplendent in highly starched shirt points and a startlingly striped waistcoat. 'Charlotte Grainger has hardly looked at me tonight. Just because Kydd is already in possession of the Court and *I'm* only my father's heir.'

But he and his friends were made happy after dinner, for Kit elected to play whist and the golden-haired beauty made such a hash of the round game which Emily had set up that she turned gratefully to whichever of her suitors could instruct her in the simplest language.

'Poor Charlotte,' whispered Emily with a gurgle of laughter in Susanna's ear. 'Seven thousand pounds and no brains at all.'

All very well, but Kydd Court was heavily encumbered and Susanna had never yet heard that men commonly rated intelligence as chief amongst a female's charms.

★ ★ ★

They had brushed through tonight pretty well, mused Kit, looking along the library shelves for something to read. To judge by the evening's performance, Susanna would do very nicely in front of Great-aunt Emma. A couple of times, catching sight of her across the table listening to Mr Caldwell with just the right amount of wide-eyed attention, he had almost forgotten she was an actress, so well had her personality fitted Nell's demure white dress. Except Nell had never in her life looked so convincingly interested in their neighbour's somewhat exaggerated opinions! Susanna seemed to have the knack of making whoever she was talking to feel that their conversation was the most engrossing she had ever heard. It had given him the beginnings of an idea. Ever since that appalling night in the pit, he had been determined Susanna should not return to the stage. When they came back from Newmarket, he would look about for some retired household in which she could be a valued companion. That would keep her safe, warm, fed and useful *and* it would stop her exposing herself to the impertinences of the riff-raff every night.

On the other hand, perhaps her demeanour at dinner had been caused by the costume. Had he not felt the same, donning those cracked shoes and the grey wig? He had bowed his shoulders and adopted a scurrying gait without even realizing he was doing it. It was an intriguing thought, almost enough to persuade him to clothe Susanna in a rich velvet carriage dress and take her driving in Hyde Park to see her play the grande dame. Or make her a present of a lace-trimmed, spider's web peignoir so she could act the — The book he was holding fell to the floor with a thud as he reined his unruly imagination to a halt. Was he mad? Quite apart from the fact that he was not looking for any sort of relationship, her feelings had been violated quite enough by Rafe Warwick. She would need undemanding friendship and a lot of time before she trusted any man again. He had not forgotten that it was his ill-thought offer which had sent her bolting for cover before. He was not going to make the same mistake twice.

Susanna was finding sleep impossible. The evening's events kept running through her head. Disconcerting as it had been to see Kit's popularity with the ladies, what alarmed her more was how much she had enjoyed herself. Never would she have imagined she could sit through a gentry dinner without coming unstuck, but as soon as she had discovered that the best method of avoiding questions was to turn the enquiries on her companions, it had become relatively simple. She had listened in fascination to Mr Caldwell talking about his work as Justice of the Peace for the district. On her other side, she had been amused by the youthful Mr Grainger's account of some private theatricals at a house party he was just returned from. She had made polite noises and all the right responses and had turned from one to the other of them as if she had been doing it all her life. Ned Grainger wanted to start theatricals of his own, he had confided, and was sure they could find a small part for her. Not too many lines, he had added, no doubt with his sister's mental endeavours in mind. When she had said that unfortunately they would be on their way shortly, and he had cried out in dismay that that overset his plans

91

completely because Kit was a *capital* actor, she had quite felt for him.

She tossed restlessly. Getting into the part was all very well, but if she wasn't careful she would be in danger of forgetting her station in life altogether. This was a role, no more. She had been born a housekeeper's daughter and not two weeks ago had been displaying her limbs for all to see on the London stage. She would do well to remember it.

She sighed, turned over, turned back again, and acknowledged the real problem: Kit. The image of him in his well-cut coat of blue superfine, his paler blue embroidered waistcoat and close-fitting cream pantaloons kept appearing in front of her eyes. 'Ridiculous,' she said aloud. He had made it plain he was treating this whole affair as a challenge and her as a fellow conspirator. She was getting things out of proportion because she was grateful to him for rescuing her. To imagine anything else was nonsensical. History was *not* going to repeat itself! She sat up crossly and groped for the water jug. Alas, its lightness revealed the fact that she had forgotten to fill it.

Susanna was immediately possessed of a positively enormous thirst. 'Oh, confound everything,' she muttered, pulling her shawl tightly around her and trying to recall where in this great ramble of stone the kitchen might be found. Thrusting her feet into a pair of much-darned satin slippers, she picked up the jug and slipped out into the dim passage.

There was an oil lamp burning low at the head of the stairs. Susanna descended cautiously, wondering why noise always sounded twenty times as loud at night. She had reached the lowest tread when a sudden thud from a room on one side of the hall halted her. She couldn't remember which room it was, but the door was open a crack, and behind it a light was moving. Mr Caldwell's dinner-table talk of intruders and lawless men at once flooded into her head. She crept across to put her eye to the gap, so intent on moving quietly that she overlooked a small table in the shadows and consequently stubbed her toe quite agonizingly on it. The resultant screech of wood scraping over stone was stupendous. Her heart racing, Susanna whisked sideways to flatten herself against the wall.

She didn't even hear the footsteps. One minute all was darkness, the next there was a dim rectangle of light where the door used to be and a strong male forearm was across her throat, pinning her to the wall. She didn't hesitate. She brought the jug round with a resounding crash on the back of her assailant's head.

'What the devil — !'

'Kit!' Susanna's hands flew to her mouth. 'I thought it was . . . I thought . . . '

The pressure across her throat was abruptly released. 'Susanna? What the deuce?'

He drew her through the open door. The room, she saw with a sinking heart, was the library and Kit was in his shirtsleeves with his neckcloth untied. He had plainly been looking for a book to read in bed. She had never felt so foolish in her life. 'Oh dear, I was thirsty, so I brought my jug down to fill it and then I heard a noise . . . ' She faltered, biting her lip as Kit brushed shards of pottery from his hair.

He glanced at her with wry humour. 'I take it you have been privileged to hear Emily's father's obsession with gangs of lawless house-breakers abroad in the land?'

She nodded unhappily.

'For future reference, breaking a jug over a person's head *isn't* the most effective deterrent against attack.'

'I'll give you the price of it in the morning — Oh!'

Kit had gripped her wrist, anger flaring in his face. 'Don't talk as if you're a servant! I don't charge *anyone* for breakages!'

'No . . . I'm sorry. I . . . ' Susanna could barely think in the face of his bewildering rage.

He dropped her wrist and took a deep breath. 'Forgive me. It is just that that was the sort of thing my uncle would have done. To tell you the truth, I have been wondering if — ' He broke off and picked up his candle and a book which had fallen to the floor. 'Come, you can have some of the water from my jug.'

'Thank you.' She followed him miserably out of the room. What had he been going to say? What was he wondering? If this whole charade was a mistake? If he should send her away and offer for Miss Grainger? A safe seven thousand must be a powerful inducement when set against the mere *possibility* of inheriting Lady Penfold's fortune. She surreptitiously scuffed the largest pieces of pottery against the wall with her slipper and trailed after him.

'Fetch your glass,' he said outside her chamber, and went on further up the passage. Returning with his own jug, he held the candle high so that he could see to pour. The light glimmered through his shirt, outlining the firm edges of his body against the softly draping linen.

'Devil take it!' he said suddenly.

Susanna jumped and glanced where he was looking. A faint discoloration encircled the slender bones of her wrist. She quickly pulled at the sleeve of her nightgown to cover it. 'I told you, I bruise easily,' she said. 'Pray do not concern yourself. It will be gone as soon.'

His eyes were stony. 'I should have had more control.' He put the jug on a side table and tilted her chin so that the light from his candle fell on her throat. She felt her night-time braid slither backwards over her shoulder. 'Here too,' he said, his fingertips tracing delicate eddies over her skin. 'Does it hurt?'

Hurt? It felt like lines of fire where he was touching her. Fire and danger and unbearable desire. 'No,' she whispered, swallowing convulsively. Her mother's warnings drummed in her head. 'Pardon me, I should be retiring. Thank you for the water.'

For an aeon more his fingers lingered. Susanna felt the pulse in her throat leap to meet them, knowing her breathing was becoming ragged. What would she do if his hand drifted lower, over her shawl, over the cotton nightgown beneath? Her legs trembled. The water in her glass shook. Did she want — or fear — his touch?

Suddenly his fingers were gone, only the memory of their warmth left on her skin.

'You're cold,' he said. 'I hope this adventure may not give you night terrors. Goodnight.'

'Goodnight,' she echoed. She watched him stride down the passage. Then she shut the door behind her, put the water down untasted, scrambled into bed and curled herself around her beating heart as tightly as if Rafe Warwick himself were after her.

5

It was as much as Susanna could do to face Kit with any sort of equanimity the next morning. He however, inquiring how she had slept, with a bland glance at her high-necked, long-sleeved spencer, seemed to experience no such difficulty.

'I am afraid,' she said with distinctly ruffled feelings, 'that I missed my footing on the stairs and broke one of your water jugs.'

He waved a generous hand. 'No matter. By the by, I forgot to say yesterday — do feel free to investigate the library should you be in need of reading matter. It is the second door on the left from the staircase.'

Susanna ground her teeth. 'You are too kind. At what time should I be ready for church this morning?'

'Oh, another hour will be ample. You will not mind if we take Lizzie and Tom up with us? It seems silly not to when the coach will hold four.'

'Kit, it is a luxury for me to travel by coach at all!'

The church was a large one and well endowed, which Susanna supposed accounted for many of the families she had met last night being present. After waiting in vain for Kit to distinguish her daughter, Mrs Grainger sailed up after the service in order to invite them both to a dinner she was holding on the ensuing Wednesday. She apologized profusely for not having sent a card, excusing this lapse on the grounds that she had had no idea Kit was back in Northamptonshire until the previous evening. Dinner at the Graingers, Susanna knew instinctively, would be *grand*. She willed Kit to say no, but infuriatingly heard him accept with every appearance of pleasure.

'Now I'll need another gown,' she said once they were in the carriage.

'You have been making gowns! You will need several anyway for the visit to Great-aunt Emma.'

'But this will have to be a superior one,' she pointed out. 'Unless you are telling me the Graingers do not stand on ceremony?'

Lizzie Olivant chuckled. 'That they do. The only thing Mrs Grainger would like better than Miss Charlotte calling the biggest estate hereabouts her own would be a title. Daresay she wouldn't be so busy over Mr Kit if she knew the true state of the coffers, eh?'

Susanna's heart thudded. Another pitfall no one had told her about. Thank goodness she had not mentioned anything at Belmont

House. 'Is it a secret, then? Does nobody know?'

Kit stared at her. 'Are you serious? Folk hereabouts are aware my uncle was mishandling the estate, but not to what extent he defrauded it. If it became general knowledge that he had taken out mortgages on the land and left us with no means of repaying them, we would be dunned by every creditor in the county and should never be able to restock our fields.'

Susanna saw now why he wanted the security of knowing that there was money coming to him. She couldn't help feeling uneasy, however, at his being considered such a fine catch. If Mrs Grainger's view was the prevailing one, Lady Penfold would never believe he had offered for a nobody like *her*.

The drive back from church was prolonged by their slowing to exchange greetings with homeward-bound estate workers and their Sunday-garbed families. At one point they stopped altogether in order for Kit and Tom to assist in freeing the back wheel of a crowded cart from a ditch at one side of the lane. To Susanna's astonishment, Lizzie made not the slightest demur at either of the men getting their good clothes dirtied. It seemed to be taken for granted that the owner of the estate worked as hard as his tenants.

'We'll have to get on and fill in these ruts now the worst of the winter is behind us, Bill,' Kit said to the man who had been driving the cart. 'If you and Old John will step up to the estate office tomorrow morning, we'll sort out priorities.'

Susanna leant back against the swabs, trying not to let her troubled reflections show in her face as the carriage resumed its uneven progress. She was beginning to think Kit really was different from the normal run of gentry, in which case she might do him a powerful disservice by going to Newmarket. Somehow she was going to have to find the words to tell him the truth.

★ ★ ★

Kit, however, was busy about the estate and Susanna herself sewing at her replacement wardrobe every spare minute. By mid afternoon on Tuesday, Lizzie Olivant was moved to suggest that she take a turn in the grounds for half an hour.

Susanna rubbed aching eyes and agreed it might be a good idea. She swapped indoor slippers for boots and tied on a bonnet against the wind. Wrapping her cloak around her, she avoided the intimidating front lawns and instead skirted the stables to go towards the shrubbery. Snowdrops and early aconites coloured the ground white and yellow; already some of the bushes were showing touches of green. She wondered how these grounds would look in summer and was briefly nostalgic for Mr Masterson's neat garden. She might have been only a maid, but the Cheltenham house had been her home all her childhood. There she had learnt to make bread and dress meat under Cook's stern eye. There she had polished silver and burnished tables to the butler's exacting standards. There she had discovered beautiful, delicate porcelain, and there her mother had taught her to read and cipher and instilled in her a love of literature. Susanna wandered on, caught by her memories, and hardly knew where she was when a voice calling her name jerked her out of them.

'I said,' repeated Kit from the back of an enormous black stallion, 'would you care to see the rest of the estate?'

Susanna looked up, her heart skipping a beat. He had evidently been working with the men all day, for he was bare headed and exuded the sort of healthy glow conferred by strenuous exertion. In Susanna's eyes, this served to make him look quite staggeringly virile. 'I don't ride,' she reminded him. She hoped she sounded calmer than she felt.

He grinned and walked the horse over to a tree stump. 'I won't tell Valiant, if you won't. Come — I'll pull you up in front of me. You'll be quite safe.'

Susanna baulked. 'Both our reputations will be in tatters should anyone see us.'

'In my own grounds? Your scruples are by far too nice. And what the devil could I do to you on a horse, anyway?'

'I hardly dare think!' But the wind was ruffling his hair, and his eyes were tempting her. Susanna climbed cautiously onto the stump.

Kit leaned down and put an arm around her waist. 'Jump,' he said and a second later she found herself flying upwards to land with a rather closer contact than she had expected against his chest. Her heart banged wildly at the proximity of his hard body, at the solidity of his arms around her, at his dancing eyes so near to hers.

'There, easy,' he said in complacent tones, slackening his hold in order to nudge Valiant to a walk.

'There are advantages in keeping limber for the stage,' said Susanna in a light manner she was far from feeling. She wriggled forward, desperate to put some space between them. Dear heaven, she must have been mad to agree to this. Her muscles were turning to water already. She must keep talking. 'Though suppleness is not a prerequisite in most variety theatres,' she went on. 'Lack of modesty is far more important. Kit, Ned Grainger's account of the plays he has seen gave me to think. What if any of your acquaintance have lately been in London and recognize me? It would cause a scandal. Some of the costumes I used to wear were revealing to say the least.'

For an instant he tensed but, 'People don't notice what they don't expect,' he said with a shrug, 'and no one would expect to find a Sans Pareil actress at a Northamptonshire dinner party.'

Would *he* not have recognized her, then? With his arms still loosely around her, she didn't quite dare ask. 'Where are you taking me?' she said instead.

'To the ridge above the house. It is a favourite vantage point of mine. Are you quite comfortable? You seem a little awkward there.'

Susanna was hard pressed not to point out that being jolted up and down on an uncomfortable swell of saddle and trying not to slide backwards against a pair of disturbingly muscular thighs was enough to make anyone awkward! 'I daresay I will become used to the motion soon,' she said repressively.

He gave a crack of laughter. 'If Nell has left one of her habits here, I could teach you to ride. You will find it much easier as soon as you surrender to the rhythm of the horse's stride.'

Susanna gritted her teeth. Words like 'surrender' and 'rhythm' sounded distinctly provocative, given her current position. 'Where are we in relation to the church?' she said, changing the subject.

He pointed south-west. 'The village is over there. And that is Home Farm, where the Coppings whom we rescued on Sunday live. There have been Coppings and Farleys at Kydd for generations.' His voice changed abruptly. 'When I left for India, all these cottages were full. Now three out of four stand empty.'

Susanna looked downwards to where the lane wound a meandering course between neat fields towards the main road. The estate seemed more manageable from this height. Until, that is, you focused on the Court, which you *knew* was a great rambling pile, and found it looking like a tumble of children's building blocks. She became aware that Kit had reined Valiant to a halt.

'It's odd,' he said, gazing over his demesne. 'When I was growing up, I hardly thought about what the estate meant to me. The only time I missed it at school was when I had a craving for Cook's plum cake or wanted to play truant for a morning and go fishing in the stream. And after I left Oxford I was happy enough to ride around with the bailiff learning land management and playing with the idea of breeding horses, but I'd still spend the Season in London without thinking twice about what was going on here. Even when I sailed for Bombay to sort out Cousin Augustus's affairs, I don't believe Kydd occupied my mind for more than five minutes together. Yet as soon as the letter reached me telling of my father's death, it was this view that rose up in my eyes and made me sick at heart that I was so far away. Because it is *not* the number of acres and the crops and the rents an estate brings in which are important. It is not the building either, even if the foundations were laid in Queen Elizabeth's time. It is the land itself that matters — the care of it, the husbandry. It is the people to whom we owe a duty — the Coppings, the Farleys, and the others who have been throwing in their lot with ours since the day the first Kydd built himself a three-roomed croft with a field of corn to one side and a couple of sheep to the other. *That* is what is crucial — and that is why I will do anything I must to save it now!'

His hands had tightened on the reins, his voice was intense, his eyes burnt with a deep and abiding fervour. He was, Susanna realized in awe, almost completely unaware of her. She leant back against his chest, too humbled to do anything except show by compassionate contact how honoured she was that he trusted her enough to speak his innermost thoughts aloud. For perhaps half a minute his heartbeat resonated through her body, filling her with an echo of his purpose. Then, nudging Valiant to a walk, he took them back to the Court.

★ ★ ★

Kit waved Johnny away and rubbed Valiant down himself, finding a measure of surcease in physical labour. What the devil was happening to him? *Never* had he given himself away so completely before! After the abysmal way he'd lost his temper the other night, he had thought it best to steer clear of Susanna as far as possible. To give her time to fashion her wardrobe and accustom herself to country routines. To plunge himself into filling in ruts and lending his weight with the ploughing — reminding himself of why he needed the promise of Great-aunt Emma's money.

If truth were told, he had been dreading Nell and Hugo's departure for Vienna. Kit might not want to settle down, but he was not cut out for a solitary life. It pained him beyond measure that his uncle's destructive policy had left so few of the estate workers at Kydd, and not just because the work was harder with less hands to help. He liked to have people around him. He liked the comfort of knowing John Farley was in the stables should he stroll down there. He liked Tom and Lizzie Olivant in charge of the Court.

But in the evenings, he had discovered, it was nice to have Susanna's company. They invented her a history, with names and dates and places. He told her about his journey to India. They argued about poems and plays. Today, going past the morning-room window, he had seen her at the table, sewing material the colour of the spring sky. The sun had glinted off her red-gold hair and she had evidently just said something to make Lizzie laugh. She'd looked happy, at one with her surroundings. Kit had felt his spirits lift.

And then this afternoon he had ridden up from the fields, pleasantly tired and thinking of nothing more than a warm tub and a tankard of ale, and she'd been walking ankle deep in the spring flowers with her thoughts far away. She'd looked so right, so at home, a million miles away from the gamine dancer she'd projected on stage. He had stopped on impulse and offered to show her the estate.

Her pluck in mounting Valiant had not surprised him. Her nervousness at their being in close proximity was only to be expected, but his teasing seemed to alleviate her fears. What he hadn't bargained for was the effect that her sitting on his saddle-bow would have on himself. He'd remembered all over again how she'd felt in his arms that first night. For a mad moment he'd wanted to hold her more tightly, to have her nestle against his chest again. To cover his lapse, he'd found himself blurting out his deepest feelings about Kydd like some blundering schoolboy.

She hadn't laughed. She'd slid softly backwards and leant against him of her own accord. The wonder of that moment had stilled him. He'd ridden back to the Court as if he carried the treasures of Christendom on Valiant's back.

Wednesday evening arrived long before Susanna was ready for it. She looked in the cheval glass and saw a stranger dressed in an ivory satin gown with a cerulean-blue silk over-robe, a pearl clip lent by Nell nestling amongst her red-gold curls. 'I cannot do this,' she whispered, feeling the familiar panic rising up in her breast.

'Nonsense,' said Kit, helping her into a warm, blue velvet evening cloak. 'Simply be the sweet girl you were at Belmont House and you will have nothing to worry about. May I compliment you on your costume? It suits you. You will dazzle everyone.'

Susanna blushed fierily. Kit had once more made the transition from farmer to buck, and was fairly dazzling himself. His flaxen locks shone in a careless Corinthian cut, his blue coat fitted him to perfection and his ivory pantaloons displayed his legs to such advantage that she had almost missed a step when first she saw them. 'Thank you. Are you sure your mother won't mind my borrowing her cloak?'

'Mama would never begrudge anyone anything. And although we have persuaded her out of black, neither Nell nor I feel she will ever stop mourning Papa. It is doubtful she will wear this again.'

'She must have loved him very much.'

'He was the lodestone of her life. I am glad he never knew the anguish it caused her when he died.'

'Better that than a loveless marriage.'

'So I was used to think. Now I am not so sure.'

Did he mean that he would prefer *not* to

wed for love? That he would settle for esteem and mild affection in his marriage partner? Then why had he shied away from commitment before? A strange pain gnawed at Susanna's chest. Improvident as it might be, she knew she wanted the ecstasy of loving and being loved, even at the risk of devastation should life turn unkind.

★   ★   ★

True to her prediction, the Graingers' dinner turned out to be far grander than the meal at Belmont House. There were twice as many leaves in the table and such an immense array of dishes laid on it that Susanna's eyes nearly popped out of her head. She was more thankful than she could say to find that she was judged of such low status that she was placed well down the table between Emily's brother and Colonel MacGregor, an elderly uncle of Mrs Grainger, whom, to judge by that lady's occasional sharp glance in their direction, she did not trust further than she could throw.

Emily's brother, realized Susanna with a sinking heart, was the lovelorn sprig who had been incensed by Charlotte Grainger's defection at Belmont House, and as her mama's thoughtfulness had caused Charlotte to be placed next to Kit today, Susanna foresaw a very difficult dinner conversation. But a small effort on her part diverted him to a description of his latest hunter, and he turned quite happily after a while to his other neighbour, who fortunately also followed the hounds, in order to reminisce about the winter's sport.

'Nicely done,' said the colonel, a twinkle in his elderly eyes. 'And what subject do you propose *I* should bore you with, eh?'

For an awful moment, Susanna wondered if he had seen through her. *Courage, Susanna.* 'Chess, sir?' she said, hoping against hope that she was taking the right line. 'Your old campaigns?'

'Ha!' The white moustache twitched. 'Battles ain't suitable talk for young ladies, Miss Fair. And I fancy it is young Kydd with whom I should be arguing chess tactics.'

Good. She had judged him aright. 'He is teaching me the game, sir. It would be immensely useful if I had a ploy in hand that he wasn't expecting.'

The moustache twitched again. 'No, no, none of that flummery. Kind of you to do the pretty, but I'm not the sort of old fool who needs flattery all day long to keep me sweet.' He shot a glance down the table. 'Not that my niece has ever grasped that. D'you see the addlepate she's put on my other side? Still, credit where it's due. Mary's got big fish to fry tonight one way or another and she ain't stinting.'

Susanna began to feel some sympathy with Mrs Grainger's attitude towards her outspoken uncle. 'It is certainly a very handsome spread,' she said hastily. 'I am sure I have never tasted half of these dishes before. I'm afraid I shall have to rely on you for guidance, whether you think it a bore or not. What is that in front of you?'

Colonel MacGregor helped her to a small portion. 'Fricassee of calves' livers in some damned Frenchified sauce. I tell you, Miss Fair, my niece pays her chef a fortune but can he do a plain coddled egg as I like it? No he cannot!'

Susanna fought to keep her face straight. 'At least we may admire the porcelain, even if we deprecate its contents. Do you happen to know the pattern of this one or must I shame myself by overturning it in order to examine the mark?'

The Colonel's shout of laughter caused heads to turn. 'Ha! That's even neater than your dealing with young Lochinvar there!' he exclaimed with undisguised approval. 'Chess indeed! Now, who told you I had a passion for china, eh?'

Susanna could almost feel her hostess's eyes boring into her. She flushed with embarrassment. 'No one, sir, upon my honour. My em — uncle has a small collection and has passed on his interest to me.'

'He has, has he? And what is the pride of it, eh?'

Susanna thought back frantically. 'There is a Meissen tureen which we are never allowed to use. And a pierced Worcester bon-bon dish which is so pretty one can quite forgive it being totally impractical. Spode is what we generally eat off.'

Reassured by this intelligence that he wasn't being gammoned, the Colonel informed her that the calves' liver dish was from his niece's Sèvres set. 'Always comes out when she wants to impress.' His eye roved the table and alighted on some plump quails. 'Ha! And what's this one, eh?' he said, cutting a generous portion.

Susanna visualized the catalogues over which Mr Masterson used to pore. 'I think it must be Worcester,' she said cautiously. 'The fabulous bird would seem to indicate it.'

'Chelsea,' boomed the Colonel, evidently enjoying himself. 'When the factory closed, the best painters went to Worcester. What about this sauceboat then?'

Susanna suffered an orange sauce to be

poured over her quail and wished her dinner companion was not quite so exuberant. 'The cream ground can only be Queensware, surely?'

By the time Mrs Grainger signalled the ladies to rise, Susanna had eaten twice as much as was her wont, their section of the table was in disarray and she and Colonel MacGregor were fast friends. The relief at getting through the dinner unscathed was almost enough to fortify her against the sight of Charlotte's beautiful face fixed admiringly on Kit, and his head inclined with courteous attention towards those shining ringlets.

'Here,' said Colonel MacGregor suddenly. 'Get them to show you the porcelain room at Kydd Court. You'll appreciate that.'

'I will, sir,' said Susanna with a smile. 'Mr Kydd mentioned his grandmama used to frequent china warehouses.'

The Colonel gave another roar of laughter. 'Georgiana? Haunted 'em, more like,' he said, and shook his head in reminiscence. 'Knew her before she was married. Wonderful woman.' Which few words left Susanna with a most unfair curiosity to find out more about Kit's paternal grandmother and no means at all of gratifying it.

★　★　★

Kit was having a trying evening. He had Charlotte Grainger chattering inanities on one side and a starched-up matron on the other, spouting on about the duty a person has to one's class and one's family. It seemed to him that he had been experiencing matchmaking dinners like this ever since he left Eton. It was precisely these sort of occasions which had spurred him into taking off for India a couple of years previously. He should have known better than to expect anything to have changed in the meanwhile.

There was a booming laugh from further down the table. Kit set his jaw and told himself for the twentieth time that he was *glad* Susanna was acquitting herself so well. Very early on, Peter Caldwell had stopped sending him dagger glances and was now conversing quite animatedly with the Master of the Hunt's niece. Colonel MacGregor appeared equally charmed by Susanna's company. Kit supposed he couldn't fault either of them. Her red-gold curls seemed designed for candlelight and the blue of her dress enhanced the intelligent depths in her grey eyes. She looked as though she had graced tables like this for ever. The Colonel laughed again. Deuce take it, Susanna need not be doing quite such a thorough job. She'd have the old fool making her an offer if she wasn't careful. At Kit's side, Charlotte was asking him something, her lovely eyes wide. Lizzie Olivant's words in the carriage came back to him. Down the table, Colonel MacGregor was putting more food on Susanna's plate. Kit's gut roiled.

★   ★   ★

With a marriageable daughter to dispose of and a second to come out next year, Mrs Grainger had no intention of letting prospective bridegrooms waste the evening at card tables. As soon as the gentlemen joined the ladies in the saloon, Charlotte and her sister sang a couple of sweet, untaxing airs, then a carefully selected plain young lady played a sonata by way of contrast and finally an impromptu hop was mooted. The Graingers' governess seated herself at the pianoforte whilst the younger gentlemen sprang forward to move furniture and roll back the carpet. Susanna was fascinated. Mama had told her such things were commonly done in the gentry's country houses, but this was the first time she had seen it for herself.

'Do you care to join in, Miss Fair?'

She looked up in some confusion. She hadn't noticed Kit come over to her shadowy corner. 'Yes . . . that is . . . ' She stopped, inappropriate joy filling her heart. 'Thank you. I should like that very much.'

'I wasn't sure if you knew the standard country measures,' he said in an undertone as he walked her to her place. 'I thought if *I* asked first, it would save you the embarrassment of telling one of the other gentlemen you did not dance.'

Quite a lot of Susanna's pleasure abruptly subsided. 'Oh. How thoughtful of you. But Mama took care to school me in the steps from an early age so you have offended our hostess for nothing. I am persuaded she expected you to lead Miss Grainger out.'

'I have been attending to Charlotte throughout what can only be described as a frankly overlong dinner. No man can reasonably be expected to do more.'

Susanna felt a treacherous glow at this statement, and was further relieved to find the dancing not of such high standard that her initial awkwardness showed. All in all, she reflected as they drove home, she had managed tolerably well, though her assurance leached away the longer Kit remained silent.

She was about to go upstairs when he laid a detaining hand on her arm. 'You do not have to be engaged to me for Lady Penfold's benefit,' he said abruptly.

118

Susanna felt her stomach drop away. There *had* been something missing in her air, some innate quality that could only be got by breeding not imitation, and seeing her amongst the company tonight Kit did not think she could carry the deception through. For a moment she had to bite her lip hard to keep the disappointment in. 'Very well, if you do not wish it,' she said quietly.

He fidgeted with the card tray on the side-table. 'Talk gets back,' he said, not meeting her eyes. 'I am persuaded it will be more comfortable for you to stay here.'

Susanna frowned. 'I am to stay?'

'Well, naturally!' said Kit impatiently. 'You cannot return to London with that devil Warwick on the lookout for you!'

Talk gets back ... *I will do anything I must to save Kydd.*

Disillusionment rose in Susanna's throat. He did not want any breath of a false engagement in Newmarket to reach Northamptonshire and cloud his chances of a match with Miss Grainger. 'Colonel MacGregor mentioned a porcelain room,' she said, suddenly wanting something beautiful to distract her. 'Is it too late to show me tonight?'

Kit didn't look surprised by the change in subject. 'Not at all,' he said, picking up a branched candlestick. 'It is off the Long Gallery.' He squared his shoulders and cleared his throat. 'You seemed to get on very well with the Colonel.'

Wasn't she supposed to have done? She glanced at Kit's set profile and reddened neck in confusion. 'I found him interesting.'

'He certainly appeared to admire you. You are to be congratulated. It is not everyone who can amuse a notoriously particular gentleman to such an extent that his laughter is heard at the other end of the table.'

Had she drawn attention to herself? Was that where the trouble lay? 'I did not realize our conversation was so loud. Next time perhaps you should arrange for me to be seated by a quieter dinner partner.'

He cast an irate look at her. 'I was felicitating you. Colonel MacGregor has a snug manor and a good pension, in addition to being intimate with a number of influential personages.'

Susanna stopped dead, unable to believe her ears. 'He is also seventy if he's a day! How *dare* you insinuate that I made myself agreeable in order to engage his affections! As well say I had ulterior designs in turning Peter Caldwell's thoughts to a less lachrymose direction or that I let Ned Grainger trample over my toes to persuade him into making me an offer! I was a *guest*! I do not forget my part!'

Kit gave a short laugh. 'I beg your pardon. No doubt the motives of everybody else there tonight jaundiced me. You play the ingénue extremely well.'

'That was what I was supposed to do!' They had reached the Long Gallery. Susanna stalked behind Kit, digesting his words. Could he really have been releasing her from their pact in order that *she* might make a match? 'You are all about in your head!' she said with disbelief. 'How were you planning to disguise my history when the Colonel enquired my uncle's name and direction that he might ask permission to address me?'

'A lot MacGregor would care for that if even half the tales I've heard of him are true.' Kit turned, looking at her with an odd expression. 'It would give you a safe home, Susanna. He was excessively taken with you.'

'Because I did not toad-eat him! If you must know, we were playing a game.'

'A game?'

She coloured. 'Identifying tableware. Not very respectful, but a great deal better than whispering platitudes in someone's ear simply because they are rich. That is why he told me I must see the porcelain here.'

'A game,' Kit repeated blankly, opening a

panelled door and gesturing her inside. 'Susanna, you — '

But the rest of his sentence was lost. All around her in the candlelight was the soft sheen of porcelain. Her dazzled eyes took in Sèvres, Worcester . . .

'Kakeimon,' she breathed, putting out her hand to stroke a delicate Japanese plate whose single asymmetric flower caught at her with its fragile beauty. In dim recesses she saw Dresden figurines, Chelsea groups . . . 'Oh, Kit,' she said, taking the candlestick from him as if in a dream, 'I could *live* in this room!'

As she moved around, awed, she heard him say, 'There used to be more. My uncle sold a lot of it. Enjoy this whilst you can.'

Sold? Shock quivered in her soul. But she herself had parted with a jasperware jug in order to buy medicines for Mama, and on a table directly in front of her was a Meissen service which would likely pay the estate wages for a two full quarters. She glanced back at Kit. He stood just inside the doorway, his face shadowed, his whole bearing ineffably strained as he surveyed the remains of the collection. She could not bear it. She forgave him his odd humours, forgave him their spat. At that moment she would have done almost anything to wipe the care from

122

his face. 'Kit, please forget this nonsense. If you still wish me to, I *will* come to Newmarket as your betrothed.'

He crossed the room slowly, cupped her face in his hands and looked at her for a long moment. 'I shouldn't let you,' he said, 'but thank you.' And kissed her light as thistle-down on the lips.

Susanna's heart stopped. The sensation which swept through her was like nothing she had ever experienced before. Hardly knowing what she was doing, she brushed a flaxen wing of hair away from his eyes. It drifted through her fingers, as fine as her own. She felt his breath warm on her cheek.

Then suddenly he was taking the candle-stick from her and leading the way back up the gallery. 'Grandmama,' he said, indicating one of the canvases. 'Lady Georgiana Kydd. The one who started the collection.'

Susanna glanced unseeingly at the painting of a dark-haired beauty with reckless blue eyes wearing a flaunting scarlet dress. She felt as if she had run from one side of the Kydd estate to the other and had the stitch in her side and a hammering pulse to prove it. Light and valedictory and utterly meaningless as that kiss had been, nevertheless, in the space of a single heartbeat, her world had been turned upside down.

It was no longer a question of whether she could act to Lady Penfold's satisfaction as if she was in love with her great-nephew. Far more difficult now would be the task of pretending to Kit himself that she wasn't.

6

The weather was propitious for their journey, even if the rutted and ill-maintained roads left much to be desired. Accustomed to the bumping and jolting of the Chartwell Players' wagons, Susanna came to the amused conclusion that she felt the discomfort far less than either her maid or Kit's valet.

'Whoa, there!' The horses came to a halt and she heard Kit's voice calling from alongside. 'Look! Isn't Newmarket the prettiest prospect? Think so every time I come!' He sprang down from the curricle and opened the carriage door.

Emerging, Susanna at once saw what he meant. All around lay the wild, empty expanse of Newmarket Heath, but in front the road fell away to reveal the elegant main street of a market town nestled snugly between one rise and the next.

'I believe you'll like it,' said Kit. 'I never knew such a town with so many things going on for its size. Why, there must be upwards of a dozen places where you can get a decent chop and a good bottle of claret.'

John Farley snorted. 'And a couple of score

more where you take your life in your hands asking for a tankard of ale, Mr Kit! Miss Susanna won't be going to any of them. Nor the mills or the cock-fighting.'

Susanna smiled. 'Mrs Belmont did say it was not a town for ladies.'

'Not when the race meetings are on,' conceded Kit. 'It is all horses, horses, horses. But I daresay it is much like any other place for the rest of the time.' He pointed. 'You cannot tell it from here but the road divides the town. The right-hand side has the larger properties: Crockford, Queensbury and so on keep houses here. Further along on the left is the warren where Johnny's doubtful taverns are situated, but there are a good many ordinary, solid villas to be found too.'

An odd tightness constricted Susanna's chest as she gazed down at the street with its carts, phaetons and carriages. She had been so busy keeping Kit at a distance in case some hint of her feelings for him escaped, that she had managed to push this moment to the back of her mind. But now she was actually in Newmarket, about to descend into the town itself, and *still* she hadn't told him about her past. Sentences surfaced and fell apart in her head.

'Worried?' said Kit, standing close at her shoulder.

'A little.' She was glad the brim of the bonnet shielded her face. 'Where is Lady Penfold's residence?' Oh, what a coward she was!

'At the far end of the town, on the road towards Cheveley. To think of the number of times I have come here and not known! I could have insinuated myself into her affections years ago! I wonder Papa did not give me her direction.'

'Perhaps she did not want the quarrel mended. She must have been deeply hurt by your great-grandfather cutting her out of the family.'

Kit's countenance darkened. 'He was far from amiable, by all accounts. It was he who forced Grandpapa and Papa to continue with the entail by threatening to cut off their allowances. Small wonder Great-aunt Emma did not desire a reconciliation with a man who would turn off his own flesh and blood out of pure spite. Thank God not all families are so brutal.' ·

Susanna smoothed her pelisse with unsteady fingers. 'Kit — '

'Lord, I nearly forgot.' Kit slid a hand inside his greatcoat and produced a small pouch. 'You ought to have a betrothal gift to make it look right and tight. This is the ring my grandfather gave Grandmama. She was wearing it in that painting if you remember.'

Susanna lifted her eyes to his in shock, quite forgetting what she had been about to say. 'I cannot possibly borrow such a thing! It is your family's property!'

'Which is why it will convince Great-aunt Emma. I *think* she will recognize it for she did not elope until after Grandpapa married.' He grinned, his open countenance not evincing any delicacy about the subject.

'But, Kit, this ring should surely belong to Nell.'

'Never wears blue. And it's only for a fortnight, after all.' Kit took Susanna's hand in his own, peeled off her glove and slid a delicate gold ring embellished with tiny chips of sapphire onto one finger.

The intimate yet impersonal action nearly overset her. A lump formed in her throat as she stared through swimming eyes at the pinpricks of blue fire. 'It's beautiful,' she whispered. 'I will take great care of it, I promise.'

Her hand still lay in his. He gave an odd smile as he let it go. 'You'll have to. I can't afford another one. Ready for the last leg now?'

Susanna felt the pressure of his fingers across the sapphire ring and knew another moment of panic. It wasn't fair to keep him in the dark. She should never have left it this long. She opened her mouth to entreat him to wait a moment more, but he was already handing her in and then vaulting to the seat of the curricle. Biting her lip, she sank back in her corner and let the carriage carry her forward.

★   ★   ★

Not bad, thought Kit with relief. Not bad at all. He'd managed not to be alone with Susanna since damn near ruining everything in the porcelain room, and he hoped he had been offhand enough whenever they did meet to enable them to resume their previous companionable footing. He still couldn't believe he had given in to the impulse to kiss her like that! It was no excuse to say he'd been out of sorts and rubbed raw by all the unsubtle flattery he'd received during the evening, no excuse to say that he'd been ashamed of the rush of pleasure he'd got when she'd been so scathing about his offer to smooth her path with Colonel MacGregor.

His hands faltered on the reins as he remembered the softness of her lips, the way her eyes had been so startled, yet so trusting. It had been as much as he could do to haul himself back from some very unacceptable behaviour indeed. He was supposed to be protecting her. They were to be partners in this charade to come. She was worth more than to be taken as a casual mistress just because she looked so beautiful by candle-light and because he'd had a difficult day.

Yes, it was much easier to go into this as friends. He'd got Lady Georgiana's ring onto her finger in an entirely businesslike manner and all he had to do for the next two weeks was to play the fond lover in front of Great-aunt Emma, which with Susanna's acting abilities to help shouldn't be a problem at all. And *then* he would get her tucked safely out of Warwick's and temptation's way as a lady's companion in time for him to make the most of the summer weather repairing the Kydd estate.

* * *

Lady Penfold's house was easily found: a square, modern building fronting the road with a neat pleasure garden behind next to a large stable block. The front door was opened by an elderly butler who announced that Madam was in the Yellow Saloon with Mrs Martha Penfold.

Susanna had been thinking of Lady Penfold in terms of the painting in the Long

Gallery. One startled glance, however, told her that the intervening half-century had wrought a number of changes in that youthful damsel. The dark hair, for example, was now snowy white and confined under an impressive lace cap, and if the determined chin still lingered, it was camouflaged by half a dozen others wobbling below it. But it was the sylph-like waist which was the most thoroughly gone. Lady Penfold had evidently embraced the fashionable discarding of stays with as much fervour as the demi-monde, though with rather less happy results. Even without the quantities of shawls wrapped about her kerseymere gown, she had to be the stoutest person Susanna had ever seen, quite eclipsing the faded, middle-aged lady next to her, industriously knitting what seemed to be a sock.

Kit recovered first. He gave a deep bow and said, 'Lady Penfold, it is most kind of you to invite us to your home. May I present Miss Fair?'

Lady Penfold subjected Kit to a penetrating stare. 'So you'll be Christopher. Hrmph. Georgiana's eyes, I see, but you didn't get the rest of your looks from the Kydds.'

Kit inclined his head. 'I am said to resemble my mother, ma'am. It is my sister Nell who has inherited the family colouring.'

Lady Penfold's gaze travelled on to Susanna . . . assessed her travelling costume . . . and hardened. 'That looks uncommonly like the betrothal ring Jonathan gave Georgiana.'

Kit turned and smiled into Susanna's eyes with so much warmth that her heart gave a startled leap and her legs nearly buckled under her. 'It is indeed. As soon as Miss Fair did me the honour of agreeing to become my wife, I knew no other ring would do.'

Susanna wrung her gloves in agitation and prayed that her blush would be taken for modesty. Many more looks like that one and she would give herself away. She hadn't realized Kit could act so well.

Lady Penfold was frowning. 'Not puffed off in the papers. Always read them, don't we, Martha?'

'Yes, indeed,' said Martha Penfold in a colourless voice. '*The Times* and the *Gazette*. We never miss.'

Kit gave a deprecating smile. 'Miss Fair's uncle prefers that I prove my attachment is sincere before we make any announcement.'

Lady Penfold looked suspicious. 'Why? Kydd of Kydd Court? It's a good match for any girl. Don't he trust you?'

Susanna spoke quickly. 'He does not think we have known each other quite long enough to be making such a decision, ma'am. He wishes to ascertain that *both* our affections are engaged before the knowledge of it is public property. I should explain that he is by way of being a recluse and thinks I may have let being in company go to my head.'

Another hrmph followed. 'Recluse? How did you come to meet, then?'

Susanna embarked on the story they had fabricated. 'My uncle was used to be a literary correspondent of Kit and Nell's papa. Nell and I have exchanged letters for ever, but it was only when I visited her after her marriage that I met Kit.' She allowed herself a shy smile at her supposed betrothed.

'Hrmph. Red hair and grey eyes. Unusual. Travelled here from Kydd, have you? Glad you didn't invite us there.'

'You and Cousin Martha would naturally be very welcome,' said Kit, 'but I understood from your letter that you wished to see me here.'

'Of course I did. Can't go jaunting about the country at the drop of a hat! Takes me half an hour to get into my carriage for a morning call!'

There was a split second's silence while everybody sought for something unexceptional to say. Susanna broke it. 'But then, you have such a lovely house, I am sure you would never wish to leave it. Did Lord Penfold build it for you, ma'am?'

'Aye, with the money he made from the candle factory that my father was so bilious about. *And* got himself knighted into the bargain!' Lady Penfold looked about her with a satisfied air. 'No expense spared, that's what Edward wanted. We've even got pillars in the stables.'

Kit let out a crack of laughter. 'I shall look forward to seeing them.'

'Aye. You do that. How many grooms d'you bring?'

Kit took this non sequitur in his stride. 'Just the one, ma'am. John Farley. Grandson to another John Farley who has been laying down the law at the Home Farm for many a year and whom I daresay you remember as a boy.'

A chuckle agitated Lady Penfold's many chins. 'John Farley! Oh my, what a long time ago that was.' She sighed suddenly. 'Ring the bell, Martha. Hibbert will show them to their rooms. Five o'clock dinner, mind. I'm too old to keep late hours.'

Startled by their summary dismissal, they were joined in the hall by Mrs Penfold. 'You will be wanting to freshen up after your journey,' she said in a lacklustre voice. Her gaze drifted to Kit. 'Or see to your horses.

Gentlemen always do. Hibbert will show you where to go. I must settle Mother.'

Susanna's brow wrinkled. 'Is Lady Penfold not well?'

Mrs Penfold looked blank. 'Perfectly. But she holds it a sign of weakness to go to sleep in front of visitors.'

A quiver ran across Kit's lips. 'Very understandable. We will see you at dinner, then.'

There was a cough behind them. 'Your room is this way, madam,' said the butler, addressing himself to Susanna. 'Washing water has been taken up. Would you perhaps like a tray of tea also?'

'That would be *wonderful*,' said Susanna. She looked a question at Kit.

Kit grinned mischievously. 'No, no, my dear. I will go and check the horses since it is evidently expected of me.'

'And find out about mills and cock-fights, I collect. Well, it is your loss. I cannot conceive of greater comfort than warm water and a cup of tea just at this moment.'

'Until later then,' said Kit.

Why did he look at her with so much warmth? She twisted the sapphire ring nervously before realizing that the butler was still in the hall. Ah, this was for his benefit. How foolish of her. She smiled at Kit and gave him her hand, secure in her part again. 'You had best warn Johnny that Lady Penfold is like to catechize him on his grandfather.'

He raised her fingers to his lips. 'I will. I might also reconnoitre the garden in case we feel like taking a gentle stroll after dinner.'

A strong thrill shook her body. He was *acting*, she told herself. 'You know what we promised my uncle.'

'Of course.' But there was an unruly gleam in his eyes and to her consternation he pressed a kiss to each finger in turn before releasing her. It gave her sensibilities no relief at all to see Hibbert hiding a benevolent smile. Dear heaven, what had she let herself in for? Why had she not ascertained beforehand what Kit construed as lover-like behaviour? She didn't think she could cope with a whole fortnight of this!

The bedchambers, like the principal rooms, were airy and well appointed. The maid (a maid of her own! She would *never* get used to that) chattered happily as she helped Susanna off with her travelling clothes and into a loose robe so that she could wash. 'Mr Kit's just across the passage. I've got a little room all to myself upstairs. Her ladyship and Mrs Penfold are on the other side of the main staircase. It's ever so genteel, isn't it, miss? Not like I thought Newmarket would be. Only Mr Hibbert, he says if we're ever here when the big races are on, then we're to do any shopping and suchlike early in the morning on account of gentlemen liking to take advantage of a pretty armful if they sees one once they're in their cups, which they is as soon as they get up, Mr Hibbert says.'

Susanna struggled to keep a straight face. 'Well, that is certainly something to bear in mind,' she said gravely.

$$\star \quad \star \quad \star$$

Considering that they sat down only four to table, there were an inordinate number of dishes set out on the board. Susanna, eating sparingly of green goose and a selection of vegetables, no longer wondered how Lady Penfold had achieved such ample proportions when she saw the enthusiasm with which their hostess sampled everything.

'Your cook is an artist,' said Kit, his mind evidently working the same way. 'Pray send my compliments to the kitchen. This duck is quite the tenderest I have ever tasted.'

'Ha!' said Lady Penfold, not concealing her gratification. 'Should be good, the amount I pay him. Edward always said there was no point penny-pinching when it came to one's horses and one's comfort.'

'He was fortunate to be able to put his theories into practice. Is that his portrait?'

Lady Penfold paused in her eating in order to rest her eyes on the florid gentleman staring down at them from the wall of the dining room. 'Yes, that's Edward,' she said with a sigh. 'He was the most handsome man when he was younger.'

'Indeed, I would call him very distinguished-looking,' said Susanna quickly. 'And was he as good humoured as his expression suggests?'

'I never knew anyone who could make me laugh so much,' said Lady Penfold simply, and for a moment there was the trace of the girl she had once been in her face. 'To me, that one trait was worth all the titles and all the Domesday land in the country. Laughed the whole way to the Border, we did, and for forty-nine solid years after. My son was quieter but *his* son, Bertrand, was another one the same. Could have joked the apples off the trees, couldn't he, Martha? Rector's always going on about how we get what we deserve — meaning, you know, that to lose all my menfolk without an easy death amongst them is down to my scandalous disregard for the family name when I was a girl — but I don't believe a word of it. No, if I ever fall into a fit of the dismals, I tell myself how blessed I was to have had such fine men in my life.'

'I wish I could have made their acquaintance,' said Kit.

Lady Penfold resumed her dinner. 'Ah, well, it was my decision, when all's said and done. Your grandfather Jonathan always wrote, and your father too when he grew up. I daresay I didn't reply as often as they deserved. Now, what did you think of my horses, eh?'

'The chestnut looks to be a real champion,' said Kit instantly.

'You think so, do you?' said Lady Penfold, highly delighted. 'Bertrand bred him. He always said Rufus would make our name, didn't he, Martha? Four years old now. We're going to enter him during the Craven Meeting.'

'By Jove I should like to see that! What are his bloodlines?'

Susanna pushed away her wine, unable to drink more. The understated grief in Lady Penfold's voice a few minutes ago had made her ashamed of all the parts she was playing. It was with relief that she heard Martha enquire colourlessly if she was proficient on the pianoforte at all and if so whether she would play for them after dinner.

'I should be glad to,' she said. 'I have my music with me. Do you or Lady Penfold have any favourite pieces?'

'Anything pretty will do,' came the reply. 'Mother is a trifle excited with all the new company, which is not good for her. A little music generally sends her off to sleep very comfortably, however, and if you play, I shall be able to finish another pair of socks for the seamen's mission.'

A lifetime of screening her thoughts behind a servant's blank facade came to Susanna's aid as she intimated her willingness to be of service. She just hoped Mrs Penfold had put Kit's strangulated cough on her other side down to his taking too large a mouthful of wine.

★　★　★

'Well,' said Kit later, 'who would have thought Great-aunt Emma to be so unstuffy as to allow us a ramble in the garden alone.'

'It was almost an instruction,' said Susanna.

She and Kit were leaning on a small ornamental bridge halfway down Lady Penfold's garden. After approving Susanna's playing and later beating Kit at backgammon twice in succession, their hostess had retired for the night with her daughter-in-law in attendance. Susanna would have rather liked to escape too, but as the whole household was expecting them to act like an engaged couple there was no option but to stroll outside. At least the lantern-lit garden seemed a safe place to hold a private conversation.

'I have been giving some thought as to what you should do after this visit,' said Kit abruptly. 'I do not like the idea of you returning to the stage.'

Susanna looked at his averted face, startled. 'Not in London,' she agreed. 'And not to leap and stretch and pirouette as I was. But a travelling company like the Chartwell Players, where I could act properly, would not be so bad.'

What she could see of Kit's expression looked mulish. 'With your knowledge of literature, you could be a governess.'

'I have tried it,' said Susanna with a faint smile. 'I believe the lady of the house's brother still walks with a limp. It will not do, Kit. Something about me attracts attention, even though I wear shapeless dresses and scrape my hair into a bun. I cannot begin to enumerate the places where I have failed to blend in as a maid.'

'I do not want you to be a maid either! A housekeeper, perhaps. That would give you seniority.'

Why was Kit making these plans for her?

Was it a hint not to make herself too comfortable in his world? In which case, why not a return to the stage? 'You will notice that I am neither over thirty nor widowed,' she pointed out.

'Nor is Lizzie Olivant.'

'She grew up at Kydd! It is hardly the same.'

'Companion, then. There are any number of single ladies who are willing to pay for a presentable girl to do their bidding and enhance their salons.'

And be bored to tears! 'Any such employer would need to be sure that past scandals will not arise to embarrass them,' snapped Susanna.

'Warwick, you mean? Tosh. In a year that will all be forgotten.'

Susanna started guiltily. She had not been thinking of Rafe Warwick at all. And tempting as it was to let him believe so, she knew the time had come. She took a deep breath. 'Not just Mr Warwick. Kit, I have not told you anything that is untrue about me, but it has not been the whole truth. My acting ability, for instance, I believe to have come from my grandfather.'

'Your grandfather was an actor?' said Kit in surprise.

Susanna gave a short laugh. 'In a way. He

was a gentleman. Mama said he was most charismatic. He was always laughing and tossing her up in the air and playing with her when she was small. Always hosting lavish parties and mingling with the best people. Always being seen precisely where he should be and never where he should not. She said he appeared gay and good humoured and without a care in the world right up until the night he came back from Brooks' and blew his brains out in the study.'

'Good God!' Kit's elbow slipped off the narrow rail of the bridge. 'Blew his brains out? Surely not.'

'It is hardly the sort of thing I would make up!' She spoke more quietly. 'It emerged that as well as having heavy gambling losses, he was in debt to two banks, three moneylenders and scores of tradesmen. Everything had to be sold to pay his obligations: the estate, the town house, furniture, horses, my grand-mother's jewels . . . Mama's betrothal had just been announced. Her suitor dropped her the very day the news broke.'

'But, Susanna, that is scandalous!'

'A scandal, certainly. It happened at the height of the London season and not one call or letter of commiseration did Mama or Grandmama receive. Nobody spoke to them at all. People they had known for years cut them dead in the street. Grandmama was so overcome with shame that she retired to her brother's house, never to be seen in public again. My mother was made of sterner stuff. She turned her back on society and got herself a position as a governess.'

'Brave of her. I can see where you get your courage. But, Susanna, this is ancient history as far as society is concerned now.'

Susanna's hands were gripping the rail of the bridge. She forced herself to loosen them. 'Not quite. Mama faced her new life conscientiously, but she was bruised in spirit. It seemed as if all the truth she had ever known in her life had been turned on its head, and everything which she had been brought up to value was a sham. She felt the loss of her engagement keenly. No matter how many times she told herself she was better off without a man who had abandoned her at the first hint of trouble, her heart would not heal. It was almost inevitable that when her employer's second son came down from Oxford for the long vacation and displayed a partiality for her company, she would fall even more deeply in love than she had the first time.'

Susanna paused in her recital, aware of Kit's physical presence next to her as never before. She swallowed, her voice dropping lower still. 'In some respects, my father — for so he would be — was even worse off than my mother. He was wholly dependent on his allowance from the family, which was all he would get until he left Oxford to take up a profession. The prudent thing as soon as he admitted the attraction would have been to move out and leave temptation behind. Instead he persuaded a friend to procure him a special licence, married my mother in secret, and they continued to see each other on a daily basis.'

Kit was as still as if carved from stone.

'You are a man. You may guess what happened next. Just three weeks after my father went up to Oxford for his final year, it became obvious to Mama that she would be unable to hide their liaison many more months. He assured her he would stand by her. By Easter, she could no longer conceal her condition. My father's parents were furious. They declared that since their son was a minor, the marriage had been invalid. They enrolled him in the Militia and had him shipped to Dublin before he could draw breath. They found my mother a post as housekeeper on the other side of the country, passing her off as a needy widow. She was told if she ever set foot in the district again, they would publish her whole history.'

'Despicable! That such people exist!'

Kit's words sparked a brief thread of warmth in Susanna's heart. 'Mama was still sanguine. Mr Masterson was a miserly screw, but my father would have his pay, and as soon as he was of age they could marry legally. She wrote to the regiment giving her direction, and again to inform my father of my safe delivery. She never received an answer. Six months later she had a curt note from his mother announcing his death during a bout of insurrection.'

It was done. Susanna gazed unseeingly down at the dark water, emptied of all emotion at having told what had been locked inside her for so long. 'I am sorry,' she whispered. 'The illegitimate granddaughter of a disgraced gambler is hardly suitable ancestry for your betrothed. If it should come out, you can bid farewell to Lady Penfold's good opinion.'

Kit's voice was harsh. 'Why should it come out? Do you think you might slip up with no lines to guide you? You have done more than adequately so far.'

Because this is Newmarket. Susanna took a painful breath to explain but he was continuing.

'And in case you have not noticed, we have only just got here. The time to draw back is past.'

'I can invent a summons from my uncle. Take a stagecoach out.'

'Don't be ridiculous. Where would you stay? How would you protect yourself from Warwick?'

'He cannot have spies the length and breadth of the country! I shall go to . . . to Edinburgh.'

'Edinburgh? Why the devil Edinburgh?'

'It is a long way away.'

'You will do no such thing. A more cork-brained idea I never heard. I will see you in the morning.' Kit turned and strode abruptly towards the house.

Susanna gazed unhappily at his departing back. He was as furious as she had known he would be. And when he found out the whole truth, he would *never* forgive her.

★   ★   ★

Kit downed a glass of brandy in one, then paced the empty saloon, angry and confused. Why had Susanna's story disturbed him? He wasn't narrow-minded enough to care about a scandal in her family's past, nor was he concerned that her parents' illegal marriage had been a hole-in-the-corner affair. Was it shock? That but for those two circumstances she would have been his equal in birth?

People's standing in society had never bothered him before. His father had brought him up to judge a person on their acts, not their possessions or the length of their family tree. If Kit liked someone, he would talk to them. If he didn't, he wouldn't.

He poured himself another brandy, staring at its amber depths. It was rather that he hadn't expected this. It had never occurred to him that Susanna was concealing quite so much. And if she had kept this history from him, what else about her might be false? He remembered her flawless performance at Belmont House and again at the Graingers' dinner party. Her fear of Rafe Warwick had been real enough, but how could he be sure she wasn't projecting an equally convincing impression now of the untouched creature he had sworn to protect?

His fingers tightened around the bowl of the glass. He didn't want to be thinking this way. He wanted to believe her candid and sincere. But . . . she *was* an actress. And she had lied to him by omission. And she had needed very badly to get away from London.

7

Susanna slept badly and was dismayed to find Lady Penfold already partaking of a substantial breakfast when she came downstairs. She had hoped to have a respite from playing her part, but it transpired her redoubtable hostess made it a practice to walk to the stables on the arm of a stout footman every morning in order to inspect her horses and catechize her grooms about their care and well-being. Today she was in high fettle with having had the Kydd animals to criticize also, and very well pleased at finding Kit down there before her, diligently checking that his horses had taken no harm from the journey.

Susanna couldn't help wondering whether information picked up by John Farley had been responsible for this circumstance, but told herself she was being unjust. She slipped into an unused place and applied herself to a cup of coffee whilst Lady Penfold swapped incomprehensible language with Kit and consumed more ham, eggs and toast than she herself managed in a week.

Across the table, Kit met her eyes. There

was no hint in his face of his mood. 'I trust you slept well,' he said.

Susanna's hand shook. 'One would have to have a bad conscience indeed not to, the beds are so comfortable.' She raised the cup to her lips.

Kit's gaze seemed to linger on the faint circles that she knew showed under her eyes. His mouth twisted in what might have been an apology. 'Then I assume you are as ready as I am to enjoy our first day in Newmarket.'

'Ha! Unlikely. We're bidden to the Fortunes this morning.' Lady Penfold gave a reprehensible chuckle. 'Fool woman's holding an 'At Home'. Just an excuse to see my lost relation, if you ask me. Never saw Adeline Fortune's nose twitch so hard in my life as when I mentioned that one of my great-nephews was coming to stay with me. One of them! She didn't know I had any!'

'You will give me leave, Great-aunt Emma, to tell you that you are a very wicked woman,' said Kit.

Lady Penfold looked rather gratified by this epithet. 'Can't abide Adeline. Never could. How John Fortune came to choose a wife the very image of his mother, I'll never know.'

★ ★ ★

It took longer to get Lady Penfold in and out of the carriage than it did to cover the short distance between her house and that of the Fortunes.

'I may suggest we walk back,' murmured Kit in Susanna's ear under the pretext of smoothing out a crease in her pelisse.

Did that mean he'd forgiven her? A treacherous frisson of excitement shivered through Susanna at his warm breath on her neck, and his hand making the slightest of contacts with her leg as he brushed down the sarsenet. It mattered not that he was acting the solicitous lover for his great-aunt. Moments like this at once doubled her resolve to leave and increased her craving for more. How had she ever thought she could stay detached?

They were welcomed into a chilly saloon by a frigidly elegant woman who might have been carved from alabaster, so little did her expression change on greeting them. 'Mr Kydd, welcome to Newmarket. You have an estate in Northamptonshire, I understand.'

'Yes indeed,' said Kit. A gleam of something Susanna couldn't quite put a name to flashed in his eye and was gone. He smiled pleasantly. 'It is somewhat encumbered since my father's death, but fortunately Miss Fair does not mind waiting until I come about before joining her fate with mine.'

There was an indrawn breath from their hostess's left, followed by the merest suspicion of a cut-off giggle. Susanna glanced sideways. A gawky, brown-haired girl in an unflattering white muslin dress sat in a window seat exuding innocence.

Mrs Fortune affected not to have heard either Kit's comment or the giggle. 'Lady Penfold, perhaps you would like to sit by the fire.'

'Such as it is,' muttered Lady Penfold. She darted a sharp look at her great-nephew before moving ponderously off on her footman's arm.

'Mr Kydd, let me present you to my daughter,' said Mrs Fortune, indicating the pretty girl beside her. As an afterthought, she also beckoned to the girl in the window. 'And to her sister.'

Names were murmured, Kit gave a small bow and allowed himself to be drawn away. Susanna was left to the company of Miss Caroline Fortune, the younger girl.

'That was splendid, what Mr Kydd said,' approved this damsel, mischievous brown eyes belying her plain looks. 'Mama has been talking of nothing but how Honoria must make herself agreeable to him for two days. She has no hopes of me at all, which I used to feel rather hurt by, but am excessively grateful for now, after seeing what the marriage mart involves. Are you truly engaged to Mr Kydd? That will be one in the eye for Mama. She has been looking Kydd Court up in her book.'

Susanna blushed and admitted that it was indeed the case. Really, it was alarming how easily she slipped into this modest-young-lady persona. She looked across the room. 'But your sister is so lovely, she cannot fail to attract suitors, surely?'

'Oh no, they buzz around her like bees to a honey pot, as my brother Harry says. It is simply a matter of finding one rich enough or grand enough to suit Mama. Oh, there is Harry, talking to Mr Kydd now. I thought he was going to be out this morning, for usually he cannot bear Mama's 'At Homes'. Isn't he handsome? He is a dreadful rake but quite my favourite brother.'

Susanna glanced across obediently, and suffered a shock so ghastly that for a moment her eyes refused to credit what they saw. She could well believe that Harry Fortune was, if not a rake, then at least dangerously attractive to women. He was tall for one thing and dressed in the first stare of fashion with only a couple of fobs and seals dangling from his chain. He also had a wide, good-humoured mouth and laughing grey eyes. But his undoubted *pièce de résistance*, and the one which struck terror into Susanna's heart, was crisply curling hair the *exact* red-gold shade of her own! Instinctively her hands flew to her bonnet to check that hers was well and truly hidden. 'He seems very pleasant,' she managed.

'He is,' said Caroline cheerfully. 'Half the girls in the neighbourhood are in love with him. It is his hair, of course. He's the only one of us to have it.'

Across the saloon, Kit's eyes left Harry Fortune to meet hers for a single, searing moment. 'I beg your pardon?' said Susanna, pressing her hands together in her lap to stop the shake in them becoming visible.

'The Fortune red hair. Sometimes it skips entirely, you know. The only one with it in Papa's generation is my Uncle Crispin. He was a great favourite with the ladies too by all accounts, but we think he must have been annoyed by the way they chased him for he has never married, not even when he came out of the army, and he was a major by then and quite old, so could easily afford a wife.'

'I see.' Susanna was hardly aware of what she was saying. How could this be happening? It was a nightmare. Of all the households in Newmarket, why did it have to be this one which might hold the key to her past?

'There's a portrait of him in the billiard room if you should care to see it, but for my part I don't think him nearly so handsome as Harry. We *hope* Uncle Crispin will help with our plans to set up a house together and train horses but Harry must needs catch him at a propitious moment. Oh — !' Caroline put a guilty hand to her mouth. 'Oh, *please*, Miss Fair, will you forget I said that? Mama has no idea I don't want to be a proper young lady.'

'Forget what?' said Susanna, somehow managing to keep the front of her mind clear whilst the back of it was reeling in shock. 'I beg your pardon, I didn't quite catch what you said. It is very noisy in here, don't you think? Your mother will be delighted that her 'At Home' is such a success.'

Caroline looked inordinately relieved. 'You *are* a great gun. I thought you would be. Shall we join Lady Penfold? I generally see her before breakfast, but Mr Kydd was there this morning and I didn't like to disturb them. Our lands back onto each other, you know, so it is only a step from our paddocks to hers.'

'By all means,' said Susanna. They moved across to the fire. Caroline sat down next to Lady Penfold. Susanna sank onto an uncomfortable sofa whose only merit was that it allowed her to turn her back on Harry

Fortune's appallingly familiar features. Beside her was an embroidered firescreen, presumably a display of the elder Miss Fortune's skill, since the meagre blaze in the fireplace hardly warranted the use of such an object. Susanna glanced at it and felt the last blow to her composure hit her. On a pale blue background, a meticulously worked letter F had been placed squarely inside a horseshoe. A commonplace design — except that its image was impressed into an irregular circle of wax in a drawer of Mama's writing desk, and for her whole conscious life Susanna had assumed the F stood for Fair and the horseshoe was the conventional symbol for good luck.

She looked at the firescreen again. There was no mistaking it. F for Fortune. And Harry Fortune had her red-gold hair.

Susanna let Caroline and Lady Penfold's chatter wash past her whilst she made stilted conversation with a matron whose name she never did catch. Even with the length of the room between them, she could feel Kit's eyes boring into her neck. It would be only a matter of time before a pair of dove-grey pantaloons and gleaming Hessians should intrude themselves into her view and her supposed betrothed would beg his great-aunt's permission to excuse them both.

'Aye, run away and take a turn about the town before luncheon,' said Lady Penfold obligingly when this event did indeed take place. 'I'm very well satisfied with Caro to entertain me. But Lord, child, what a dreadful dress! Could Adeline not find something more becoming for you?'

'It is ugly, isn't it? It was meant for Honoria but Bridget cut it wrong so they made it over for me and added this horrid flounce to cover the mistake. Goodbye Miss Fair. It was very nice to meet you.'

Susanna's lips found something equally pretty to say but she could hardly concentrate, so aware was she of Kit's towering anger. Once outside, he set a furious pace towards the town. 'Oh, please, Kit, say *something*!' she begged after five minutes of stumbling to keep up with him.

'I assure you my present thoughts are best left unuttered!'

'I *knew* I should have made a clean breast of the whole last night! I meant to, but I was too much of a coward. It really isn't as iniquitous as it seems.'

He turned, his eyes blazing blue fire. 'Is it not? Harry Fortune's eyes and hair are a perfect match for yours! Tell me, has there been a single moment since I met you when you have *not* been scheming?'

Susanna clenched her hands in anguish. The unfamiliar weight of the ring seemed to underline the accusation. 'I *knew* that was what you would think!'

'It is the obvious conclusion. And as I have already had cause to observe, you *are* an accomplished actress.'

'Truly, Kit, it is not as bad as you suppose. Won't you please listen?'

'Is there reason for me to?' he said, an uncompromising expression on his face.

Susanna's words tumbled out. 'You have already guessed that Mama must have been employed by the Fortunes. So I think also now, but I *swear* all she told me was that the family resided in Newmarket. 'Fair' is the name she took when she left. I don't know either her true identity or my father's. She always said what I didn't know couldn't hurt me. I am not wholly convinced she was right.'

'You expect me to believe you came to Newmarket with no ulterior motive?' Kit's voice was raw with disillusionment.

'I promise that my first thought was to help you, but yes the locality was an inducement,' said Susanna. 'At least it was to begin with, before I knew you all properly. And afterwards I still thought it might be safe. All I was hoping was that I might get a feel of the town and absorb some of my father's background. I did not expect to run into his image on my first morning call!'

'You knew what he looked like! You came to Newmarket *knowing* that with such unusual colouring, the family would not be hard to find!'

'No! That is, I knew I favoured him, for Mama had his picture in a locket, but it never occurred to me that other relations might share the same traits. Truly, Kit, it was the most horrible shock when Miss Caroline Fortune pointed out 'my brother Harry'.'

'I had some pretty murderous thoughts myself.'

'No more than I deserve. It was very wrong of me not to tell you.' She put her gloved hand on his arm. 'Please, you must help me take the next stagecoach out of town. I cannot possibly stay. It is clear Miss Caroline is on terms of considerable intimacy with Lady Penfold. If there is frequent concourse between the families, someone *must* remark the likeness soon.'

He looked at her, his blue eyes stony. 'You mean you don't want to know more of your family now that you have found them?'

'Not at the expense of exposing myself and affecting your relationship with your great-aunt! And, indeed, I never wished to know *them* precisely, whoever they were. I merely wanted to feel a little less of a nobody. It was all very well for Mama to invent herself anew and discard the past, but it is no very pleasant thing not to have *any* idea about one's history, I can tell you.'

'I cannot let you go,' said Kit shortly. 'I promised I would keep you safe.' But he tempered these brusque words by tucking her hand into his arm.

Susanna leant on him, almost faint with relief. He had stopped hating her. Her heart pounded with gratitude. 'But I must leave, Kit. You heard Lady Penfold talking about red hair and grey eyes. If she is not to make the connection, I shall have to do something perfectly ridiculous like purchase extra bonnets and make myself eccentric by never taking them off inside the house.' She focused on the narrow street they were traversing. 'Oh, a milliner's shop. How appropriate.'

Kit seemed to see their surroundings for the first time since he had marched her out of the Fortunes' house. 'Good God, Susanna, we are in the Dukeries! Don't ever come here alone.'

'I won't have the chance. Were you not listening? I'm going to leave Newmarket as soon as it may be arranged.'

'No! That would be worse than anything, for how would it look if I let you set off unattended?' He swerved her around a noxious puddle in their way. 'Mind your shoes. The sooner we are out of these lanes the better.'

'It is no worse than the old parts of many other towns. That was a perfectly good linen-draper you just dragged me past.'

'Yes, and it was next to an alehouse where you would lose your purse as soon as sneeze. I know these alleys, Susanna. The Pelican opposite your old lodgings is the height of respectability compared to some of these drinking dens.'

Susanna was so startled she let him hustle her past another three taverns. 'How ever do you know of the Pelican?'

A tinge of colour stained his cheeks. 'I observed it, that is all. Ah, this is better.' They had emerged from the oppressive lane with its overhanging upper storeys to a large green with a church at the far end. 'Promise, Susanna?'

'I think you are making a great fuss about nothing. All I could see were respectable townsfolk going about their shopping.'

'I assure you, you would see far worse at night,' said Kit grimly.

'I should not be going shopping at night! Oh, very well, I bow to your superior knowledge. It was your feet took us there, and you did say you knew the town.'

'Vixen.' He turned to face her, taking her hands in his. 'I apologize for losing my temper.'

Susanna's heart flipped end for end. 'You were justified,' she said in a shaky voice. 'I am sorry I did not disclose the whole last night.' She saw his mouth soften, felt her own lips part. Merciful heavens, was he going to kiss her? Out here in the open? After the gamut of shocks she had sustained in the last hour, she would never be able to stop herself responding! 'Perhaps if I wear my hair straight and off my face,' she gabbled desperately, 'any resemblance to Harry Fortune will not be too marked. What do you think? It will make me look shockingly plain, of course, but that will be all to your credit with Lady Penfold. She cannot doubt your devotion to someone who employs no subtle arts to keep you by her side until the knot is tied.'

There was the oddest look in Kit's eyes. 'Subtle arts? Just at the moment I would compound for knowing what you are going to spring on me from one moment to the next.'

★   ★   ★

Susanna kept the door to her room open whilst Kit examined the miniature of her

162

father. The locket itself was long sold but the tiny painting had been kept safe in the writing desk.

'And there is this also,' she said, showing him the impressed sealing wax. 'It must have come off a letter which Mama subsequently destroyed. The same emblem is embroidered onto a firescreen in the Fortunes' saloon.'

'I saw it.' Kit looked at the miniature again. 'This man and Harry Fortune could be twins.'

Susanna groaned. 'I must have been cork-brained not to have considered the possibility. The colouring does not occur often, apparently. Miss Caroline said her uncle is the only red-head in the previous generation. I suppose Papa died before she was born and the rest of the family have tidily forgotten him.' She put the tiny oval painting back in the smallest drawer of her writing desk along with the sealing wax. 'It seems such a waste of both their lives.'

Kit laid his hand on hers. 'Susanna, I — '

But a bustle downstairs announced Lady Penfold's return. 'Go down,' said Susanna, hoping her instinctive jerk away from his touch would be put down to panic. 'I must restyle my hair and then, I suppose, there will be food again. I almost dread to imagine your great-aunt's idea of a light luncheon.'

If not as hearty as the previous night's meal, the repast was still substantial. Their hostess looked disapprovingly at Susanna's small portion. 'Don't know how you young girls survive. What did you think of the town?'

Susanna reviewed the shops and houses which had streamed past in the blur of Kit's rapid passage. 'The main street is remarkably handsome.' She summoned up her acting ability and threw a roguish look at Kit. 'Although I was not allowed to examine the shops as closely as I would have liked.'

Lady Penfold chuckled, her chins wobbling alarmingly. 'Aye, it's well enough, and what you can't buy here can always be got in Bury St Edmunds or Cambridge. It will be livelier still soon. Caro tells me there is a theatre company due. She always contrives to be first with the news. Comes from hobnobbing with the grooms so much, I daresay. Been in and out of the stables, right from a child. My god-daughter, you know. I did wonder whether she and Bertrand might — ' She broke off. 'Ah, well, all water under the bridge now.'

'It cannot be the Norfolk and Suffolk Company who are coming,' stated Martha Penfold. 'They were only here last year and would never repeat so soon.'

'Then it's some other troupe,' said Lady

Penfold impatiently. 'What does it matter? A play's a play.' She chuckled again. 'Always gives me a laugh to see how everyone gets togged up in their finery to go and watch — and then they have to spend the evening holding their dresses above their ankles so they don't get trod in the dirt!'

Susanna laughed aloud at the vivid recollection Lady Penfold's words brought to mind. 'And the way the tallest folk *will* always sit on the front benches so the people behind have to bob up and down in order to see. Where do the companies play, ma'am? Is there a theatre in Newmarket?'

'No, they generally hire one of Marshall's barns over on the St Mary's side of town. The Fishers stay two months or more, but Caro tells me these people only plan on a fortnight. They are engaged to give a performance for the Duke of Rutland at Cheveley, but will do shows in the town as well.'

Susanna nodded. That was sound business sense for a travelling company. It was not unusual for the gentry to bespeak a particular play once a troupe was in the area, but the knowledge that they were high enough in the local nobility's favour to be performing at a house party did wondrous things for ticket sales as long as their repertoire lasted. She closed her mouth on saying as much, however, for fear of giving herself away. She had been almost too unguarded in her enthusiasm as it was. No sheltered ingénue would be near so well informed.

Fortunately, Lady Penfold had other fish to fry. She fixed Kit with a basilisk eye. 'What were you saying to Adeline about Kydd Court being encumbered? A hum to stop her foisting that bloodless chit Honoria on to you, was it?'

Kit ducked his head ruefully. 'Only in part. I imagine it is well known by now that my uncle shockingly mismanaged the estate whilst I was in India.'

Lady Penfold's gaze narrowed. 'Mismanaged? In what way?'

Kit shrugged. 'Oh, turning off men to cut down on costs and then not having sufficient labour to get in the harvest. Saving on fires and then discovering that damp had rotted the carpets and ruined the furniture. It is nothing which hard work and application cannot put right, but until it is I cannot afford to draw the bustle overmuch. That is another reason why Susanna and I are not making a formal announcement just yet.'

Susanna looked down at her plate, her brief animation at the memory of her travelling days gone. They had discussed how much of Kydd's financial plight they should disclose to her ladyship. Nell had been all for making the whole known, in order to expose the perfidy of their relations, but Kit had favoured a softer, bravery-in-adversity approach, saying that he didn't want it to sound as if he was whining and if Great-aunt Emma initiated enquiries, as she was bound to do, she would think the better of him for making light of his difficulties.

That was good sense, they had all agreed. It was simply that now, hearing Kit give exactly the explanation they had rehearsed and managing to sound beautifully open and natural about it, his calculated presentation had turned a tender slice of beef into boot leather in Susanna's mouth. What in the world was wrong with her?

8

Kit reined his horse to a walk, a hard gallop across the heath having relieved his feelings somewhat. 'I tell you, Johnny, I was within an ace of strangling her.'

John Farley eyed his master from where he rode alongside. 'As to that, I disremember you giving Miss Susanna a chance to tell you aught of her history before you bustled her out of London.'

'Oh, you're making it my fault, are you?'

'Stranger things than this tale of hers have been true before now.'

'For sure. But I cannot help remembering she is an actress.'

'So you got on your high ropes as usual. It's my belief you're in a way to liking her more than half, Mr Kit, and *that's* why you're at outs with yourself.'

Kit felt a tide of red suffuse his face. 'The devil fly away with you, Johnny! Any more of that and you'll be looking for another position.'

'I'm in the right town, then, aren't I?'

Was he really finding fault with Susanna because he liked her too well? He had been so angry this morning, in a rage that had almost frightened himself, yet the moment she said wildly that she must leave, his instinct had been to haul her back to his side. And when she'd persisted he'd had to find reasons for her to stay. 'All the horseflesh about us has addled your wits,' he growled.

'Daresay that'll be it,' agreed Johnny. 'It wouldn't be that you've spent so long avoiding parson's mousetrap with the grasping females at home, that you're running scared at the thought of being sweet on a maid who *don't* want the Court.'

'It scares her half to death,' said Kit ruefully. *And now Johnny will assume he's right simply because I haven't denied it.* 'Heigh ho,' he said. 'Best get back. Another dissipated evening of backgammon and penny-a-point piquet lies before me.'

★   ★   ★

The after-dinner pattern was a repeat of the previous night. While Lady Penfold talked over Northamptonshire neighbours with Kit, Susanna played the pianoforte, blessing her mother's shade for insisting that she continue to practise even after she had turned twelve and was working full time in Mr Masterson's household. 'You may be a servant now,'

Mama had scolded fiercely, 'but you are a gentleman's daughter no matter how shabbily they treated us, and I won't have your only accomplishments that you can dust a drawing room to perfection and wash an entire dinner service without breaking a single piece!'

'Do you sing as well as play, Miss Fair?' said Lady Penfold when Kit stepped outside to stretch his legs. 'There are some of Bertrand's favourite airs with our music. It would be pleasant to hear them again.'

'Certainly,' said Susanna with a smile, and went to the cherry-wood cabinet to sort through the sheets. Her eye was caught by the free-standing portrait of a young man in regimentals. 'Is this your grandson?'

'Yes, that's Bertrand.' For a moment there was a quaver in Lady Penfold's voice. 'I always knew I'd see Edward out, what with his fondness for brandy and his gout and all. We never thought to see our son carried off in his prime, though, and none of us dreamt when we waved goodbye to Bertrand after his last furlough that he wouldn't be coming back.'

'I'm sorry,' said Susanna gently. 'Perhaps I shouldn't play after all.'

Their hostess rallied. 'No, no. Keeping silent is no way to remember loved ones. Sing that ditty about foreign adventures. He used

170

to enjoy that, didn't he, Martha?'

'He did. It is a hard thing to lose your only child, Miss Fair, but life must go on.' And Martha Penfold bent her eyes back to her knitting as if by ceaseless endeavour she could ensure that other mothers' sons would at least have dry feet wherever they roamed.

Susanna located the robust sea shanty, along with several more songs that she could imagine appealing to a vigorous baritone. She played it quietly through to familiarize herself with the tune, and then began to sing. All at once a stillness descended on the room, even Martha's knitting needles faltering. Out of the corner of her eye, Susanna saw her clasp her mother-in-law's hand as a tear rolled down the aged face. She had to redouble her efforts to keep the requisite gaiety in her voice. It was perhaps fortunate that Kit returned as she finished the final refrain.

'Capital,' he said, strolling over to the piano and investigating the sheets of music. 'Do you feel brave enough to essay a duet?'

'Only if you do not drown out my voice,' she replied, taking the piece he handed her. In truth she had never heard him sing, but as always when they were in company, her spirit lifted to the challenge and she found herself playing to his lead.

He looked affronted. 'Are you intimating

171

that I bellow, Miss Fair?'

She glanced at him archly. 'Surely that is for the audience to judge.'

Lady Penfold chuckled. Kit stationed himself next to Susanna, one hand resting on her shoulder as she played the introduction. Instantly, a tingling warmth shot through the thin muslin of her capped sleeve and coursed around her veins. Confound him! How was she to even read the lyrics with the distraction of his physical presence so close, let alone sing in tune? This was going to be a disaster.

But extraordinarily, magically, their voices blended as if they had been performing together for years. Had Mr Scott been present, he would have put them on the Sans Pareil stage every night of the season. By the second verse, Kit's hand on her shoulder was not so much anchoring her to the stool as whirling her through the heavens. She felt dizzy with the exhilaration of their close harmony. And yet beneath everything there still ran a thread of unease. Had Kit guessed these were Bertrand Penfold's favourite songs? Was this another opportunity to charm his great-aunt? Surely nobody could really be this perfect.

★ ★ ★

Next morning, Lady Penfold was scrutinizing her post when she uttered a 'Ha!' and waved a letter at Kit. 'This is from your cousin James. Seems they've reviewed their commitments and find they can visit me earlier than they thought.'

'Then I fear we shall have to cut our own stay short,' said Kit. 'It would generate too much awkwardness for us to be under the same roof.'

Oh yes! Susanna looked up from her sewing. She could be packed in half an hour if need be.

'Nonsense!' said Lady Penfold, blighting her hopes. 'Martha will write back saying it might be convenient for him, but it ain't for me. Didn't show any eagerness when I first contacted him, so he can't expect better treatment now. Did I tell you he wanted me to traipse halfway across England to visit him instead of them coming here?'

'I daresay he thought it would be easier for you to meet all my cousins at the same time.'

'Didn't think that at all,' said Lady Penfold roundly. 'Wanted to show off his fine estate and didn't fancy the cost of transporting the lot of them over here. Why won't you be in the same house with him, eh?'

There was a second of agonizing silence. Then Kit said quietly, 'Because I detest him,

173

ma'am. Both him and his brother. I know it was my uncle who did his level best to ruin Kydd, but from James and Dick's attitude I am convinced they were at least partly in his confidence.'

Susanna let out a silent breath. Whether such honesty had been a calculated risk or not, Kit's speech had had an unmistakable ring of truth to it and she could see Lady Penfold was impressed.

What she said, however, was, 'Changed your tune, haven't you? A couple of days ago it was mismanagement. Now it's ruination.'

Kit's lips tightened. 'Fortunately, Kydd is not in quite the state it would have been had my uncle's regime continued. That fact, however, does not incline me to look with any very friendly eye on the perpetrators.'

'Well, well,' said Lady Penfold noncommittally, 'you won't be required to. I'm too set in my ways to cope with a lot of new acquaintances all at once.'

No more was said on the subject. Kit, recalling aloud that Susanna had expressed the intention of purchasing another bonnet, offered her his escort should she wish to walk into the town.

Lady Penfold's chins shook. 'Easy to see you ain't been engaged for so very long,' she said. 'Shopping, indeed!' She waved them off with instructions to stop by the baker in case he had a batch of the cinnamon pastries she liked.

'What did you want to say?' asked Susanna. In normal circumstances it would have been quite comfortable strolling down the High Street in the spring sunshine but, given yesterday's furious passage through the town and all the concentrated charm that Kit had lavished on his great-aunt since, Susanna still had the feeling that she was walking a knife-edge. If he was going to question her about her history or scold her for singing warm songs, or if there was some other little thing he'd thought of that he wanted her to remember, she'd rather he got on with it.

His blue eyes looked down at her, puzzled. 'What did I want to say when?'

Susanna stared. 'Now. I assumed that was why you offered to escort me.'

'Oh! No, I just felt cooped up. And I thought you might like a chance to be yourself.' He frowned at her. 'Did I tell you how much I dislike this frumpish way of dressing your hair?'

Susanna turned her face up to him, deeply pleased — despite her better judgement — that he objected to her new plain style, but incredulous that he had forgotten why she was adopting it. 'It is hardly for my own enjoyment! You have no idea how much persuading my wretched curls take to lie flat like this, but as long as it makes me appear sufficiently unlike Harry Fortune, we will both have to endure it. And as we said yesterday, it will do you no harm with Lady Penfold.'

'Dammit, will you stop thinking of everything in terms of Great-aunt Emma! I don't like to see you looking a dowd!'

Susanna stared at him, almost doubting what she was hearing.

He coloured and turned his eyes away. 'Milliner,' he said gruffly, pointing at a shop window. 'Try on that straw affair with the yellow and blue ribbons. I'll come in with you and make sure you aren't stung.'

Susanna recovered herself. 'Unless Newmarket is quite unlike any other town, the presence of a gentleman will push the price up.'

He raised his eyebrows. 'Is that a challenge? I'll wager I can get you two bonnets for the initial asking price of that one.'

'Taken,' said Susanna instantly. 'What are we betting?'

'Tell you later,' he said, the gleam back in his eyes as he pushed the shop door open. Too late, Susanna reflected that she had possibly been unwise to encourage him.

Inside, she took a moment to adjust to the dimmer light. A stout, grey-clad woman with a rigid coiffure emerged from an inner door to ask their pleasure. Susanna cast a quick glance at Kit in case he wanted to open the proceedings and had to stifle a choke of laughter. He had changed persona the instant they crossed the threshold and was now staring at the displayed hats with an air of terrified fascination. 'The bonnet in the window,' she said shyly, untying her own ribbons. 'With the blue and yellow ruffles. May I try it on, please? My betrothed thinks it might suit me.'

'Ah, the Angoulême.' The woman brought the bonnet out and arranged it over Susanna's bun. 'Very fetching, madam. The gentleman has excellent taste.'

Susanna studied herself in the mirror and turned hesitantly to Kit. 'It is nice. What do you think?'

'Charming,' said Kit in a hurried voice. 'My sister has one like it, has she not? But we are only *looking*, remember?'

'Of course, my dear,' said Susanna and smiled at him.

Kit gulped and eased his cravat. 'How, er, how much is it, if you please?'

The milliner, pained at this unnatural

attention to business, named a number of guineas.

Looking at Kit out of the corner of her eye, Susanna saw him blench. 'Surely not,' he said. 'Why, my sister never paid so much for a hat in her life. Are you sure you have not made a mistake?'

Susanna gave an infinitesimal sigh and began to take the bonnet off.

The woman shot her a sharp glance. 'Oh, how stupid of me, I was confusing it with another. It should be two guineas less.'

Kit looked aghast. 'Is that all? Why, we could buy a couple of ells of ribbon and re-trim her old one far more cheaply.'

Susanna smiled bravely. 'Yes, that would be much better. How clever of you to think of it. I wish my fingers were as nimble as your sister's, but I daresay my efforts will not look *too* inferior to hers when I am finished.' She cast a last wistful glance at the ruffled hat and drifted over to examine a very dashing creation in silver net, which must have been made as an advertisement of the milliner's skill rather than in expectation of a sale, for she could not imagine any of the ladies she had seen so far in the town wearing such a frivolous affair.

'Inferior?' said Kit with a frown. 'No, I never meant for you to — '

178

Susanna lifted the clever wisps of net, held together with a single white rose, and moved to the mirror. Kit's eyes followed her.

The proprietor hurriedly reduced the Angoulême bonnet by another two guineas and adjusted the rose to perch more becomingly over Susanna's right eye. 'Beautiful, madam. This design is all the mode in London. Of course the hair should be arranged a little more . . . ' She made an expansive movement with her hands.

'What is wrong with her hair?' demanded Kit. 'It is very neat. My mother likes it particularly.'

'Nothing, sir, nothing at all,' said the woman at once. 'It is as exactly befits a young lady. But for a ball where one might wear such a pretty trifle as this, it would naturally be styled with a few curls framing the face.'

'A ball?' said Kit, sounding horrified. 'We are not going to a ball! We are buying a new bonnet suitable for church!' But it was noticeable to both Susanna and the milliner that he was, not to put too fine a point on it, goggling at the enchanting picture she presented.

'And for morning calls,' put in Susanna demurely. She took off the silver net with a sigh of regret and laid it aside.

'Church?' said the milliner, a martial light

in her eye. 'Well, and if you had said so before, I have the very thing.' She brought out a broderie anglaise bonnet with an audaciously high brim, trimmed with deceptively innocent cream flowers. 'And a very reasonable price it is too, sir. Why that and the Angoulême together wouldn't come to much more than I charged you mistakenly at first.'

Susanna tied the cream ribbons beneath her chin and smiled at Kit in the glass. 'This would go delightfully with the white muslin your sister was kind enough to make over for me,' she said.

'It does look rather . . . both for the same price? Oh, oh well if that is so . . . ' Kit visibly struggled with himself before taking out his notecase. 'But we're not buying that thing with the rose.'

'No, my dear,' said Susanna soothingly. 'For even if we do go to the concert your mama was talking of, I daresay a hat like that one would be quite out of place. I should hate to feel that everybody was admiring *me* rather than listening to the music.'

'Exactly.' Kit handed over the money and drummed his fingers while the woman packed the hats into boxes.

'And the blue and yellow ruffled bonnet will be just the thing for the play. I am convinced that only very smart ladies would wear anything else.'

'Mmm.' Kit's eyes rested on the wisps of net uneasily as the milliner replaced the frivolous confection on the shelf. He was still casting backward glances at it as they left the shop.

They continued down the road for some minutes before both dissolving into laughter. 'Oh, Kit, that poor woman!' said Susanna, leaning on his arm as she wiped her eyes. 'I shan't dare go in there again!'

'Nonsense,' said Kit robustly. 'All shop-keepers are thieves and robbers. She'll still have made a profit out of us.' He adjusted the boxes dangling from his hand and squinted down at her. 'You were extraordinary. Have you done that before?'

'Done what?' She looked inquiringly into his face, then realized what he meant. 'You mean cheated a tradesman out of an honest price? No, I have not! What do you take me for?' She pulled away from him, furious.

'Susanna, I — ' Kit broke off, swearing under his breath. 'I'm sorry. It is just that you were so good. Better than I expected.'

She kept her eyes on the swell of the Heath rising beyond the town. 'So were you,' she said in a choked voice. 'One would think you were the actor, not me.'

In front of them, an extremely dapper

gentleman alighted from his coach and strolled into a nearby coffee house.

'That's where the Jockey Club does their business,' said Kit absently.

'Perhaps you should follow him in then,' snapped Susanna. 'You will no doubt find it a simple matter to convince them you are a gentleman trainer. I understand large sums of money can be won on horse races.'

Kit pulled her arm firmly back inside his. 'That is pure foolishness. I admit I like to act, but what happened in that shop was as much your doing as mine. I had no intention of playing it that way until you peeped up at me so provocatively.'

'I was not provocative!'

'You gave a perfect impersonation of a woman who was about to wind some poor sap about her little finger. Of course I played along.'

'I — ' Susanna stopped and hung her head. 'Something happens when we are together,' she said helplessly. 'I have never acted opposite anyone like you.'

They crossed the road by mutual consent and began to walk back along the other side. 'Ah well,' said Kit. 'If I lose Kydd Court, at least we know we can always make a living as adventurers.' He sounded quite cheerful at the prospect.

But he wouldn't lose the Court, thought Susanna despondently. Because if Lady Penfold hadn't succumbed to Kit's charm yet, it wouldn't be very long before she did. How could she avoid it when the wretch never put a foot wrong? Those cousins of his didn't stand a chance. There was no need for Susanna to have come to Newmarket at all, no need to have disclosed her scandalous history, no need to have incurred his rage and risked exposing them all to the world's censure.

She was jerked out of her gloomy thoughts by catching sight of an engraved plate on the building they were passing. 'Cocks and Biddulph!' she said. 'This bank draws on Cocks and Biddulph in London. If we go in now, I can write them a draft and repay you for the hats.'

'I beg your pardon?' said Kit, looking startled.

Susanna pointed to the sign. 'Hammonds Bank draws on Cocks and Biddulph in London,' she said slowly and clearly. 'So I may get some of my money out here. I have almost nothing left of what Mr Scott gave me.'

'Ladies do not have bank accounts.'

'Oh, do they not? Then what was I supposed to do with my small savings, pray?

Leave the coins in a leather purse in my trunk for every light-fingered inn servant to find? Sew them into the hem of my cloak and never dare take the wretched garment off? Ladies of *your* acquaintance may not feel the need for a secure place for their money, Mr Kydd, but women in *my* position most certainly do! Adam Prettyman, the manager of the Chartwell Players, opened the account for me some weeks after I joined them. The Sans Pareil's man of business undertook to transfer it to London. I assure you that the peace of mind it engenders makes it worth putting up with the stares I get whenever I enter such an establishment.'

Kit appeared thoroughly put out. 'But dammit, Susanna, I can't go into a bank dangling a couple of band boxes!'

'Then give them to me.'

'And have everyone think I am too high in the instep to carry them myself? No thank you.'

'You will have to wait to be reimbursed, then.'

Kit flushed. 'I'm not quite in Queer Street yet. I can afford to stand you a paltry bonnet or two.'

'That's not what it sounded like in the shop.'

'I was *acting*! Besides, I offered you this

184

job. Suitable clothing is part of it.'

'You did not expect I would have to hide my hair so much.'

Kit looked uncomfortable. 'Oh, well, I may have said some things yesterday I did not mean. I daresay no one else will make the connection.'

'No one else will . . . ?' Susanna shut her mouth with a snap. 'How anyone can have reached the age of five-and-twenty and still be so idiotically optimistic about the world I simply don't know!'

'Sunny disposition. Pray accept the bonnets with my compliments, Miss Fair. You've got the vagueness of fate to save your guineas for. Tilly at your lodgings told me.'

Susanna stared at him, then let out a peal of laughter. '*Vagaries* of Fate. Oh, Kit, you are ridiculous.'

He smiled down at her. 'Better that than an ogre, which I seem to have been doing a good impression of recently. Susanna, I am profoundly ashamed of the way I behaved yesterday.'

A queer feeling wriggled through Susanna's chest. 'That is no reason to lay out your blunt on my hats,' she said, rallying. 'Besides which you had *cause* to be cross.' But his smile was already working on her, weakening her defences.

He saw it. His eyes danced in triumph. 'Very true, and as reparation *you* may buy the pastries for Great-aunt Emma. What shall we try for? Fifteen for the price of twelve?'

Susanna let him tow her along, helpless in the face of his immense charm. Quite why he had decided to forgive her she wasn't prepared to speculate. He was such a mixture of parts that it could be for any reason, or none at all. For the nonce she would simply be grateful and continue to play her part.

* * *

It was when she went up to dress for dinner that she found a third box outside her door. She hesitated a considerable time before opening it. She was almost sure she knew what it contained and didn't want to deal with it.

True to her fears, inside lay the silver net confection with the white silk rose. Susanna's chest grew so tight that she could hardly breathe. The note read, *This is to make amends to both you and the milliner.*

The maid bustled in with a can of hot water. 'Ooh, miss, I thought you only bought the two hats. My word, that will make folk sit up and take notice, that will.'

'Yes. I — ' She heard Kit's voice in the

passage and darted to her door just as he opened his own one opposite.

'Ah,' said Kit. 'Settling day. Five minutes, Motson, please.'

His valet cast him a look of deep disapproval from the stand where he had set out soap, steaming water and a lethal-looking razor. 'As you wish, sir,' he said, stalking past them.

'Kit, I cannot accept the hat,' said Susanna without preamble.

There was a disquieting mischief in his eyes as he drew her inside his room. 'Then you had best pass it on to Great-aunt Emma, for I certainly cannot return it, not after the performance I gave of a man buying it against all his better principles. That milliner thinks she has a customer for life. I swear she was reaching for *La Belle Assemblée* even as I left.'

'But, Kit, why?' wailed Susanna. 'Something so frivolous must have set you back far more than you can afford. And I cannot even wear it here! The silver net will draw attention to my hair, not hide it!'

The laughter faded from Kit's face. He clasped her hands and looked straight into her eyes. 'Because I too was taken aback at our success. I felt guilty.'

Susanna didn't know whether to laugh or

cry. Was he telling the truth? Or simply getting her back on his side?

'And also,' he said fairly, 'having once seen it on you, I could not bear to think of it gracing someone else's head.'

'Oh, don't,' implored Susanna. 'Don't pay me such ridiculous compliments. There is not the least need. No one can hear them here.'

Kit grinned. 'Nor they can't,' he agreed. 'They can't see me kiss you either.' And before she could protest, he took possession of her mouth for a swift, piratical second. 'Let's call that the payment of the bet, shall we?'

The tingling was far stronger this time. It flared instantaneously over the whole of her body, from her toes to her shoulder blades. 'Kit!' she said, shaken to her very core.

He put a finger on her lips and propelled her gently from the room. His valet was hovering meaningfully at the end of the passage. 'Hush. Motson is ready to shave me and I daren't incur his wrath by leaving it a minute longer. You have no idea how unnerving he is with a razor in his hand.'

'You, unnerved?' said Susanna bitterly. 'I wish I may live to see it!'

★ ★ ★

Susanna went down to dinner with her lips still in shock, her heart palpitating, and hitherto dormant parts of her anatomy waking up and demanding more. She was, however, forced to assume a calm air on discovering there were guests. As the introductions were performed, with casual qualifications from Lady Penfold such as 'the local doctor, you know' and 'my man of business', it crossed Susanna's mind that Kit was being put on show. She also realized that as these were all local people who were likely acquainted with the Fortunes, she had best be even more shy and uninteresting than normal. She couldn't hide her hair, but she could at least keep her eyes lowered and not contribute to the conversation unless she had to.

Fortunately it was an informal meal and everyone else seemed more than happy to talk.

'Rutland's getting a house party together,' said Dr Peck, tutting at all the rich food on Lady Penfold's plate. He pointedly selected a *small* portion of quail in butter sauce for himself. 'Word is he's stirring up interest in this filly he's entering for the One Thousand Guineas.'

'Hrmph,' said Lady Penfold. 'Who's training her? Boyce again, I suppose. Seen her in action?'

Dr Peck scratched his chin reflectively. 'Not personally, but my informant tells me there aren't many three-year-olds faster. Will you be back for the races, Kydd?'

'Sadly, my estate has to take priority over my own pleasure,' said Kit. 'It's possible I might be able to spare a few days during the July Meeting. There is little to rival the sight of half a dozen matched horses running free as they were designed to do.'

'Very true. How's that chestnut of yours?' asked another guest.

'Rufus?' Lady Penfold sounded surprised. 'Oh, fair to middling. My god-daughter takes him out for a hack once in a while to stretch his legs. We thought of entering him this year. Would have done it last year except for being in black gloves over Edward. What do you think to this cod, eh? Ever seen one such a size? Damn nuisance fish come with so many bones.'

'Perhaps if you took a smaller helping . . . ?' murmured the doctor.

9

'By the by,' said Lady Penfold at breakfast the next morning. 'It is the monthly assembly at Bury St Edmunds on Monday. Very smart, the New Subscription Rooms. Edward gave a subscription when they were rebuilding. Always go, don't we, Martha? Don't dance of course, but it does us good to get out.'

Susanna's knife clattered to the plate. She was horrified. She had never been to a ball in her life. It would be worse by far than the impromptu dance at the Graingers' house. So much for Kit's assertion that Lady Penfold no doubt lived quite retired. She looked at him for reassurance but his face was so ingenuous she knew exactly what he was thinking. She glared, daring him to say a single thing about it being just the occasion for silver-net hair confections. 'It sounds delightful,' she said mendaciously. 'Do many of your neighbours attend?'

'Adeline Fortune will be there for one. Trying to get Honoria off her hands without the expense of a London season. Daresay the chit'll take well enough, but Lord, give me Caro over that insipid miss any time.'

Too perturbed to sit still, Susanna poured herself another cup of coffee from the sideboard, only remembering afterwards that she should have let someone do it for her. 'I liked Miss Caroline Fortune very much when I met her the other day,' she said, bestowing a smile on the slightly mollified footman as she sat down.

Lady Penfold chuckled. 'Always says what she thinks, does Caro, which don't endear her to Adeline above half.' She sighed and tackled a large slice of ham. 'Only just seventeen, you know. Often thought if she'd been older, Bertrand might have sold out early.'

Was *that* why Caroline didn't want to be a 'proper young lady' and join the marriage mart? She concealed her heartache very well if so. 'Don't you think she would rather have followed him to the Peninsula, ma'am?' said Susanna.

Lady Penfold stared, her fork held halfway to her mouth. 'Stap me if you ain't right! I can just see her doing it too. I'd have lost them both! Well, blow me down.' She finished her breakfast looking much more cheerful.

Kit smiled at Susanna, which made her feel bad all over again, for she'd said what she felt, not something designed to please.

During the course of the morning the ladies sustained a visit from Caroline herself, in attendance on her mother and sister and looking very gawky and unfinished in comparison to either of them.

'I hear you have bought that tremendously fast hat in Mrs Roger's shop,' she whispered in Susanna's ear. 'Do wear it to the assembly on Monday. It will be wonderful to see Mama forced to be polite to you because you are Lady Penfold's guest.'

'Certainly not,' said Susanna in an undertone. 'What an unnatural daughter you are. Mr Kydd purchased it as a . . . that is, he bought it for a wager. I should not dream of embarrassing anyone by actually wearing it.'

'Pity,' said Caroline, unabashed. 'Especially as everybody will be expecting you to.'

'Now see what you have done,' said Susanna to Kit when she encountered him on the stairs later that day. 'The whole of Newmarket is talking about that wretched hat. I am become infamous!'

He grinned unrepentantly. 'You should be thankful it was not me who had the dressing of you. Who knows what indelicate garments might now be languishing in your closet.'

'I have worn enough indelicate garments these last few months to last me a lifetime,' she said, refusing to be diverted by thoughts of what else he might like to buy her. 'Why are you so cheerful? Did you back a winner at the cock-fight we are not supposed to know you attended this afternoon?'

He smiled even more widely. 'I did, but that is not all. It may interest you to know that afterwards, I was invited back to play billiards with Harry Fortune.'

Susanna's hand flew to her breast. 'Oh, Kit, you did not go? I wish you had not. You have not been saying anything to him, have you?'

'I have not given away your secret, if that is what you mean.' But his eyes danced so disquietingly that Susanna felt quite sick with apprehension.

'Then what?' she begged.

But he refused to say any more, merely flicking her carelessly on the cheek and telling her not to worry, before taking the remaining stairs two at a time in order to change into clothes which did not smell as if he had spent the entire day in the company of the lower orders.

* * *

As Kit shut the bedroom door behind him, his demeanour underwent an abrupt change. His new-found acquaintances would never have recognized him as the same sporting blade who had been so free with his friendship that afternoon.

What to do for the best? That was the question hammering at Kit's brain. How to balance Susanna's present safety and future prospects with his own unfolding desires.

He grimaced at his reflection. It shouldn't have taken Johnny to point out what a blockhead he was being. Susanna was the perfect foil, quick and clever and unafraid to rake him down when she felt herself wronged. As soon as he'd acquitted her of using him, he'd realized it. And she was right — something *did* seem to happen to them when they were together. He had only been half-joking when he'd made that remark about not wanting to see the silver-net hat on anybody else's head. The comedy they had enacted in the shop had bound it to her and he wasn't at all sure that it hadn't worked on him the same way.

What he emphatically *hadn't* intended to do was kiss her again, but her reaction had taken away the last of his doubts. He had felt her quiver, had known better than she did herself what her response would have been had he let it go on even a second longer. He'd stood there, a golden shaft of realization drying his tongue and petrifying his brain. In Susanna he might actually have found someone with whom it *wouldn't* be a penance to share his life and his home. But how to convince her of it? He hadn't forgotten her reaction the first time he had tried to help. *Look around you*, she'd said, *the world I live in is not yours*. He might disregard her background, but she most certainly would not!

Which brought him full circle to what he might have discovered this afternoon. Would it make a difference to her? And if the answer to that was yes, then ought he to pursue it? Kit changed his clothes slowly, revolving possible plans of action in his head. Only one thing was definite: for once in his life he wasn't going to do anything in haste. He had a God-given opportunity to spend ten days of enforced idleness persuading Susanna into a more flexible frame of mind regarding what she saw as an unequal alliance. If he couldn't turn the circumstances of this false engagement to advantage in that time, then he didn't deserve to succeed.

★ ★ ★

Monday evening saw the party embark for the Assembly Rooms at Bury St Edmunds. As it was a journey of some fifteen miles with rain threatening, it was felt by the ladies that Kit would be far better off riding in the coach than taking his curricle as originally planned.

All the ladies except Susanna, that is. The Assembly necessitated more-formal attire than she had yet seen Kit wear, and the sight of him at dinner in a tail coat, silk knee-breeches and clocked stockings had affected her so powerfully as to reduce her appetite to a mere trace. Personally, she would have preferred him *anywhere* other than sitting opposite her, his blue eyes resting on her much more than was comfortable and his thinly clad legs brushing hers whenever they hit a bump in the road.

'Not wearing your hat?' he had teased in the hallway.

'It would not have matched the ivory satin,' she had said repressively.

'And a plain chignon with the pearl clip does?'

'Yes,' Susanna had snapped. 'And furthermore it is exactly what I wish. This is the first public assembly I have ever attended. It will be a lot easier if my every mistake is not instantly taken note of. I wish you had let me cry off.'

'Deuce take it, Susanna, it is only a country assembly, for all we look so fine. We will dance, make polite conversation, eat an indifferent supper and come home again. How difficult can it be?'

Now she shifted on the seat, trying not to make contact with his knees. He had no notion. It was all very well for him, he had grown up with occasions like this. She hadn't even seen them from the other side of the baize door. All the description in the world could not prepare her for what to expect.

She also had another source of worry: the growing warmth in Kit's eyes and the tendency he had shown over the last couple of days to seek out her company, apparently for no other reason than to fleece her at piquet, argue about Scott and Byron, and teach her the finer points of billiards. This last seemed to involve an unconscionable amount of laying his arm against hers and his hand over hers in order to fractionally change the position of the cue. Lady Penfold might approve, but it had got so that he had only to stand behind her for her legs to buckle and her aim to go wildly astray! He was dangerous when bored, Nell had said, and if Susanna knew nothing else about Kit, she was as certain as it was possible to be that kicking his heels in polite attendance on an elderly lady was chafing him to no small degree. If only this deception could have been played out at Kydd Court, where he could channel his spare energies into the regeneration of the estate, Susanna would have felt far more sanguine. As it was, she couldn't escape the suspicion that he was looking to *her* to inject a little excitement into his life. Given the way she felt about him, whether it was love or gratitude or just an unseemly attraction, she couldn't afford to let him succeed.

Meanwhile, there was tonight to get out of the way. The Assembly Rooms were on Angel Hill. Lady Penfold had talked glibly of the famous abbey and its Roman arch and the botanic gardens laid out inside, but all Susanna could glimpse in the gathering dusk was old stonework and paler, newer houses. She hoped fervently that the overcast sky would cause Lady Penfold such anxiety on behalf of her horses that they would have to leave the assembly early. Impersonating a gently bred young lady in the closed world of a private house was one thing, stepping boldly into the public arena was quite another.

They entered the vestibule (too grand, panicked Susanna) and were made known to the Master of Ceremonies. In far too short a time, Lady Penfold and Martha were ensconced on the sturdiest of the cushioned benches around the wall and Susanna was lining up opposite Kit for the first country dance. She was in such a state of nerves that his was the sole face which stood out amidst the wash of people surrounding her. The chandeliers might have been tallow dips and the elegant panelling so much painted scenery for all the impact they had. The music started, only its familiarity prompting her hands and feet to make the correct moves. But gradually her head translated the orchestra into the old pianoforte in the housekeeper's room, her mother calling out the steps as she played, and she began to relax.

'That's better,' said Kit's voice from a long way off. 'I was afraid you had been summoned by some malignant spirit into one of those gothic trances which are scattered so widely amongst novels these days.'

Susanna focused on him, and realized with a start that they had nearly reached the end of the progression. 'Oh my goodness,' she said, darting a glance at their neighbours. 'Have I offended anyone?'

Kit grinned, taking her hand as they changed places. 'No,' he said. 'What is worrying you? You were not this tense at the Graingers' house.'

I had had two glasses of wine with the meal to give me courage there, thought Susanna, but did not dare say so aloud lest he abandon her to go and procure some. 'It was

'. . . cosier,' she said inadequately.

Kit looked highly amused. 'Cosier? Mrs Grainger would be mortified.'

They switched places again. 'You know what I mean,' she said.

'Yes, I do,' said Kit, relenting. 'Are you able to go down the progression? I should hate to lose you before we reach the bottom.'

Their fingertips touched briefly together, then they wheeled in opposite directions and walked down outside the long line. Susanna was aware of Kit keeping pace with her all the way. They had just clasped hands again when the music came to an end. She felt a wave of utter relief.

'Refreshment,' said Kit. 'I prescribe a glass of champagne, topped up at judicious intervals with lemonade.'

'Adding physicking to your other accomplishments?' She disengaged her hand and let him steer her across the room.

'Evening, Kydd!' A cheerful voice halted them. 'You got pressed into this bun-fight too, I see.'

Kit turned around. 'Fortune,' he said affably. 'I don't believe you have made my betrothed's acquaintance. Miss Fair, might I introduce Mr Fortune to you?'

Susanna's first feeling was to wish they had reached the champagne first. Her second was sheer, enormous gratitude that Kit was with her. His arm next to hers was rock-steady, his very presence infected her with some of his own bravado. 'I am pleased to meet you,' she said, extending her hand to Harry Fortune and dropping him a small curtsey.

'And I you. Would you care to stand up with me for the next dance?'

Susanna felt a stab of horror. 'Thank you,' she said helplessly, 'that is most kind.'

'Steal my partner, would you?' said Kit with easy address. 'Then I'd better offer my services to your sister.'

'Honoria?' said Harry. 'Not unless you want to be bored stiff for the next half-hour.'

'I was thinking of Miss *Caroline* Fortune.'

Harry's expression cleared. 'Oh yes, Caro's a great gun.'

Caroline professed herself delighted. Her ready chatter made other conversation unnecessary and Susanna was more than ever grateful to Kit for his thoughtfulness — until she realized that he was using the opportunity to discover why the girl was so often to be found in their stables in the early morning.

'Oh, that is the only time I can talk to Lady Penfold without having to mind my words in front of company,' replied Caroline with artless candour. 'It didn't used to be a problem before it was decided I should come out in Honoria's wake, so as to save the expense of launching me properly. I could always slip away from our governess on the flimsiest of pretexts. But these days Mama insists on knowing where I am all the time in case anyone comes to call. It is a dead bore, I can tell you.'

Susanna smiled as the four of them circled in time to the music. It did not seem to her that Caroline Fortune was any more fettered by convention than her brother. She peeped up at Harry as they danced to the centre of a four-point star and back again, apprehensive that he would now join in the conversation and expect her to bear a part. To her relief, however, his attention was directed at someone over her shoulder.

'Louisa Taylor,' said Caroline knowledgeably. 'I have known her for ever and poor Harry is smitten, but unfortunately her father is the most prominent goldsmith in Bury St Edmunds.'

'Why is that unfortunate?' said Susanna, noticing with some indignation that Kit's eyes had also turned towards the blonde beauty in the next set.

'Because Harry has no expectations and a quite dreadful reputation into the bargain. Louisa would have to be out of her wits to do more than stand up for a country dance with him.'

'One day,' said Harry amiably, 'someone is going to throttle you. I beg your pardon, Miss Fair, was I neglecting you?'

Heavens, his eyes really were the same grey as her own. Susanna kept hers downcast and said, 'Not at all. It is I who might seem uncivil. I have to concentrate so hard on the steps, you see, that I have often been accused of wool-gathering whilst dancing.'

'There,' said Caroline, 'what a good thing it is that Mr Kydd asked me to make up the group. I have never had the least difficulty in talking and dancing at the same time. Do you think as a reward you could contrive to procure me a glass of champagne before Mama realizes?'

Kit looked amused. 'Certainly. I regret I cannot draw you away from her for supper, but that dance is promised to Susanna.'

'Oh, I daresay I shall manage something,' said Caroline.

At the end of the dance there was a general move towards the refreshments. Harry took advantage of Louisa Taylor's partner's disappearance in search of lemonade to enter into a spirited conversation with her. Susanna just had time to feel grateful at having got through the set without exciting any interest in him when a booming shout rocked her stability once again.

'Miss Fair! Well, by all that's wonderful!'

Utterly dismayed, Susanna saw Colonel MacGregor, of all people, pushing towards her! Whatever was he doing in this part of the world? The evening was going from bad to worse. She looked desperately for Kit, but he was several crowded feet away. 'Colonel,' she gasped, 'how, er, unexpected.'

'Staying with Rutland!' he boomed again. 'Over at Cheveley, you know.'

'Why, that is quite close to us,' piped up Caroline at once. 'Oh, I do beg your pardon. I am forever getting into conversation with people before being introduced. Mama is always scolding me about it.'

After which Susanna had perforce to present the Colonel in the sure knowledge that five minutes of conversation with her young friend would acquaint him with all there was to know about her and Kit's situation. So much for news of the false engagement not getting back to Northamptonshire! Kit would be furious.

'Lady Penfold?' said Colonel MacGregor, looking astounded. 'Kydd's great-aunt is Lady Penfold?'

'Yes,' said Susanna. 'She is on that settle with her widowed daughter-in-law.'

Colonel MacGregor's bushy eyebrows shot up his forehead. 'Good God!' he yelled, scattering all and sundry as he made a bee-line for Lady Penfold. 'Emma! I should never have recognized you!'

Kit came up behind them, carrying three glasses. 'An old acquaintance, do I gather?'

Susanna took her champagne gratefully. 'It would seem so. He mentioned at the Graingers' house that he used to know your grandmother. It appears he was familiar with the whole family.'

'I think it's lovely,' said Caroline. 'Thank you *very* much for my champagne, Mr Kydd. If Mama asks, I shall tell her it was lemonade.' Her hand was then solicited by a friend of her brother, no doubt to disguise the fact that Harry himself was leading the vivacious Louisa into the same set.

'It seems Miss Caroline is made use of by everybody,' said Kit, looking after her.

'I do not think she minds,' said Susanna, resting her hand on his arm as they moved to a quieter part of the room. 'Do you suppose there is *any* chance that we shall be leaving soon?'

Kit looked down at her, his eyes laughing. 'My poor girl. Are you hating this so much?'

'Yes,' said Susanna, unsettled by the careless endearment. She struggled to express her misgivings, the ones which *weren't* bound up with the fact that even standing next to him made her pulse behave erratically. 'Firstly, I am convinced every moment that I will do something wrong. Also, Colonel MacGregor now believes us to be engaged, so you will have to explain to your whole neighbourhood when you get home that I have jilted you. And third — oh Kit, the more we mix in public the more aware I am that this sham does you and your family and your friends a gross disservice.'

There was the tiniest of pauses. 'What if it were not a sham?' he said.

Her brow creased. 'Not a sham? How do you mean?'

'If you were at this assembly legitimately with the man you truly loved. Would it be as trying an experience then?'

Afterwards, Susanna could only put her reply down to too fast an ingestion of champagne. 'If I knew, without question, that the man I loved, loved me — then it would not matter where we were,' she said. 'Together or apart, the world would cease to hold any terrors.'

'That would be something,' said Kit, 'to be that man.'

She looked up into the intense blue of Kit's eyes. For a heart-stopping moment time stilled around them. Then someone bumped into her and the spell was broken.

It was the gentleman who had been dancing with Miss Taylor before. He was carrying a glass of lemonade and looking hot and bothered. 'I beg your pardon,' he said, 'I was searching for my partner.'

'Aren't we all,' murmured Kit.

Susanna felt herself blush flame red. Champagne, it seemed, was a vastly more dangerous drink even than Madeira. 'I had best sit with your great-aunt a while. I would not want her to think I am neglecting her.'

Kit's lips twitched. 'She won't thank you for it.'

Susanna glanced across the length of the room to where Lady Penfold and Colonel MacGregor were roaring with laughter, drawing pained expressions from all those within earshot.

'Alternatively,' said Kit as the musicians started up again, 'you could dance the waltz with me. You do know the steps?'

Susanna's mouth dried. 'I . . . well, yes, but I — '

'Honoria! Caroline! Over here, if you please!' Adeline Fortune's voice issued from nearby, sharp and commanding.

'Kit, I do not think it is proper for young ladies to — '

But his hand was on the small of her back, propelling her forward. 'If you sit it out, you will be hard pressed to avoid Mrs Fortune,' he warned. 'Of course, if you believe her to be as unobservant as her son as regards hair and eye colour . . . '

'There is no need to sound so smug,' hissed Susanna, hastening to the other side of a concealing group of dancers.

He chuckled reprehensibly in her ear. 'Is there not?'

His arm was already about her, his other hand holding hers. As she laid her palm on his upper arm, his clasp tightened in a disturbingly proprietorial manner.

The satin and silk of her costume was no bar to her being quiveringly aware of every part of him. Which meant, she realized with a rapid thumping of her heart, that he could almost certainly feel the curves and planes of her body too. The appreciative smile as he shifted his hand fractionally lower did nothing to dispel this impression.

'I am sure it is not necessary to hold me so close,' she said, making a valiant effort to sound disinterested.

His breathing rate had increased as they started to dance. 'I am considering your dignity,' he said. His hand moved again, less a hold than a caress. His voice grew huskier. 'You would not want to go wrong in such an interesting dance and embarrass yourself in front of all these people.'

They would be embarrassed far worse if she didn't do something right now! 'Small chance of that,' she retorted. 'My feet are all but stepping on your toes!' *And my thigh is hard against yours and if my bodice is not brushing against your waistcoat it is only by severe restraint upon my part!*

Her prosaic tone had its effect. She felt the moment he came to his senses, when he remembered they were in a public ballroom with people all around them and his great-aunt only a few turns of the dance away. He loosened his grasp until a respectable handspan separated them. 'Is this better?'

Contrarily, Susanna's body informed her that it was not better at all. It was as if something unbearably wonderful had just been wrenched away from her. 'Much more conventional,' she said.

After the waltz, she recovered her equanimity by standing up with Harry's friend for an unexceptional country dance, then repaired to Lady Penfold's side to drink a much-needed glass of lemonade.

'Extraordinary,' her hostess greeted her. 'Meeting Randolph MacGregor again. He had quite a tendre for Georgiana in the old days you know, but he was far too young, even if it hadn't been clear to the entire county that Jonathan was the only man who would ever be able to control her. To think he's been staying at Cheveley off and on all this time and me not knowing. I daresay Edward met him often enough during the race weeks, but Randolph had already gone into the army by the time I met Edward, so neither of them would have had any idea who the other was. I've invited him to dine. Ten to one he'll look at Edward's portrait and say he's been acquainted with him these twenty years.'

Susanna sipped her lemonade. 'But surely, forgive me if I am speaking out of turn, but I understood that you didn't want to be reminded of your life before you met Lord Penfold. Kit told me that his father said you did not seek closer family ties.'

Lady Penfold hrmphed and drank some of her wine. 'I'll tell you,' she said gruffly. 'When Edward was alive, I didn't need anyone else. He had a way of filling the whole horizon. It is only since he's been gone that I realize how my world has shrunk. Makes me wonder if I've been a bit too stubborn.'

'I cannot believe you would have derived any more enjoyment from your life by forgiving your father's harsh treatment than by throwing your lot wholeheartedly behind your husband.'

Lady Penfold chuckled and patted her hand. 'You're a good girl.' She was silent for a moment. 'But you're not as happy as you could be. Just because I'm old, it doesn't make me unobservant. Uncertainty, is it? Want me to write to your uncle telling him I'm making young Kit my heir? Think that'll do the trick?'

Susanna met her eyes, startled. 'No!' she said before she could stop herself. 'I mean, it is very good of your ladyship, and you do Kit great honour, but you must not decide before you have met the other branch of the family. The fact that Kit himself does not get along with them, does not mean you won't either.'

'Ha!' said Lady Penfold, obscurely pleased. 'Had a notion you'd say something of the sort. Meant it, too, didn't you? Well, well, here the boy comes to claim you for the supper dance. Mind you tell him to keep a respectable distance between the pair of you this time!'

Susanna escaped, conscious that Lady Penfold saw a good deal more than was comfortable, and conscious also that her words gave Susanna the assurance that her own physical presence in Newmarket was no longer necessary for Kit's advancement. Which was good, very good. It was merely weak-willed sentimentality to imagine that there was nowhere else she would rather be.

10

It had to be done. During their morning walk, Susanna screwed up her courage and told Kit it would be best for all concerned if she were to leave Newmarket.

'You cannot!' he said, stopping dead in consternation.

Susanna gripped her reticule. His reaction, gratifying though it was, only strengthened her determination. That waltz had shown how dangerously close Kit was to finding her more than attractive. Given the susceptibility of her own feelings, she would never be able to hold out against him. Before she knew it, she would be in her mother's predicament. She would rather go now before she discovered that Kit had feet of clay. 'I must. On Friday it will be March and I shall be free of Mr Warwick's wager. Lady Penfold is disposed to look favourably on you now, and you must see that each day I remain increases the danger of my being exposed as a fraud.'

'I do not see it at all!'

Every shred of acting ability Susanna possessed went into her good-humoured answer. 'The fact of the matter is that *you* are so realistic a dissembler you have persuaded yourself I am indeed a gently born young lady who has the right to live in the society you inhabit. But I am not, Kit, and it is not only me who would be shunned if the truth were known. You may be careless of your own standing in the world but Lady Penfold would be made to look ridiculous. I am persuaded you would not want that.'

'Nor do I want you taking off with no money, no destination in mind and no man to protect you!'

'You do not have the right to stop me.' The strain of sustaining the light-hearted tone was making it difficult to concentrate. Susanna felt more wretched with every word. The sapphire ring weighed down her finger, reminding her that she had agreed to play this part for the whole visit. It was scant comfort that she would further the deception far better by leaving than by staying; she knew what she was doing was running away.

There was a long silence as they cut across the top of the town and walked towards the church. 'Would you consider returning to Kydd then, until I am free to escort you somewhere else?' said Kit at last. 'It would ease my mind knowing Tom Olivant and the Coppings were nearby, and there is ample scope for employment in the house should you need occupation.'

Susanna felt weak with relief. From Northampton she could take a stage to anywhere she chose and he would never know. 'Very well,' she said.

'And you will not go until Friday?'

'If you insist.' She felt so guilty at betraying his trust that she made no demur about taking his arm as they crossed one of the paths traversing the green. She did not even object when he pulled her out of the way of an urchin who was thrusting printed bills at every gentleman he could see. Friday would be soon enough to regret no longer having this evidence of his care. No doubt by nightfall she would be enumerating each tender bruise, each remembered touch.

Kit looked at the paper he'd been handed. 'The theatre company are opening on Thursday night,' he said. 'They respectfully request our attendance at *Hamlet or The Prince Of Denmark*, followed by the first showing outside London of *Whackham and Windham, The Wrangling Lawyers*. Great-aunt Emma will be delighted. Not only a play, but a wonderful excuse to set dinner forward since the doors open at five.'

He spoke in a forced likeness of his usual tones. Susanna bit her lip. Be strong, she reminded herself, he will thank you in the long run. '*Whackham and Windham?*' she said. 'That is one of Miss Scott's. There was some talk of reviving it whilst I was at the Sans Pareil. May I see?'

'I daresay one of the company was in the Strand when it was put on before and conned enough to make a copy,' said Kit. 'It is often done, I believe.'

'Very frequently. They were rehearsing *A School For Scandal* when I asked at Drury Lane for work, and I was astonished to see how different it was from the performance we had been offering with the Chartwell Players.' Her eyes dropped to the playbill. She found she had to blink to clear them. As the bold black print swam into focus, the blood thrummed in her veins. 'Oh!'

Instantly, Kit's arm was around her waist, supporting her. 'What is it? What's wrong, sweetheart? Are you ill? Tell me!'

The endearment caught on her mind to be remembered later. For now she pointed shakily to the legend at the top of the paper. 'The theatre company — it is the Chartwell Players.'

For a moment there was silence. 'Is that bad?' asked Kit. 'Would they give you away?'

'No,' said Susanna. 'Certainly not Adam and Mary, the actor-manager and his wife. They were the best of people, and very good to me. It is simply that I would have liked to see how they go on, but . . . '

She stopped. She *could* now visit them. Her feelings for Adam — the small, pale, gratitude-fed longings that she'd thought such a threat to his marriage she'd fled to London rather than give in to them — had vanished. They'd been extinguished in the strength of her love for Kit.

Love.

She'd said it in her head without thinking. It must be true.

'But?' prompted Kit.

She was still standing in the circle of his arm. She stepped away hastily. 'But one of Lady Penfold's acquaintances might see us enter the company's quarters and wonder why. Word would travel back to her quicker than we'd get there ourselves. It isn't worth the risk. I had best wear a close bonnet and sit in the shadows when we watch the play. Any of the company will know me else and be offended when I do not go round.' Even as she spoke, an idea formed. She opened her mouth to advance it, then stopped with sinking heart when she saw Kit was frowning. He had not liked to be reminded that she was an actress.

They walked on a little way. 'I have been thinking,' he said, and she could see how much the words cost him. 'It is not right that you should be prevented from seeing your friends because I involved you in my affairs. If you plead a headache tonight, I daresay I could smuggle you out of the house for a short visit.'

'Thank you.' She moistened her lips. 'It occurs to me that at the performance the Players may announce where they are to go when they leave Newmarket. I might await them there and rejoin them. That would give me a purpose and save you the awkwardness and expense of my travel to Kydd Court. It is not as if I would be staying beyond your own return anyway.'

Far from being relieved that at least she was not now thinking of setting forth into the unknown, Kit's looks grew even blacker.

At the house, Susanna found her bonnet strings had tied themselves into a knot. 'Go on,' she said, as she wrestled with them. 'I will be there as soon as — '

'You are making it worse,' said Kit. 'Here, let me.' He tilted her chin to the light and studied the snarl of ribbons.

Oh this wasn't *fair*! What use was it trying to be strong and doing the right thing when circumstances repeatedly conspired with Fate to put her into situations like this? Susanna hardly dared breathe as Kit's fingers brushed her throat. She looked into his face, bent close to hers and with golden eyelashes down-swept as he teased apart the tangle, and knew how little it would take to give herself away. *Friday*, she told herself, trembling. She had only to keep her feelings for him hidden until Friday.

'A letter came for you in the post,' said Lady Penfold. 'What's that you're holding?'

'Oh, it is the playbill for the theatre company. They are arrived already and advertising their first show.' He gave it to his great-aunt and started to open his letter. 'I daresay this will be my sister, to say they are arrived in . . . ' His voice tailed off.

Susanna saw his face change and was assailed by a stab of worry. 'What is it? Is something amiss with Nell?'

Kit screwed up the paper and threw it on the fire. 'No, it was from my cousins. Felicitating me on my betrothal and express-ing surprise that they had heard of it from Lady Penfold, not myself or the *Gazette*. It seems they have more family feeling than I credited them with. They long to know all about you, Susanna.'

Susanna gripped her hands together tightly, feeling more and more ill. She hadn't given a thought to Kit's cousins testing the story they had fabricated. They would certainly lose no time in exposing the charade to Lady Penfold should they discover her real history. She watched Kit leave the room, anxiety filling her.

★ ★ ★

For Kit, his cousin' letter was an irritant, no more. They would be paying their own visit soon; what happened during it was beyond his control so it was pointless to worry. Now he had got to know her, he trusted entirely to Great-aunt Emma's intelligence to see through James and Dick. Far more pressing was the problem of how to keep Susanna here. His mind must have been disordered indeed to have ever imagined she was trying to entrap him. Every time he got near the girl she skittered away! He knew perfectly well that she had had no intention of staying at the Court. He had made the suggestion in the desperation of the moment purely to give himself an extra couple of days in which to persuade her to accept him. And now she had this appalling plan of joining her previous travelling company again! One thing was certain — she wasn't going anywhere until Kit had seen the conditions with his own eyes.

He paced irritably up to the paddocks. On

the other side of the boundary, Harry Fortune was putting a young filly through her paces. Kit leant on the rail and watched, liking his gentle hands and patient instruction. 'Thunder and turf, Fortune, you're never working?'

Harry grinned. 'Louisa's father paid a visit, cutting up rough about my waltzing with her and muttering stuff about idle whelps and horsewhips which my revered papa found himself in complete agreement with. In consequence, and especially with a bill arriving from my tailor, I thought it might be wise to be blamelessly occupied for the day.'

Kit laughed. 'And the evening?'

Another grin. 'Louisa knows I'm not much of a catch, but she don't like to be driven, d'you see. Her father happens to be hosting a masquerade at the Bury St Edmunds Guildhall tonight and she bribed his groom to palm me an invitation. Plain brown domino and mask, and no one will know me except for a certain delectable Columbine.'

Kit reached up to fondle the filly's neck. 'Sounds like the sort of thing a man might like an alibi for . . . '

*   *   *

At dinner, observing aloud how little Susanna was eating, Kit was solicitous in suggesting that she was possibly unwell and that she should go and lie down for the rest of the evening.

Her eyes widened, then as he had known she would, she agreed that she was a little overtired and would benefit from an early night if Lady Penfold did not mind excusing her.

'Oh,' said Kit, 'that is very true. I had forgot that I am engaged with Harry Fortune myself this evening. I had better cancel so you are not completely bereft of company.'

'None of that,' chuckled his great-aunt. 'Young men will be young men as well I know. As for you, miss, get yourself to bed and let me see some more colour in your cheeks in the morning. Martha will tell you I ought to be retiring early myself tonight with all the racketing around we've been doing recently.'

★ ★ ★

Susanna felt very conspicuous hurrying along by Kit's side towards the barn that the Chartwell Players had hired. There seemed to be an unconscionable number of men abroad, all of them on pleasure bent. She was glad of her concealing blue cloak, no matter that underneath she wore a modest spotted muslin with a lawn fichu tucked into the bodice for warmth and decency.

'Perfect,' Kit had said when he'd tapped at her door to tell her the hallway was clear. He himself was dressed in riding coat and top boots as if intending to while away the last few hours of Shrove Tuesday in the company of Harry Fortune. This, he informed her cheerfully, had done him no disservice at all in Great-aunt Emma's eyes when he had popped his head around the door to make his goodbye.

'Oh, Kit, this gets worse and worse. Have you thought what will happen when Caroline tells Lady Penfold tomorrow that her brother spent a blameless evening at home?'

Kit slanted a mischievous look down at her. 'Ah, but, he won't. I happen to know he has a clandestine assignation with the fair Miss Taylor. Thus he is only too willing to let it be thought he is acquainting me with the more dubious diversions that the countryside has to offer.'

Susanna narrowed her eyes at him, a sudden suspicion crossing her mind. 'Kit, can it possibly be that you are *enjoying* this?'

He grinned happily in the lamplight and tucked her arm closer into his. 'You have to admit, it beats playing backgammon for chicken stakes. Now, are you sure these players of yours will be at the barn? Will they not rather be ensconced snugly at the Market Inn for the night?'

Susanna shook her head. 'Not on the first evening in a new town. Adam always stays with the wagons. They will be surprised to see me, for I'm sure they thought I would be a fixture in Mr Kean's company by now.'

'I have wondered that myself,' said Kit.

Susanna flushed. 'It transpired that the actor who said he could get me a place at the theatre had a rather different idea of my role than I had. So I left.'

'You cannot be held responsible for everyone's good taste.'

'Well, really!' she said, pulling away from him. 'I am sure I do not know what it is about me which makes certain gentlemen so very determined. It is not as if I ever encourage them — and if you saw the way some of the dancers at the London theatres flirt with their admirers, you would think me positively straight-laced!'

'I have seen them,' said Kit. 'Far too obvious. *You* hint at depth beneath the surface.'

'Fudge!' said Susanna. 'I wish you would not talk such nonsense. I am too pale and too thin. You told me so yourself. Oh, there are the wagons! We have found the place! You will like Adam, Kit, but take care. He has only to meet a person once before he can copy their actions and mimic their voice.'

'A useful attribute in an actor.' Kit closed the gate behind them. 'And did it never occur to you that some people find pale and thin attractive?'

'Then some people,' retorted Susanna, her pace increasing as she spotted familiar forms and faces across the field, 'have windmills in their head.' She waved energetically to a burly fair-haired man just emerging from the lit doorway of the barn. 'Adam! Adam!'

The man peered in their direction and strode forward. 'Susanna?' he said incredulously. Then he gave a great laugh and bellowed, 'Mary! Susanna is here!' before enfolding her in a resounding hug, giving her a smacking kiss and swinging her around. 'Plague take it, girl, whatever are you doing in these parts? Has our luck changed? Are you coming back to us? We thought you'd be lording it over them all at Drury Lane by now!'

Susanna faltered. Faced with plain, honest, hard-working Adam, dedicated to his art and forever struggling to keep his company solvent, her reasons for being in Newmarket seemed horribly shallow.

'Miss Fair is bearing my great-aunt company for a few days,' said Kit in an odd, clipped voice.

Thank you, thought Susanna fervently. She laid her hand on his arm. 'Kit, this is Mr Prettyman, the manager of the Chartwell Players.' She paused. Adam had a peculiar look on his face and Kit seemed to have turned to ice. Surely he hadn't been bothered by Adam's exuberant greeting? She hurried on. 'I, er, found myself in difficulties, Adam. Mr Kydd and his sister rescued me.'

'Good of them,' said Adam, in tones which intimated that it was anything but.

Susanna's temper snapped. 'Well, and so it was, for the alternative was not to have been borne.'

A small girl tugged at Adam's leg. 'Papa, Mama says if it is indeed Susanna, then why does she not come inside?'

'I beg your pardon, Lottie,' said Susanna, turning from the men with a distinct sense of deliverance. 'Do bring me to your mama. Is she well?'

The little girl skipped along beside her. 'No, for first there was the fire and she got a cough, and then the new baby grew wrong and made her ill, but he is in Heaven now and soon Mama will be better again.'

A horrid presentiment gripped Susanna. 'Mary?' she called as her eyes adapted to the lantern light in the barn. At the far end a familiar, rudimentary stage had been erected. Her heart gave a strange pang. She had forgotten the peculiar pleasure of every new place being home as soon as the Players unpacked.

Next to the stage, tucked into a bed made of hay bales, a brown-haired woman was propped up darning a rent in the stage curtains. Her face lit up, emphasizing its gauntness. 'Susanna!'

Susanna hurried forward, past the men building up the boxes. 'Lottie tells me there was a fire and you lost the baby. Oh, Mary, I'm so sorry.'

Mary Prettyman gave a strained smile. 'Lottie's tongue runs on fiddlesticks. However, she is a good girl and if I ask her to go to Mrs Jackson and bring us back two bowls of broth, she can do it without spilling a single drop.'

'That would be capital,' said Susanna, 'for Mrs Jackson's broth is fit for the queens and duchesses she plays and so you may tell her, Lottie.'

Lottie beamed with pride and trotted off on the errand. Out of habit, Susanna threaded a needle and began work on the far side of the tear. 'You do not look well. Tell me everything. Should you have come so far?'

The thin shoulders shrugged. 'I had no choice. Our takings started to fall off soon after you left. Then the barn we were playing in towards Gloucester caught fire and a lot of stock had to be replaced, but even with new scenery the audiences were not so generous as they had been. We were near desperate when the Duke of Rutland saw us play at Bath. His Grace is very fond of Shakespeare and fortunately I was well that day. He offered us a handsome fee and travelling costs into the bargain if we would act for him here. There would never be another chance to change circuits so profitably.'

'But your health! Could you not have waited behind until you were recovered and then come on later?'

Mary's lips compressed. 'Where Adam and the children go, I go.'

There always had been this streak of obstinacy in her. Grateful as Susanna must ever be to the older woman for taking her in and befriending her, she had never quite got over the feeling that such ruthless self-subjection in pursuit of her husband's livelihood could not be beneficial to either party. It was one of the reasons she had left, the knowledge that she herself could have shaken Adam into being a man, not just an actor. She bit her tongue, however, and told Mary circumstances had necessitated her leaving London, but that she was making a short visit in Newmarket so would be able to watch the plays. It was a welcome distraction when Kit's shadow fell across her.

'Oh, Mary, I must introduce Mr Kydd to you. He and his sister have been so kind to me.' She looked up at Kit. 'Mary is the best Shakespeare actress I know.'

'Enchanted,' murmured Kit, bending low over Mary's work-worn hand. 'I would quiz you on your favourite parts, but I foolishly asked your husband if there was anything I could do to help and he has enlisted my aid with the seating for your admiring public.' With which astonishing statement he stripped right down to his shirtsleeves, laying the discarded garments next to Susanna before striding over to the nearside of Joe Jackson's long bench and hefting it into place with him.

'Very comely,' commented Mary. 'You have done well for yourself.'

Susanna hauled her attention back from Kit's splendid physique, displayed to mesmerizing advantage by the lack of conventional clothing. 'Too comely,' she said with feeling. Then the other woman's words sank in. 'It is not like that,' she said, her cheeks flaming.

'He is a friend, no more.'

Mary's raised eyebrows made plain her disbelief.

'I will prove it! Where are you to play after Newmarket? It is possible I might rejoin you there, if you will have me?' *And that was it. The die cast. Forgive me, Kit.*

'If we will have you? Why, there is no need to wait until we get to Ely. Your Ophelia will be just as acceptable to the people of Newmarket as mine.'

Susanna bit her lip at the sick woman's eager tones. It was a wretched trick to use her friends as a means to distance herself from Kit. 'I cannot, not yet. I am Lady Penfold's guest. It would cause too much . . . that is, there are reasons why . . . '

But Mary had already subsided against her cushions. 'It is of no account,' she said, the hope in her voice quenched. 'I daresay I will manage. I still have tomorrow to rest.'

'Oh, Mary, will you not see a doctor?' Susanna took the other woman's hand. 'Lady Penfold's man is very good. I can give Adam his direction and I have the fee should you not — '

'Nonsense. Repose is all I need.' Mary shook Susanna off and reapplied herself to mending the curtain.

'I would help if I could,' said Susanna,

trying to explain, 'but I have an obligation to Mr Kydd. He rescued me when I was in sore need, and now I aid him by pretending to be his betrothed. For his sake, I cannot run the risk of Lady Penfold or her acquaintance recognising me on your stage.'

The arrival of Mrs Jackson's lively eldest daughter, Lucy, and the other young actresses put an end to more confidences. All of them were agog to hear of the wonders of London. Susanna downplayed her sojourn in the capital and grew more concerned than ever to see the effort Mary put into swallowing her broth. When Kit came to retrieve his outerwear, she made her farewells, still troubled.

'I mislike her looks,' she said as they traversed the dark path to the gate. 'I wish she had let me go to Dr Peck for her.'

She heard the frown in Kit's voice. 'Surely that is for her husband to do?'

Susanna gave a vexed laugh. 'You do not know Mary. She sublimates herself for Adam's work, and he is so driven by the company that he does not query her.'

'You cannot interfere between husband and wife.'

'No.' She cleared her throat. 'It was good of you to help with the benches.'

'I could hardly stand idle when everyone

around me was working. Also I felt somewhat impelled to prove that not all the gentry are merely decorative.'

'They thought I was your mistress, didn't they?' said Susanna in a low voice. 'That is why Adam was so cool.'

Kit said nothing.

She moistened her lips. 'Mary too. And your cousin implied as much in his letter. It is what everybody will think if the truth comes out. You must think me a simpleton for not having seen it before.'

Kit stopped and turned her to face him. 'I think it very much to your credit. And the truth is not going to come out.'

Oh, Kit, would that I was as sanguine. Susanna looked away. 'The Chartwell Players travel next to Ely. Mary said I am welcome to join them. I would be truly useful. None of the other actresses get on so well with Shakespeare, so my being there would free Mary from the longer roles until she is better.'

She could almost feel the intense blue gaze boring into her. 'When?'

'They play at Cheveley on Monday and are to do two or three more performances in the town after that before they go.'

He exhaled the slightest of breaths. 'Then you may stay as originally planned until our visit ends. I will escort you to Ely myself.'

Susanna stamped her foot. 'Oh, how can you be so obstinate? Every day I remain is a day closer to discovery. Do you *want* to be pointed out as the man who introduced his doxy into his great-aunt's household?'

'You are not my doxy! And as if the *ton*'s views matter when I have taken away your good character in your friends' eyes! Susanna, I may be a knave and a fool, but I will *not* abandon you to unknown lodgings in a strange town. Good God, I do not even want you to act again, let alone be friendless and scared and a prey to every passing blade.'

Tears blurred Susanna's eyes. 'But, Kit, I do not know how much longer I can keep up this pretence. I wish I had never come.'

He put up a hand and traced the line of her cheek. When he spoke, his voice was husky. 'Sweetheart. Has it been so very difficult?'

His features were impossibly handsome in the moonlight. Susanna's heart twisted. 'Don't,' she whispered. 'Don't do this.'

As they stood on the green by the church, trembling on the brink of either disaster or delight, two gentlemen emerged from one of the passageways which gave on to the Dukeries. 'Deuce take it, Rafe, that was the worst excuse for a cock-fight I ever saw! The Blue was blind in one eye and that Grey positively squeezed to make him fight! I'm embarrassed to have been seen there.'

'You must comfort yourself, Vere, by reflecting how rich you have made the locals' lives by your presence.'

At the smooth, sarcastic tones of the second man, Susanna froze. This couldn't be happening! Rafe Warwick couldn't be here in Newmarket!

The following moment Kit had whipped her into the nearest alley, cursing fluently under his breath. 'That settles it. You do not go to Ely, you do not go to Kydd, you do not even stir from the house without me by your side. We'll have to cut through to the High Street from here. For God's sake stay close.'

Susanna needed no further exhortation. The cockpit must have finished business for the evening, for there were men of all stations pushing through the narrow lanes towards their favoured inns, from country swells to disgruntled bucks to discontented townsfolk — and all of them spoiling for a fight.

Kit swore again and slowed his pace, scanning the crowd for a way through. The overhanging alleys with their occasional flaring torches and patches of black shadow took on a grotesque, nightmare aspect. A carter reeking of drink jostled against Susanna and went into a semi-crouch, a knife appearing in his hand.

'Clumsy mort,' said Kit in a loud, coarse voice. 'Put your chive away, mate. She can't help it.'

'Who are you calling clumsy?' shrilled Susanna without conscious thought. 'Find someone else to warm your bed if that's how you feel!'

The carter mumbled an oath and swerved off.

'Well done,' breathed Kit.

Susanna's heart was beating twice as fast as usual. 'And you,' she returned. 'How do we get out of here?'

'Not that way,' said Kit, as a fight broke out in the cross-alley to their left. Ahead of them the carter lurched into someone else, a farm-hand as ready with his fists as the carter was with his knife. 'Damn, and not that way either. We'll double back and hope the coast is clear.'

Susanna twisted to look over her shoulder. 'No!' she said with horror. A tall, horribly familiar shadow preceded its owner along the wall. 'It's Warwick! They must have taken a wrong turn themselves!' She clutched at Kit's arm with real panic. 'Kit, I know you would like nothing better than to mill him down again, but if that cane is truly a swordstick we must either get away or hide. He has a friend with him this time and as soon as he sees us he is like to kill you and abduct me!' She felt Kit's muscles bunch in instinctive rejection of such a cowardly action and shook his arm to make him attend her. 'Oh Kit, *think*! Nothing could be easier in this crush. Winnings and revenge in one stroke and the pair of them would be away before the hue and cry was even raised!'

Kit nodded reluctant acquiescence. 'I suppose so. Come on then.'

But by now all the tavern doorways within reach were blocked by belligerent townsfolk. 'How?' said Susanna helplessly.

Kit darted a look at the alehouse closest to them where a blind passage formed a squalid yard outside with several couples congregated along it. His face was grim. 'Down here,' he said. 'There's no other way. Deuce take it but I'm sorry, sweetheart.'

Sorry? What was he sorry for? And how were they to hide in plain sight? There was no egress through the high overhanging wall. But as Kit pulled her past the other people to the shadowy far end where the stink and the grime were worst, Susanna realized what it was the couples were doing and understood.

11

Within seconds Susanna found herself pressed against the rough timber wall of the tavern.

'You're wearing the wrong clothes for this. Quick, take your cloak off,' said Kit, ripping off his hat and greatcoat and throwing them onto the filthy cobbles. 'And your gloves. Oh Lord, your hair!' He wrenched the fichu out of her bodice and twisted it about her head in concealment.

'What of yours? It is at least as noticeable as mine.' Susanna hastily scooped up a double handful of muck, plastering it over those moon-bright locks. Her dreams jeered at her: all this time longing to run her fingers through Kit's hair and at her first legitimate chance, she was smearing it with gutter slime!

His eyes looked into hers, desperate. 'Forgive me, Susanna, but in order to be convincing, I fear we shall have to pretend to — '

Susanna felt as if her cheeks were on fire. She forced herself to answer prosaically. 'Pray disregard it. I haven't spent the best part of my life below-stairs without knowing what goes where.' She raised the front of her skirts, her heart hammering as he adjusted his own clothing. Icy apprehension shot through her as he moved closer and the top of his naked thighs met hers. She swallowed. 'Do you not need to — ?'

'No!' he answered explosively. He cleared his throat. 'It is enough to look the part. Our clothes will hide the details.'

Someone to Susanna's left was emitting loud grunts. The wooden wall flexed rhythmically. As mortification threatened to overwhelm her, the shadow of a gentleman in a tall hat and carrying a cane fell across the entrance to the yard. 'Kiss me,' she whispered, fear slanting through her chest.

Instantly, Kit's mouth was over hers: safe, warm, all-enveloping. The cold shaft of terror receded. Susanna's hand rose of its own volition to cradle his head. His hold on her shifted, became possessive. His tongue gently parted her lips.

Astonishment filled Susanna like warm honey. Instinctively, she arched towards him, careless of the sudden rush of night air on her skin as her loosened bodice caught on his waistcoat.

Kit's hand slid up her waist, over the swell of her breast, an odd sound in his throat as his palm caressed the exposed flesh. He started to rock against her, his thighs pressing hers, causing an exhilarating sensation that hinted at far-off wonderful things. She forgot all about Rafe Warwick, forgot the tavern wall at her back, forgot the greasy, stinking cobbles under her feet. There was just her and Kit and a great burgeoning promise of paradise.

'My God,' drawled a fastidious voice in the background, 'what a town, where men take their pleasure upright in *alleys*!'

'They do in the more interesting parts of London too. And one could hardly lie down,' came the amused reply.

'There I agree. I shall have to throw away these boots as it is. But outside a *tavern*, Rafe, where everyone can see. It doesn't bear thinking about.'

'Oh, I don't know,' said Rafe Warwick's smooth, dispassionate voice. 'It's quick and cheap. No bedbugs. No getting rid of the doxy next morning. And there is a certain roughness to the proceedings which cannot but add spice. I confess, I find it almost exciting. What do you say, Vere? Shall we take over a couple of harlots when they are finished and enlarge our experience?'

'God, Rafe, the things you suggest! I daresay you find the thought of the pox you would contract rather endearing also?'

Warwick laughed silkily. 'I see what it is. You cannot practise any of the diversions you enjoy so much against a wall.'

'You will not draw me, Rafe, I have known you too long. Away and let us meet this man who may have information about the Duke's new horse. I swear, if I had known how dreary Newmarket is when there are no races on, I should never have let you drag me up here, no matter how great your need to rusticate.'

As Rafe Warwick and his companion left, Susanna felt the tension ebb from Kit's body. He did not let her go, for which she was grateful. She might have been shocked back to her senses when the conversation interrupted them, but between Kit's powerfully real embrace and the fear which Warwick brought with him, she did not think she could have stood unaided.

They remained entwined in the stinking shadows as whistles and shouts announced the arrival of the parish constable to clear the fights. Susanna's heart pounded as Kit's arms curved still more protectively around her; she felt him smile as his kiss deepened. Her mother's warnings seared her brain. Her father's painted image shrieked the inconstancy of the gentry. She should move, pull tactfully back, shake down her skirts, make some amused, deprecating remark about their combined acting ability.

But even as her mind framed the words, her body rebelled. It was tired of being told what to do. It *knew* it loved. It trusted entirely to Kit's safe, strong arms and intoxicating kisses, and responded with a lack of inhibition which made him squeeze her tight in jubilation. Susanna surrendered as completely as tinder to a roaring fire. In a way it was a relief: no more heart-wrenching decisions, no more struggling to keep him at arm's length. The world, after all, was full of mistresses.

'And that,' he murmured at last, 'is the true reason I would not have you leave.' He cupped her cheek, gazing deeply into her eyes. 'You won't, will you?'

'No,' she said simply, and rested her head against his chest. 'Oh, Kit, what a coil.' She wondered when he would come to her tonight and how she was going to keep this new knowledge of him safe within her breast.

His lips brushed her forehead. 'We will resolve it.' He looked around. They were alone. With the fighters being rounded up, their neighbours had speedily concluded their business lest they too be accused of breaching the peace. The alleys were relatively quiet once more. Kit shrugged himself tidy, pulled

Susanna's clothes straight and restored the lawn fichu to her shoulders. 'Home,' he said, picking up her cloak and his greatcoat. 'Tomorrow will be time enough to talk.'

She looked up at him, doubting. 'But — '

He placed a kiss on his finger and transferred it to her lips. 'You are worn out. I shall smuggle you inside and then find John Farley and put my head under the stable pump before *I* brave the house.'

★   ★   ★

She was his! His! For two pins he'd have danced on the cobbles. Had any lips ever tasted so sweet? Had any response ever been so breathtakingly innocent, yet so deliciously wanton? The scent of her hair, the swell of her breast under his fingers. Oh God, the feel of her thighs against his. For a bewitching moment Kit had honestly forgotten where they were and the danger they were in. He had walked her back to Penfold Lodge and had kissed her again before she slipped in through the side door, feeling himself harden with triumph and desire. It was fortuitous that a dog barking in the kennels had brought them both back to their senses.

Johnny was just coming through the archway when Kit reached the stable yard.

His eyes widened. 'Stap me, Mr Kit, what happened to you?'

'Paradise, Johnny. Work the pump, will you?'

The groom complied, rather too vigorously for Kit's comfort. 'Paradise, is it? Tom Olivant reckoned you'd met your match at last.'

'Oh, did he? Be damned to you both for your cheek!'

He went inside, still remembering the feel of Susanna in his arms, and immediately encountered Hibbert.

'High-spirited young gentleman, Mr Harry Fortune,' murmured the butler, and offered to send a brandy up to Kit's room along with his valet. The implication was that he would need the fortification once Motson viewed the wreck of his hair and his cravat.

Kit accepted with a good grace, casting Susanna's door a rueful glance as he passed. Perhaps it was as well that there would be no opportunity to give in to temptation tonight.

★   ★   ★

'Morning.' Lady Penfold waved a forkful of ham from a strangely scanty plate as Susanna sat down at the breakfast table. 'Martha's writing letters and Kit went riding early.' She chortled. 'Don't know where he finds the energy. Hibbert tells me he came in last night looking like a water-rat.' She cocked a mildly challenging eye at Susanna. 'Shocked?'

'Not at all. I am aware that gentlemen have sources of pleasure unavailable to us females. It has always seemed unfair that we cannot retaliate.'

Lady Penfold chuckled. 'You're the wife for him, no doubt about that.' She cast a jaundiced eye at her empty plate. 'I suppose it is good for one, fasting for Lent.'

Of course, it was Ash Wednesday! That was why the streets had been so busy last night and why the Chartwell Players were not opening until tomorrow. 'It will certainly make us appreciate the evening meal the more,' Susanna said diplomatically.

She thought she would later jest to Kit that only Lady Penfold could call four eggs, five rashers of ham and six slices of toast fasting. For now she changed for church, worried about going out in daylight, but thankful to have an unexceptional excuse for choosing her very plainest gown and bonnet. Her caution was superfluous, however, for no sign of Rafe Warwick did they see. She prayed far harder that he and his friend had obtained their information and gone than she did for the enlightenment of her own immortal soul.

By next morning Lady Penfold was in a better humour, bewailing that she and Martha were engaged to dine with friends in Bury St Edmunds the following day. 'Not that I will not enjoy tonight's plays, but Caro tells me it is to be *As You Like It* followed by a melodrama tomorrow. You'll have to tell us how you find it. I do love a good rant. You feel you're getting your money's worth when they shout and storm about so on stage.'

Kit lifted an eyebrow. 'Getting your money's worth? I don't believe *you* were ever sold short measure in your life.'

Lady Penfold's chins quivered. 'Once maybe, never twice!'

★ ★ ★

Susanna wore her white muslin for the play and arranged her hair so it would be easily covered by the blue-and-yellow ruffled bonnet. It was still too modish for her inclinations, but Lady Penfold would be certain to wonder what was afoot if she wore a plain poke on an occasion when the rest of Newmarket was dressed for display. Having seen the barn, Kit was confident he could screen her from all comers. All she had to do was to sit in the shadows and keep her head averted should Rafe Warwick hove into sight.

All the same, she was in a flurry of agitation until she had satisfied herself that the cruel countenance which still haunted her nightmares was nowhere in the audience.

Lady Penfold looked over her shoulder. 'You are not placed very well there, girl. You won't be able to see.'

'Indeed, I am quite comfortable,' Susanna assured her. 'It is kind of you to be concerned, but I have a slight headache, so I would as lief not be any nearer the lanterns. I will be perfectly well able to hear the actors and Kit can tell me anything I may miss.'

Beside her, Kit squeezed her hand in a comforting grip. It was only after scanning the faces in the barn fully as keenly as her that he started to trace patterns on her palm. She drew her hand away reprovingly. Now was *not* the time to have her insides turn to the consistency of an unwhisked syllabub.

The Prince of Denmark started to a bustle of settling down and shifting on benches by the audience. Susanna experienced an unexpected jolt at being here in the shadows of the box, rather than in the makeshift greenroom, waiting to come on as one of Queen Gertrude's ladies.

Kit rubbed his arm against hers as if he guessed, which was how she knew he stiffened at Adam's first entrance as Hamlet.

'Stupid,' she whispered, and wondered at herself all over again.

He relaxed, looking only a little sheepish.

Susanna was on tenterhooks for Mary's appearance. She leant forward as Ophelia bantered with her brother, noticing that her friend was using Joe Jackson's arm for a lot more support than was customary.

'The girl looks half-mad already,' said Lady Penfold in a penetrating whisper.

Susanna bit her lip. Mary was indeed pale, but still she managed to carry the scene. Maybe it would be all right. It was hardly as if Ophelia was a long part.

But as act succeeded act, this hope faltered. Adam had cut down Mary's speeches, but it was plain to the most inexperienced theatregoer that the actress playing Hamlet's ill-fated lover was unwell. When, at the conclusion of her 'mad' scene, Ophelia fell to the floor in an apparent ecstasy of grief, there was a quite spontaneous silence from the audience, who were waiting to see whether she would get up again.

She didn't. She was lifted and borne offstage and her appearance at the funeral in the last act was implied by a cloth-wrapped body. Susanna sat through the closing scenes in increasing frustration.

'Would some air help your headache?' asked Kit almost as soon as the curtain fell.

'Yes, yes I believe it would,' she answered as civilly as she could manage, and within seconds they were hurrying out of the doors and around to the back of the barn where the company was congregated.

Mary was conscious, but very weak.

'Why didn't you *tell* me you were so ill?' fumed Adam, pacing the cramped space like the beasts at the Exeter Exchange.

'Because you wouldn't have listened,' retorted Mrs Jackson, the matriarch of the company, imposing even backstage in Queen Gertrude's robes.

'Dr Peck is in the audience,' said Susanna, pushing her way through. 'Do find him, Kit, and if he cavils at attending a travelling player, tell him you will give him a draft on Hammond's bank in the morning.'

'You'll do no such thing,' said Mrs Jackson roundly. 'We'll pay his fee out of tonight's takings before we divide it up, the same as we did when my Joe broke his arm getting the horses free during the fire.'

'I didn't *know*,' repeated Adam, looking haunted. 'I didn't *know*!'

Dr Peck bustled in, took one look at Mary and summarily banished everybody about their business. Susanna returned to Lady

Penfold's box with Kit, feeling helpless and useless.

Mr Furnell came on stage to do his comic monologue. The Jackson girls followed with a dance and then their father sang a popular song. At last the curtains opened on the farce. Susanna recognized it as having the lightness of touch which characterized all Miss Scott's comic creations, but so worried was she about Mary that she was hard pressed at the end of the evening to remember a single speech.

★ ★ ★

Next morning she was dressed long before the maid brought the washing water. Creeping down to the side door, Susanna hoped the rest of the indoor servants were equally dilatory. The grooms she knew would be up. John Farley would not mind riding out to the Chartwell Players' barn to inquire after Mary. Outside she heard hoofbeats thudding up to the rear of the stable block. There was a clink of harness and a soft whinny.

'For shame, Rufus, you know I will be back later, but for now I must go,' said a familiar voice.

Susanna stopped dead in amazement. Whatever was Caroline Fortune doing here at this hour of the morning? She peered around the corner of the wall. Her eyes widened. A figure in breeches and short coat was loping swiftly away towards the stile which marked the boundary between Lady Penfold's land and that of the Fortunes.

Susanna moved slowly back to the stable arch. Only Lady Penfold's head groom was abroad inside, a rubbing-down cloth in his hand. 'Good morning,' she said with a smile. 'I know it is shockingly early, but could you please give this note to John Farley? I would like him to run me an errand as soon as it is convenient. Mr Kydd or I will come down after breakfast for the answer.'

The groom took the folded paper, his face impassive.

'It is a lovely morning, is it not?' Susanna chattered on. 'If it were not for seeing you, I could fancy myself the only person awake in the world.'

She could feel his eyes boring into her back as she returned to the house. It seemed she wasn't the only one with secrets.

★   ★   ★

Mary had passed an equable night, said Adam's short note, but on the back of it was written, in a firm hand which Susanna

250

recognized as belonging to Mrs Jackson, 'Important you come soon.'

'People of few words, these travelling players of yours,' commented Kit when she showed him.

'I must go, Kit. Will you accompany me?'

He smiled wryly. 'I already warned Johnny to ready the curricle.'

But when they got to the barn, Mary was nowhere to be seen. Mrs Jackson made her request without apology. 'We need you to play Rosalind tonight.'

Susanna sat down on the nearest hay-bale, her hand to her chest. 'Rosalind? But can Lucy not — ?'

'Lucy,' said her mama, 'is playing Celia, I'm too old for the part, and there's none of the other girls will touch such a long role with only half a day's warning. You've played it before and done it well.'

'Ridiculous!' burst out Kit. 'Change the programme if you have no other actress capable of taking over.'

Mrs Jackson looked at him without expression. 'We are doing so for the remainder of our stay, but the bills for *As You Like It* have already been printed and handed out. The Duke has bespoken seats on the strength of it, and even if he hadn't there'd be a full house tonight with all the drama yesterday. We stand together in the theatre. Susanna was one of us, and now we need her again.'

'It is true, Kit,' said Susanna in a low voice. 'I could not square it with my conscience if I let the Players down. You are always telling me people see what they expect to see. If we can manage it without my being recognized by all the people who know me through your great-aunt, I think I must do the part. It is fortunate she herself will be absent.'

There was anger in his face. 'Does Mr Prettyman not have the decency to ask this boon of Miss Fair himself?'

'He don't know about it,' said Mrs Jackson. 'He's away settling Mary at the Wheatsheaf. Half out of his mind with guilt, he is, and not before time. I said I'd arrange the female parts, but dressing my Lucy in breeches when there's a Duke in the audience is what I won't have!'

'Breeches!' yelled Kit, even more explosively.

Susanna laid a placating hand on his arm. 'For when Rosalind pretends to be Celia's brother. I have worn them before, Kit. They are perfectly decent.' She looked at Mrs Jackson. 'I will need the black wig too.'

Kit handed her up to the curricle without a word and they left the field at a spanking trot.

Susanna looked at his set expression, feeling sick at heart that she was the one who had caused it. 'You are angry with me,' she said.

Kit swung around a laden cart with two inches to spare. 'Angry, yes. With you, no.'

'Then with whom?'

'That fearsome battleaxe for asking you in a way you could not refuse. Your wretched Adam for dragging a sick wife across the breadth of the country. Myself.'

'He is not my Adam.'

Kit let the bays slow to a walk. 'I know. I knew it as soon as I kissed you. And I know acting has been your trade and you feel guilty about the Chartwell Players because they are your friends. If you must know I am mostly cross with myself for being so unreasonable as to wish you had never set eyes on them.'

Susanna looked down at her lap. 'If I had not, I would surely have died or been in a Magdalen long since.'

Kit turned his head with a wry look. 'Making *me* feel guilty now?'

'I do not mean to.'

He turned a corner, the curricle's springs compensating for the ruts in the lane. 'Devil take it, why did it have to be a *breeches* part?'

He was jealous! He wasn't even thinking about the danger of her being recognized. He was angry because he did not want other men to see her legs! The knowledge at once uplifted and exasperated her. 'Adam always has a breeches play on the second night,' she said, as if taking his question literally. 'One with a love element so it will bring both gentlemen *and* ladies back to the theatre a second time. The third evening generally incorporates a phantasmagorical effect — usually a pantomime or an allegory — along with a comedy that folk will be familiar with. You have no notion how much hard planning goes into enticing people to return and fill the coffers time and again.'

There was silence, apart from the bays' hooves. Susanna looked at the burgeoning hedgerows. 'Always,' said Kit, 'always you unbalance me.' He glanced sideways at her, his lips twisting. 'I confess I could almost wish there was a part for me too. I am envious of the activity at the barn. I do not like to be as idle as I am forced to be here.'

Susanna gave a small laugh. 'I noticed. I had your character all wrong that first night I saw you at the Sans Pareil — Kit!' She gripped his arm and stared at him, aghast.

He checked the horses immediately. 'What is it?'

'Rafe Warwick! Suppose he is still in town? What if *he* should see me?'

Kit's eyes narrowed as he started the bays

moving again. 'All the more reason to have Johnny standing by with the carriage, ready to spring the horses the moment your part is finished. We will tell the servants you suffered a recurrence of your headache so I was obliged to bring you home from the play early. But Warwick was not there last night. I assumed he had left for London.'

'I hope so,' said Susanna in a fervent voice. 'Kit, can they really have come all this way out over a *horse*?'

'When she is rumoured to be the fastest since Eclipse, yes. I got a brief sight the other morning. The betting on her for the One Thousand Guineas is extremely heavy. And fond as the Dishonourable Rafe is of a wager, I fancy he is fonder still, the more hard facts he has before risking his blunt.'

Susanna was silent. 'It has just occurred to me — it is March. I am free of his bet.'

Kit snorted. 'Well enough if you think him so sporting as to bear you no ill will for making him pay out instead of collect.' He transferred both reins to one hand and reached across with the other to lightly clasp her fingers. 'Call me cynical, sweetheart, but I do not think we should take that risk.'

Sweetheart. That was the third or fourth time he had addressed her thus. And he touched her hand or her arm or her waist ever more readily, and there was a breath-snatching smile in his eyes sometimes when he looked at her, but he had not kissed her again like he had on Tuesday night, nor come to her room as she'd expected. What did he mean by it? What was in his mind? It was . . . disturbing.

She looked about her at the bustling hamlet they had just entered. 'Where are we?' she said, changing the subject.

'Cheveley village. Three more miles and we will be back at Great-aunt Emma's.' He too surveyed their surroundings: the church, the baker's shop, the neat cottages, the school where a master's voice issued from a half-closed door. He gave a sigh. 'It's snug enough, but it makes me long to be at home.'

'Another week and you will be,' said Susanna.

And what of her? Where would she be?

12

The midday meal was more substantial than ever, on account of Lady Penfold needing to muster her strength in case her host's table this evening fell short of her own. Susanna ate what she could then, struck by inspiration, offered to read *As You Like It* aloud to make up for Lady Penfold and Martha missing the play later.

Outwardly she was calm. Inwardly, she was shaking with nerves. She hadn't acted properly — with words — for six months or more. *And what was she doing now if not acting, pray?* Thinking of which — suppose she *was* recognized? The whole deception would come tumbling around their ears. And then there was Kit. Though she had as good as said she was his now, he still didn't want her to act again anywhere, ever. Yet how could she stand aside and not help her friends? Would it sour things between them before they had ever begun? Was this, in short, one final chance for her to make the break?

Susanna's mind continued to reel between three sorts of panic until she stepped onto the Chartwell Players stage that evening. Then, abruptly, she *was* Rosalind, enamoured of the youth Orlando and about to be banished to the Forest of Arden. The relief was tremendous.

Until, near the end of the last act, she looked up and saw Rafe Warwick in the audience, his quizzing glass raised as if branding her with his attention.

Terror. A shaft of darkness in a painted world. But Shakespeare's words continued and she had perforce to follow. Be Rosalind. Any other thoughts and she would be undone.

'Quick,' said Kit as she came off for the final time. 'Before the Duke congratulates you in his box for all Newmarket to see.'

'There is no need to dissemble,' said Susanna as they scrambled into the carriage. 'I saw Mr Warwick. I thought I should have died right there on the stage. I have warned Adam he may come looking for me, and if so to tell him I have packed and left. I hope to God he does not threaten them as he did the Sans Pareil.'

'They asked you to play. Their risk.'

'No, for we did not tell them the whole, did we?'

'Well, you will not act again, at any rate.'

He sounded preoccupied. When Susanna fixed her eyes more closely on him in the hurrying shadows, his face was a mask of calculation. Her heart hammered in her chest. 'Kit, what are you planning?'

'What I should have done three nights ago. I am going to borrow Johnny's coat, mingle with the townsfolk and follow Warwick to his lair. I mislike being at a disadvantage.'

'Oh, Kit, can we not simply return to Kydd? He only came in towards the end. He might not be sure it was me.'

'I am tired of running away.'

'But . . . the danger — '

'No!' He let out a frustrated-sounding breath. 'Forgive me. I daresay all that will happen is I track him to the King's Head, where he eats an expensive supper and repairs to bed. Here we are. Out you get and remember you are ill.'

It wasn't difficult to pretend. Susanna leant on his arm and pressed her hand across her lips, nodding weakly to Hibbert and hastening up the stairs. She pressed her forehead to the window and waited until she saw a figure slip back outside. In common clothes and a shapeless hat, Kit looked more shabby and nondescript than she would have thought possible. A memory teased her, but vanished when she tried to pin it down. 'Take care,' she whispered, though she knew he could not hear.

Much, much later, she heard movement from the passage. She waited, breath taut, but Kit did not enter her room. Cursing all men who thought themselves above explanations, she fell into a troubled sleep.

In the morning there was no sign of him. 'Riding,' said Lady Penfold.

Susanna hardly ate anything, so sick was she with apprehension. And when he *did* put in an appearance, the ladies were sustaining a call from Mrs Fortune and her daughters, so she still could not find out if he had discovered anything.

'What did you think of the play last night?' said Caroline. 'Did you not think the actress taking the part of Rosalind very good?'

'Disgraceful,' pronounced Mrs Fortune. 'Had I known it was that sort of play, I should never have gone.'

'But, Mama, it was Shakespeare,' said Caroline in an innocent voice.

'Which does not mean that sections of it were not extremely improper!'

Lady Penfold's eyes snapped happily. 'Would that be because one of the actresses wears breeches?'

Mrs Fortune's countenance suggested that only impeccable breeding enabled her to ignore the introduction of an item of gentleman's apparel into the conversation.

'Too stuffy by half, that's your trouble, Adeline. Why, I wore breeches myself when I eloped with Edward. Only way to travel fast enough to Gretna so that my dratted father didn't overtake us.'

Susanna couldn't like Mrs Fortune, but she almost felt sorry for her. To be obliged to suffer a discussion of breeches *and* elopements during the same morning call! 'I hope the melodrama was more to your taste, ma'am,' she said. 'Unfortunately I had the headache so had to leave without seeing it.'

Mrs Fortune agreed stiffly that the second offering by the Chartwell Players had indeed been more acceptable.

Susanna turned back to Caroline to find her smothering an attack of unfilial glee. 'Poor Mama. She is *so* often disappointed with the world. What a great gun Lady Penfold is, don't you think?'

'Certainly,' said Susanna. She eyed the younger girl and went on smoothly, 'There is a portrait at Kydd Court before her marriage. I can imagine nothing more likely than that she should have borrowed her brother's clothes when she ran away. A man's costume must have made an excellent disguise, besides affording such useful freedom of movement.'

Her quarry grinned. 'I don't suppose anyone will offer for me no matter what I wear. Shall we see you at the play tonight?'

'Does your mama risk going again then in view of yesterday's performance?'

Caroline's brown eyes danced. 'Oh yes. If there is one thing worse than being shocked, it is *not* being shocked when the rest of her acquaintance are. Only think how disagreeable it would be if the dancing in the pantomime were indecent and she was obliged to listen to accounts of it at second hand.'

'Dancing?' said Lady Penfold, catching the word. 'Now if you'd ever seen the dancers at Covent Garden, Adeline, you'd be right to be affronted. Mere strips of gauze, I promise you. The play could have been in Greek for all the attention the gentlemen were paying to the words.'

Inside Susanna a tiny flicker of hope died. Her past would always damn her in these people's eyes. Lady Penfold's elopement fifty years ago might have been the scandal of the *ton* then, but at least she had been high-born and her lover rich. With front enough, those assets were easily sufficient to re-establish yourself. *She* had nothing.

The Fortune ladies left. Susanna tried to catch Kit's eye, but a booming shout from the hall announced Colonel MacGregor's presence.

'Ha! Emma! Just the person I wanted to see!'

'Naturally, Randolph, else you would not be here. Hibbert, refreshment for the Colonel, please.'

'Thank you, just a little of the Madeira,' he said, watching with satisfaction as a generous measure was poured. 'Your health, ladies. Now then, what do you all say to coming over to Cheveley on Monday for dinner and to see the play, eh? Rutland's invitation. He was vastly pleased with the performance last evening and thinks the actors deserve a bigger audience.'

'We should be delighted! Will you stay for a nuncheon, Randolph?'

'Don't mind if I do. What are you serving it on, the Worcester or the Wedgewood?' He winked at Susanna.

She smiled back, but reflected that his company would make it impossible to talk privately to Kit. From porcelain, matters turned to Northamptonshire. The Colonel was surprised to learn they were returning soon and not staying until the race meeting.

'Another six weeks? I think not,' said Kit easily. 'I must get back to Kydd Court. There is enough and more to do there.'

'I might ride with you then. Save going post by myself.' He helped himself to another slice of beef. 'Yes, I was forgetting the state of your land. Bad business. My niece's husband mentioned the trouble with your uncle.'

Kit looked a little grim. 'Indeed? I had thought better of him.'

'No need to get on your high ropes, lad. Only told me because he knows I'm not a gabster. Think — if my niece knew, she wouldn't have been throwing Charlotte at your head, now would she?'

Kit's jaw tightened. Lady Penfold's eyes were going from one to the other of them, sharp as a bird after a worm. Susanna didn't hesitate. She turned to Colonel MacGregor. 'Is the house party at Cheveley not very large, that his Grace needs more people to see the play?'

'So-so. We sat down twenty to table yesterday. But the actorman was there this morning to look over the saloon where they are to perform and it struck the Duchess that it might be a touch thin. Believe she's inviting the Abbey people and parties from the Grange and the Towers as well.'

Lady Penfold raised her eyebrows. 'We shall be exalted. I shall wear my ostrich-feather headdress for fear of feeling crushed.'

'Ha! You were never crushed in your life! Do you remember the time you . . .'

Susanna finished her bread and butter and

toyed with her wine, trying to rationalize the change in herself. Ten days ago she had been embarrassed when Kit made light of his financial problems in front of Lady Penfold. Today she had unhesitatingly changed the subject for him. Was this what love did? Made you want to smooth their path no matter how uncertainly they were behaving? She stole a glance sideways, relieved to see that the stormy look was gone from his face. Had he forgotten or deliberately altered his part? She wanted so much to believe that this was how he genuinely was. He met her eyes and smiled. Her heart turned over.

Kit accompanied Colonel MacGregor back to Cheveley to give thanks for the invitation in person. Susanna bit down her frustration at still being no nearer finding out about Mr Warwick, put aside the pattern for a silver-threaded white silk reticule and instead got out of her work-bag a peignoir which she was trimming with ivory satin ribbon. When she became Kit's mistress she wanted the occasion to be memorable, not squalid, no matter that her reputation would be irretrievably lost afterwards. Filmy gauze slithered over her arm, her pale skin clearly visible beneath it. She felt again the insistent tug of promise in his body the night they had kissed outside the tavern. She bent to her sewing, suddenly breathless.

The whole household was to attend the pantomime that evening. It was the very last thing Susanna wanted to do, but for the life of her she could not see how to get out of the party without arousing suspicion. She dressed as plainly as possible and kept tight to Lady Penfold's great bulk. She saw Rafe Warwick as soon as he entered the barn. Kit's hand tightening on her shoulder told her he had spotted him too. She watched how the man scrutinized every face on the stage and how his hard eyes then turned to the audience. Her reticule slipped to the floor; she bent to retrieve it, waiting for Kit's nudge before she lifted her head.

'I fear you are unwell again,' said Kit in a voice calculated to reach his great-aunt's ears. 'Shall I take you home at the interval and then return?'

'I . . . I do not wish to be a nuisance,' she whispered.

'Stuff and nonsense, girl, I can feel you shaking from here and I'd as lief not catch it, whatever it is,' said Lady Penfold. 'No need to come back, Kit. I've footmen and coachmen enough here to see Martha and me safely home.'

Susanna gasped her thanks, and took advantage of the candles being doused for

Columbine's song to creep out.

'Kit, he was looking for me,' she said once she was wrapped in a rug on his curricle and they were under way. 'Do not deny it, I know he was.'

'He was,' said Kit, his voice grim. 'Good thing Great-aunt Emma don't want me. I searched the town for him last night to no avail, so I'll disguise myself again and follow him for certain. I daresay your Players can supply the necessary.'

Which made it even more impossible for Susanna to rest easy. She lit working candles and laid out her pattern pieces, but after stabbing herself innumerable times with her needle, repaired to bed. The rest of the household returned and still she lay in the darkness, shivering and sweating by turns, listening to the quiet sounds of the night as alert as if it had been midday. Eventually she was rewarded by the stairs creaking and a light tread coming along the passage.

Her heart beating a rapid staccato, Susanna gripped her shawl close and slipped out of her room. Kit's door stood slightly ajar. As she pushed it further open, she saw he had taken off a jerkin and was bending down to unlace a pair of working boots. He spun around at her entry.

A huge jolt of memory hit her at his stance.

'The sailor,' she gasped. 'You were the sailor outside my lodgings!'

He straightened up. 'Guilty.' There was a wary look in his eyes. 'And at other times a soldier, a city clerk and a drunkard.'

She gazed at him, bewildered. 'Why?'

'It was not my impression that Rafe Warwick would be so easily baulked of his prey.'

'He wasn't. He came back. But there was a fight and — oh!' She sank down on the edge of the bed, clutching a fold of shawl to her chest. 'You started it! You started the fight to protect me. But why, Kit? Why would you do such a thing? You hardly knew me. I don't understand.'

He sat beside her and traced the side of her face with the back of his hand. 'Nor did I, then,' he said softly.

And suddenly she was in his arms, feeling his lean, hard body through the linen of his shirt, and his fingers were loosening her night-time braid, and his mouth was claiming hers as surely as if he had put a seal of ownership upon it.

The intervening days since their embrace outside the tavern might never have been. Susanna made a tiny moan of relief and gave herself to his kiss.

Sweetheart. It was in her head as clearly as

if he had spoken the word aloud. He held her tighter, his lips locked to hers, his tongue teaching hers what to do. Then his hand was under her shawl, moving round to caress, to stroke, to release the ribbon at the neck of her nightgown. Susanna's eyes flew wide open as a wave of new and entirely unexpected sensations assaulted her.

'Beautiful,' murmured Kit. He pulled away to look at her, his eyes luminous. 'If you only knew how much I have longed to do this.'

'Mr Warwick,' Susanna managed to say. 'What of him?'

'Not staying in Newmarket. He scrutinized everyone leaving the barn, had a chop and drank his fill at the Golden Lion, then was in his curricle and away up the Bury Road before I could get to mine. Sweetheart, if you do not go back to bed now, I am going to do so much more that we will both regret it come the morning.'

She couldn't help it. 'There's more?' she said.

He tipped up her chin and laid a line of kisses down the column of her throat. 'A whole lifetime more. Which is why I have heroically held off thus far and do not intend embarking on anything here in my great-aunt's house with nothing settled between us.' He drew up the front of her nightgown and tied the ribbon. 'Sweet dreams, my love. Believe me, this is much more difficult for me than it is for you.'

★ ★ ★

Sunday. A day of rest. A day for quiet contemplation. *My love.* Susanna fixed her eyes on the rector and tried to concentrate on what he was saying. Never had she felt less devout. Beside her, Kit's sleeve of blue superfine brushed against hers of watered silk. She was aware of every breath he took, every shift of his muscles as he eased long legs cramped by the confines of the pew. He moved again and his thigh touched hers. She let the sermon wash over her. Moments such as this were made to treasure.

The churchyard afterwards was full of the chattering dawdle of neighbours. Susanna smiled to herself, soothed by the ineffable Sunday-ness of it all. Whatever class you were, whatever church you attended, in whatever town or village, the afterservice ritual was exactly the same.

Lady Penfold was so very slow and so very respected in Newmarket that it took her fully as long to get from the porch to the lych gate as it had to get out of the church. Having walked too fast and got ahead, Susanna stood a little apart whilst Kit attended his great-aunt, exchanging greetings and gossip on her ponderous way through the crowd.

'Lady Penfold, I presume,' murmured a smooth, dangerous voice in her ear.

Susanna whirled, feeling the blood drain from her face.

'The rich, elderly Lady Penfold, with no immediate family to leave her money to, but with a quaint faith in the power of love. I congratulate you, my dear. Who would have thought the tiresome hothead would have such interesting prospects?'

'Don't touch me,' she whispered through a mouth dry with terror. 'It is March. Your bet is lost.'

Rafe Warwick's eyes glinted. 'I had not forgotten, my dear. It is the reason I am currently ornamenting the area. Certain consequences of my ire on discovering your disappearance called for a judicious with-drawal from London. Another grudge to add to your tally. But don't fret that beautiful head, I have no intention of touching you yet. I shall save the pleasure for when it can do you and your lover most harm.'

Thoughts jostled frantically in Susanna's brain. Mislead him. Misdirect him. Out of the corner of her eye she kept track of Lady Penfold's progress. 'How did you find me?'

'I am not likely to forget the man who floored me in that filthy alley,' said Rafe Warwick venomously. 'Having drawn a blank in every club in London, imagine how my heart lifted when I saw him strolling as careless as you please down this abominable town's excuse for a main thoroughfare. He led me straight to the door. A few idle enquiries to my host and his good lady and the story was mine. And then you made the incalculable error of playing Rosalind. One might almost think you *wished* me to have my revenge.'

There was a ringing in Susanna's ears. They had been so careful hiding *her* from sight that they had clean forgotten Kit. Away down the path, Lady Penfold moved another yard. 'What do you want?' she heard herself say.

Warwick almost purred with satisfaction. 'Well now, that all depends on the stakes, doesn't it? How much is the pretty-boy paying you to act the milk-and-water betrothed?'

Hope flared in Susanna's breast. She kept her voice indifferent. 'I daresay you already know he has nothing but mortgages. He offered me his protection and a change of identity.' She forced herself to glance up under her lashes. 'I was glad enough to take it.'

Warwick's eyes narrowed. 'Doing it a little too brown, my dear. What about the baubles and the new wardrobe?' He ran the head of his cane down the watered silk of her sleeve.

She couldn't prevent her instinctive flinch away from him. 'On tick. I could hardly play the part in my Sans Pareil clothes.'

'Your altruism is charming. You will forgive me mentioning that I imagine the thought of the blackmail should he not pay up once in possession of his inheritance influenced your decision. Which leaves me with an interesting dilemma. Much as I would like to revenge myself immediately, the thought of having you *both* in my power for as long as the old lady lives is a powerful inducement to stay my hand.' He gripped her wrist, his fingers digging mercilessly into her flesh. 'One thing you don't do. Not if you wish to live. You do not disappear again. I am perfectly capable of combing every theatre troupe in the country for you. With force if necessary.'

Susanna allowed sullen resentment to creep into her voice. 'You make it very difficult to do aught but obey.'

'I am glad we understand each other.' He released her arm. 'We will meet again, my dear.'

He sauntered away towards the line of carriages. Susanna stayed where she was.

Freed from the desperate need to appear insouciant, her body felt as if it might shatter at a single touch. She massaged her throbbing wrist, feeling unclean and contaminated. What was she to do? Not only was Rafe Warwick here, he knew her direction, her circumstances and that she was still acting. And *she* knew her flight had done nothing but harden his determination to violate her.

An acquaintance of Lady Penfold nodded politely. Susanna just managed to drop a brief curtsey in reply. Her mind was a terrifying blank. All she wanted was the security of Kit's safe, strong arm under her own and an end to the creeping numbness in her soul.

13

Kit hurried to catch up with Susanna before she followed the others into the saloon. 'Dr Peck was at church,' he said.

For a moment, her eyes were blank. Then: 'Yes, I overheard him telling Lady Penfold that she should take more exercise and less dinner unless she wanted a commemorative plaque put up to her in the nave soon.'

Kit frowned. What was the matter? She'd been fine in the church, enjoying the intimacy of sharing a prayer book as much as he had, not moving away when he'd alleviated the sermon's length by brushing gently against her side. Yet just now she had looked at him as if she couldn't remember who he was. 'It appears that Mrs Prettyman is still far from well,' he went on, trying to divine what was wrong. 'If you wish, I could drive you to the Wheatsheaf this afternoon to visit her. Susanna, are you all right? Has something happened to discompose you?'

But she was gazing at him, startled. 'I thought you wanted me to have nothing more to do with the Chartwell Players?'

Kit felt a twinge of guilt. 'I never said so.'

'You did not need to.' She hesitated. 'What of Mr Warwick? What if he should be abroad and see us?'

Ah, *that* was what was bothering her! She felt exposed outside the house, and no wonder. What a clodpole he was not to have realized. He spoke with extra heartiness. 'On a Sunday? The Dishonourable Rafe? Unlikely! He will be criticizing his host's library or punishing him at billiards.' He raised her hand to his lips. 'By the by, you were right in the milliner's shop. The broderie anglaise bonnet *does* go beautifully with that dress.' He had the satisfaction of seeing a blush rise to her cheeks as they entered the saloon.

★　★　★

So Kit had not observed Mr Warwick at the church. Relief and regret warred in Susanna's breast. Relief because Rafe Warwick was dangerous and she did not want Kit involved with him. He had been lucky once, he was unlikely to be so again. Regret — shamefully — because whatever the consequences to himself, Kit would have insisted on bearing his part. The realization pulled her up short, a reminder of how easy it had become to depend on him rather than relying on her own wits. Would this be her life from now on?

The curricle had barely set off when Kit gave a loud holler and wheeled across the road to pull up next to another one, drawn by a pair of matched greys.

'Hello,' said Caroline Fortune cheerfully, while the men engaged in a comparison of their respective vehicles. 'Harry is taking me for a drive around the town because I felt a little faint indoors.'

Susanna raised her eyebrows. A more healthy countenance than Caroline's would have been hard to imagine. 'It seems to be effective,' she said drily, 'and unless I am sadly turned about, that is the road to Bury St Edmunds.'

'I suppose it might be,' agreed Caroline. 'You would think Harry ought not to mistake his direction by now, wouldn't you?'

'I fancy your brother knows exactly where he is going. Do you never object to being used in this way?'

'Lord, no, his intrigues are by far more amusing than being confined to home with Mama and Honoria.'

Susanna couldn't help chuckling. 'I daresay I would find them so too. Do you go to Cheveley tomorrow for the play?'

Caroline's eyes twinkled. 'Alas, no. Mama has been telling everyone how fortunate it is that we are not on sufficient terms to be invited, since she would have had to risk giving offence by declining. It is *Twelfth Night* you see.'

'Ah,' said Susanna. 'Breeches.'

'Just so. But it is a shame, for we heard this morning at church that my Uncle Crispin arrived last night to stay with the Duke, so I could have asked him about backing our stables project. Harry will have to take me to call instead. Uncle Crispin does not visit us at home as a consequence of some long-ago falling out with Papa. Oh, we appear to be off. Good day.'

Kit looked distracted as they went on their way. Twice he glanced at Susanna as if to speak, then appeared to think better of it. When they pulled into the yard of the Wheatsheaf Inn, he tossed the reins to an ostler as he dismounted, asking him to hold the bays for a minute or two.

'Do you not come in?' said Susanna in surprise.

'No, I . . . that is, I have just had word . . . in short, there is someone I must see. Will an hour suffice you here, do you think?'

'Yes, of course. I had not thought to have so long.' She put a hand on his sleeve, struck by a stomach-churning thought. 'Kit, it is not Mr Warwick?'

'Who? No, nothing like that, I promise you.'

When Susanna was shown into Mary's chamber, she was taken aback by the reactions of the inhabitants. Adam, writing at the table, looked up in amazement. Their son Will, whittling a piece of wood into a stage dagger, seemed piqued. Lottie jumped up from her mother's bedside saying, 'She has come! Susanna has come!' and Mary sank back against her pillows whispering, 'Oh, thank God.'

'Did you know, then?' said Adam in wonder, putting aside his pen to greet her. 'Did you know I was just now writing you a note?'

'No, how could I? I am come to see Mary.' Susanna laid her basket on the table and took her friend's hand, trying not to wince at its dry, papery feel. 'Dr Peck said you were not going on as prosperously as he would like. I had thought you would be better by now.'

'I am, very nearly,' said Mary, which was a patent falsehood if ever Susanna had heard one.

Lottie beamed with the unshakable confidence of the very young. 'Mama is worried about the Duke and Viola, but now you will act instead and she can sleep easily again.'

'I?' Susanna turned in alarm to Adam. 'But

you have had three full days to arrange this! Why does Lucy Jackson not play Viola? Or Grace? Or Ann Furnell?'

'That is why I was writing.' Adam looked down at his unfinished letter, then bent and fed it to the fire.

'And I was to deliver it and get a penny from the butler,' said Will.

'Oh, Will, I do beg your pardon. Perhaps slices of cake from Lady Penfold's cook for you and Lottie will make up for the disappointment. There is a small bottle of Madeira in my basket for your mama as well.' She busied herself unpacking these items, then looked across at Adam. 'You had best tell me the whole.'

'Little to tell. *Twelfth Night* is what was bespoke. Lucy wanted to do Viola, she was wild for it, and had the performance been anywhere but at Cheveley, I believe her mother would have relented. But you know how Mrs Jackson is, Susanna. She constantly has Mrs Jordan's dread example in mind. She is convinced members of the nobility have only to see Lucy in breeches before sweeping her off to a cottage in Richmond and fathering ten children on her. No amount of reasoning will persuade her otherwise. So Ann Furnell has been learning the part but it will not stay in her head and what words do stumble from her mouth are so lifeless it is like trying to act with a block of wood! Meanwhile Mary gets no better and I have a temper like a bear.'

'And the Duke was so *pleased* on Friday,' said Mary fretfully. 'He sent a message commending your performance and a special purse for you besides.'

Susanna sat down in a rush by her friend's bed. 'Oh, what a coil. Lady Penfold has accepted an invitation for us all to attend the play. I can have the headache again, I suppose, but she is no fool. With the best will in the world, I do not see how she can fail to recognize your leading actress as the same person she has been facing over the breakfast table these past ten days.'

Young Will's spirits had risen with the advent of the cake. 'It is a fine big room,' he said helpfully, if indistinctly. 'I went to see it with Papa. There are windows to the terrace all along one side and we are only to use a third part of it for the stage. Lady Penfold might sit at the back.'

'We need the Duke's patronage,' whispered Mary. 'We can barely feed the horses as it is.'

There was a dreadful hurry of thought in Susanna's mind. She distractedly pressed the glass of Madeira into her friend's hand. 'Sip this. It will do you good. And a piece of the

cake too, if Lottie will crumble it for you.'
What to do? What to do for the best?

'The truth is that we are near at fiddlestick's end,' said Adam in a shamed voice. 'Receipts have been down so I have not been taking the manager's or the company share in order to leave enough for the others. Then there has been the cost of replacing what was lost in the fire, Joe Jackson's broken arm, Mary's illness — '

Susanna put her hand over his. 'Stop. I will do what I can, though I cannot promise anything until I have explained the whole to Kit.' *Oh Lord, he was going to be so angry.* 'But you must change the shipwreck scene, Adam, so I am in breeches the entire play. If I appear dressed only as a boy and in the black wig besides, and if Lady Penfold is seated as near the back of this 'fine, big room' as possible, I might yet escape detection. We return to Kydd Court on Wednesday. I pray she will be too involved with Kit before that to pay overmuch attention to me.'

Adam met her eyes. 'You are not rejoining us? But Mary said — '

Susanna felt herself blush. 'I am sorry. There are . . . reasons why not.'

He unlocked his travelling chest and handed her a leather purse. 'Then you had best take this now.'

'Why, what is it?'

'The gratuity the Duke sent after *As You Like It*.'

Susanna shook her head. 'I would not profit by Mary's misfortune. I acted Rosalind in thanks for your past kindnesses. Keep it. Use it to pay your shot here or to feed the horses.'

She turned the talk firmly to the Players' new tour route, but Mary's illness hung like a pall over the conversation and Susanna's heart gave a glad jolt when she heard a clatter of hooves and Kit's voice in the inn yard. 'I must go. Look after your mama, Lottie, and make sure she eats. Will? Do you carry my basket down and meet Mr Kydd's horses?'

'Take the children, Adam, and tell Mr Kydd that Susanna will not be a moment,' said Mary.

Adam raised his brows but made no demur.

'What is it, Mary?' said Susanna.

'You. You said he was simply a friend, but I saw your face just now when you heard his voice. Is he the reason you do not come with us when we go?'

Susanna felt herself blush. 'In part.'

'Despite what happened to your mother?'

'It has passed the point where I could leave. I am not fooling myself, Mary. I know the best I can hope is that he settles me in one of his empty cottages and invents a perfectly sound reason for me being there. I am still not sure I can bear it, but whenever he kisses me I feel my heart fall into place.'

'You love him, in other words. Have you *made* love to him?'

Susanna's blush became red fire. 'No. He said he wouldn't, not under his great-aunt's roof.'

'A moral man. There's a rarity. Susanna, there is nothing to worry about. I was scared myself the first time Adam . . . ' Mary broke off. 'But it was wonderful.'

Susanna already knew it would be. The act, whenever it came, no longer bothered her. What racked her by night and day was whether she was strong enough to bear the pain when Kit married someone who wasn't an illegitimate maidservant-turned-actress.

Mary pressed her hand a moment longer. 'We make our own destiny. It is up to us to make it well.'

In the inn yard, Susanna took leave of Adam. 'I shall send word tonight, one way or the other.'

Adam went to help her up to the curricle seat. 'He does not deserve you, girl.'

Susanna thought of Rafe Warwick and his twisted desire for revenge. She thought of her appalling likeness to Harry Fortune, of the scandal which could ruin Kit if the *ton* got even a hint of her introduction into Lady Penfold's household. She thought of how Kit's cousins would leap on his fall from grace. 'Nobody deserves me,' she said bleakly.

⋆ ⋆ ⋆

That Kit's errand, whatever it had been, had not been wholly satisfactory was evident as he drove back to Penfold Lodge. Twice he asked how Susanna had found her friend, and appeared to take in her answer no better the second time than he had the first. At the house, he followed her into the empty sitting room and said, 'Susanna, there is something I must tell you.'

'No, Kit, there is something I must tell *you.*' She clasped her hands together, felt all her carefully chosen words tangle together on her tongue and finally said baldly, 'They have asked me to play Viola in front of the Duke of Rutland at Cheveley tomorrow.'

'*What?*'

She flinched. 'I know. Indeed I know, Kit, and I am sorry, but I do not quite see how to refuse. They are desperate.'

Kit raked both hands through his hair, wrecking his valet's best efforts. 'How can they be desperate? I counted at least six actresses on that stage last night.'

'Yes, but Kit you must see that neither Mrs Jackson nor Mrs Furnell could play a young woman masquerading as a stripling. As for the others, only Lucy has the ability to undertake the part and she is not permitted to.'

'Then let them change the play, or put it off a week until Mrs Prettyman is better and can take the role herself. If you act at Cheveley, it will ruin all!'

Susanna experienced an incredulous moment of disappointment, so intense that it hurt. She had not thought Kit could be selfish. Had Lady Penfold let fall a hint about her intentions? Did he not want to risk annoying her? 'It is not so simple,' she said, hearing and hating the reserve in her voice. 'Adam is on his beam-ends. It has always been Mary who managed their money, but she was ill even before she lost the baby and did not realize he was cutting their take to help the others and so . . . ' She swallowed and continued in a more resolute tone. 'To be blunt, if the Chartwell Players do not please his Grace tomorrow, they are all of them in danger of ending the quarter in the sponging house. Kit, I do not ask this lightly, but perhaps if we tell Lady Penfold that I am unwell again, and you settle her as near the back of the room as possible, we may yet come out of this unscathed.'

'But you have to be there as *yourself* tomorrow! You have no notion how important it is!'

Tears sprang to Susanna's eyes. 'No, you cannot be this selfish! I will not believe it of you!'

'Selfish? What the deuce are you talking about?'

'Oh, Kit, I know you are desperate for capital to restore Kydd and feed your estate workers, but at least they will still have their homes. Adam and Mary are like to lose all they possess if I do not help them!'

'What the devil has Kydd Court got to do with — ?' He broke off suddenly, his eyes blazing. 'God in Heaven, you think I'm talking about Great-aunt Emma's money! Susanna, surely you know me better than that? That has been the last thing on my mind for . . . for *days*! She can leave it to the foundling hospital for all I care! I am talking about *you*. It is imperative that *you* go to Cheveley.'

Part of Susanna wanted to cry with relief. 'Don't be ridiculous,' she said in a shaky voice. 'What could be more important than saving Adam and Mary from ruin? If I will not abandon them for you, I certainly will not for myself.' She took an unsteady breath. 'Viola is my best part. I know I can act it sufficiently well for the company to keep his Grace's favour. And if I am recognized, I am no worse off than I was before you rescued me from Mr Warwick. I will take the guilt on myself. I shall say I deceived you as to my respectability and I will go right away and perhaps the scandal will not be so very great and Lady Penfold will forgive you.'

'Scandal? What do I care for scandal?'

'Now you are being foolish. I know how banks function. If there is even the least hint of unpleasantness you will never be able to raise any capital for Kydd.'

Kit strode across the room and gripped her arms. 'How many times do I have to tell you that Kydd no longer occupies the forefront of my mind? *Hang* the damned bank! I can sell off the rest of the porcelain. For that matter I can sell every stick of furniture in the place and we will sleep in the stables! It is you I need, Susanna. I love you to distraction and if you do not come back with me to Kydd and marry me in the parish church as soon as I can procure a licence, I will likely go clean out of my wits!'

'And I suppose,' said an awful voice from the doorway, 'having disturbed my rest and shaken the house to its foundations with your rumbustifications, you are going to tell me exactly why it is that she might not?'

Vaguely, very vaguely, Susanna registered Lady Penfold's presence. Her eyes were locked into Kit's stormy blue gaze. 'You love me?' she whispered.

'Simpleton,' he said, and folded her into his arms.

'A fine mode of address to one's betrothed,' said Lady Penfold, making her way ponderously across the room with the help of her favourite footman. She subsided into a massive wing chair and pointed to the sofa with her stick. 'Sit,' she said, in accents not to be disobeyed. 'And talk.'

'Very willingly,' said Kit. 'Though what we have to relate is likely to mortify and distress you. You would be within your rights to dismiss us from your roof within the hour.'

'I'll be the judge of that.'

Susanna took a deep breath. Stunned as she was by the magic words 'marry me', she had to ease her conscience by telling Lady Penfold the truth before she did anything else. 'I am not the niece of a literary gentleman, ma'am,' she said. 'That was a fabrication to give me a veneer of respectability. The truth is that my grandfather shot himself after gambling away his inheritance, and my mother's union with my father was unlawful. When it was discovered, Mama took the post of housekeeper in a gentleman's establishment in Cheltenham where I was brought up to be a maid of all work. After she died I found it impossible to keep another position because of being constantly importuned or suffering from fellow servants' jealousy, so I became an actress, first with the Chartwell Players in the west country and latterly at the Sans Pareil theatre in the Strand.' She took a further deep breath. 'Dancing. In strips of gauze.'

'Where I fell in love with her,' said Kit. 'And rescued her from a would-be abductor.' He picked up her hand and kissed it. 'And have hardly dared let her out of my sight since.'

'Then why the devil didn't you tell me?' said Lady Penfold.

Susanna barely heard her. Kit had fallen in love with her all the way back then? Her hand trembled in his. She looked at him wonderingly.

There was a rueful light in his eyes as he looked back at her. 'I cannot blame you for not knowing,' he said. 'I wasn't even aware of it myself.'

'How could I know? You were so offhand.'

'Because you had been frightened by

Warwick. I thought you would never trust a man again. I was trying to show you that all men are not like him.'

They were recalled to the present by Lady Penfold's stick thumping on the floor. 'I repeat,' she said, a martial light in her eye, 'why the devil didn't you tell me?'

'*Tell you?*' Kit's face was horrified.

'Lord above, boy, you surely didn't think I'd be shocked? I eloped with Edward to Gretna in breeches, remember? I was at Kydd when Georgiana led Jonathan such a merry dance that it ended in him damn near killing — ' She broke off at Kit's perplexed expression. 'No, perhaps you weren't told about that. The fact remains that of all the people in this town, I am the least likely to cavil at my great-nephew wanting to tie the knot with an actress whose grandfather shot himself. You young people! Just because I won't see sixty again, doesn't mean I'm too straight-laced to view the world in perspective. Age doesn't guarantee respectability, it just makes living dangerously a damn sight more difficult!'

'You are, without doubt, a diamond amongst great-aunts,' said Kit. 'How many times should I apologize?'

'Hrmph.' Lady Penfold turned her basilisk stare on Susanna. '*Now* I know who you are.

Aye, and why you've been at such pains to hide yourself and dress so damned plainly. You're the child that was born to the Fortunes' governess.'

Susanna swallowed. 'I believe I must be, though all I knew for certain when I arrived in these parts was that Mama had been employed in a Newmarket household. She never told me her real name or what my father was called. But that is ancient history if you please, ma'am. The marriage was not legal and since both my parents are dead I would not want the scandal raked up to discompose Mrs Fortune or her daughters.'

'But your father is *not* dead,' burst out Kit. 'That is what I have been trying to tell you! Why do you think I have been spending so much time with Harry? My suspicions were kindled the moment I saw his uncle's portrait in their billiard room. Sweetheart, Harry's father only ever had one brother. The same Major Crispin Fortune who is even now staying with the Duke of Rutland at Cheveley. I tried to see him today, but the gentlemen were all engaged.'

The room spun about her. Her hand clutched at her breast. 'It cannot be true,' she whispered. 'His parents wrote to Mama that he died in an uprising.'

Lady Penfold spoke in the grimmest tone

Susanna had yet heard her use. 'And they told *him* that *she* died in childbirth along with you. It's true enough, girl, I've lived here forty years.' She turned to the footman standing impassively by the door. 'Tea, Thomas, and something stronger too. Miss Fair has sustained a considerable shock.'

The footman bowed and withdrew. The 'something stronger' was forthcoming immediately. Susanna gasped as Kit persuaded a mouthful of fiery spirit between her lips. But it did jolt her out of her daze, and when the tea arrived she drank it gratefully.

'Want to hear more?' asked Lady Penfold.

Susanna nodded, feeling Kit take her hand in his own.

'Haven, that was your mother's family name. Big scandal when her father blew his brains out, but fresh news soon drives out old and after a couple of months no one paid heed to it any more. No one apart from Maria Fortune, a poisonous woman if ever there was one, who positively revelled in telling everybody how saintly she was being in employing poor, disgraced Fanny Haven as governess for her three youngest brats. Served her right when Crispin fell in love with the girl. Fine young man, Crispin, nothing like his mother or elder brother. All of us saw it coming and hugged ourselves to think of Maria getting her comeuppance, but none of us dreamt what she'd do when she found out.'

'Which was to send your mama away and enrol your papa into the army,' murmured Kit.

'No, the Militia,' said Susanna, rousing herself. 'They were stationed in Ireland at the time.'

'As I said, a poisonous woman,' repeated Lady Penfold. 'It *was* the regular army and he embarked straightaway for *France*. And she told Crispin that your mother had taken up a post in Newcastle. Misdirection all the way in case they should be determined enough to try and find each other again. When the news came that mother and babe had died in childbirth, it never occurred to anyone to disbelieve her. Crispin hasn't set foot in the Fortune house from that day to this. Maria paid a heavy price for her meddling.'

Alive. Her father was alive. Susanna's head felt like an empty, cavernous house, echoing and dusty. She looked instinctively at Kit. 'What should I do?'

'Have another cup of tea and a macaroon,' said Lady Penfold with gruff practicality, 'whilst my scapegrace of a nephew explains to me why you must act in this play tomorrow and risk all my neighbours finding out about you.'

Alive. And she would act in front of him tomorrow. *He never married*, repeated Caroline's voice in her head . . . *Some sort of falling-out with Papa . . .*

Alive. The fact that he would not know her was immaterial. That he had been faithful to Mama's memory was the sweetest comfort Lady Penfold could have imparted.

Alive . . . But she became aware that Kit had finished his explanation and that Lady Penfold's eyes were more gleeful than a septuagenarian's had any right to be and, moreover, that she was beating her stick in a triumphant tattoo on the floor.

'Caro,' she said. 'That's who we need. She comes as my guest, dressed in one of those awful outfits Adeline provides. You, on the other hand, will wear the most dazzling costume we can contrive, along with that hat from Mrs Rogers.'

Susanna was moved to protest. 'But everybody will look at me!'

Lady Penfold nodded. 'They will indeed. And no one at Caro. So when you change for the play and *she* dresses in *your* clothes and conceals herself in plain sight surrounded by me and my family, nobody will realize she ain't you!'

'Then, after the play, you both change back and no one can accuse you of acting Viola because they all saw you watching it throughout,' finished Kit. He kissed Lady Penfold's hand with an extravagant flourish. 'Great-aunt Emma, I salute you. A magnificent solution. But Miss Caroline Fortune is very young and not at all discreet. Are you sure she will not give us away?'

Susanna gave a disbelieving laugh. 'Not discreet? Kit, that girl has more secrets in her head than Hoare's bank vault. Why, she has been training Rufus at dawn for years without anyone but Lady Penfold and her head groom being any the wiser.'

Kit's mouth dropped open in comical dismay. Lady Penfold studied Susanna with grim amusement. 'And how do you know that, missy?'

'I saw her one morning. But it was no concern of mine and I too can hold my tongue.'

'She was there at his birth,' said Lady Penfold. 'Climbed out of her window, shinned down the ivy and sat up all night with Bertrand. Rufus has always been as much her horse as his. She'll have him when I'm gone.'

'That is a splendid thought,' said Susanna. 'I'm sure your grandson would have approved.'

Lady Penfold hrmphed. 'Know he would. Lord, look at the time. Should have been dressing half an hour ago. Thomas!'

Kit stood up as his great-aunt left the room and then pulled Susanna to her feet. 'A redoubtable lady,' he said.

'To whom we are much indebted.' Susanna looked shyly up at him. 'So much has happened this afternoon that my wits are quite addled. Have you really loved me that long?'

He stroked her hair. 'I rather think I must have fallen in love the first moment you smiled at me from the stage. I give you fair warning, sweetheart, if you do not agree to marry me, I am prepared to force you to the altar at pistol point and then spend the rest of my life persuading you to love me.'

She brought his hand to her lips. 'Oh, Kit, I already do. Since the first moment I saw *you*, smiling down at me from the box. But I thought you would be arrogant and untrustworthy like all the gentry . . . And even though I now know you are not, you *cannot* marry me. Think of your reputation.'

He held her closer. 'I don't need a reputation, I need you. And if you were not going to marry me, my girl, what the devil did you mean by agreeing to come back with me to Kydd?'

Susanna blushed. 'I thought you intended installing me in one of those empty cottages. I

297

thought you would make me your mistress.'

'Thus ruining my reputation far more comprehensively,' said Kit. 'You are quite shameless, love. There is nothing for it, one of us is going to have to sacrifice their principles.' He smiled into her eyes, his own clear and loving. 'Will you marry me, Susanna?'

She felt as if her heart would burst with happiness. 'Yes,' she whispered, 'if you really will not mind when people shun us or refuse to recognize me.'

'Not at all. It will mean fewer tedious evening parties to do the pretty through.'

Her lips quivered. 'I suppose you could always say it was cheaper to marry me than to employ a housekeeper.'

'A housekeeper? By the time our wedding night is over, you will be in no condition to count sheets, I assure you.'

14

Susanna looked at herself in the glass with something very like panic. She wore figured white silk with an over-dress of spangled silver gauze (a relic of Lady Penfold's younger days, and altered overnight with reverent fingers), white satin slippers with silver roses, her silver-threaded reticule and the infamous silver-net hair confection. 'Too dazzling,' she said. 'By far too dazzling.'

'No one,' added Caroline with conviction, 'is ever going to take me for you.'

'Both wrong,' said Lady Penfold cheerfully. 'You are as fine as fivepence and since the house party will have ample time to fix *Miss Fair* into their collective consciousness during dinner, it will never occur to them that the black-haired youth on stage is also you. And they will glimpse Caro during the performance, dressed in white and silver, with a ginger wig from the Chartwell Players and that deliciously visible hat, and never doubt that the person they are seeing is Susanna.'

'If you say so,' said Caroline dubiously.

'I do. Try it on, try it on.'

299

Ten minutes later, Susanna was hard-pressed not to laugh as Caroline stared in profound disbelief at the mirror. 'Dearest Susanna, should any gentleman wishful of setting up a training stable come to call on me, please may I borrow this outfit?'

'With pleasure,' said Susanna, 'but if you think your mama will let you wear it whilst your sister remains unwed, your wits must have gone begging. You look magnificent, Caroline.' She spoke no less than the truth. Stripped of the flounces and frills and furbelows which delighted Mrs Fortune and her elder daughter, and standing straighter and taller in consequence, Caroline exuded an almost Amazonian grace.

'Thank you,' said Caroline in heartfelt tones, though whether she addressed Susanna or some invisible deity was unclear.

'It will do,' said Lady Penfold. 'Trust me.'

As the day wore on, Susanna had to pray she was right. The impossibility of any rehearsal with the Chartwell Players worried her, but she had played Viola often enough that once on stage the moves would come back. The only new lines were in the rewritten shipwreck scene which was delivered (and this time Will did get a penny from the butler) along with the ginger wig for Caroline. The state of this last so horrified Lady Penfold's maid that it was whisked away and not returned until the ladies were dressing. Susanna had no doubt that as soon as Mary saw its lustrous condition, all the other stock hairpieces would be bundled into a basket and sent to Penfold Lodge too.

★   ★   ★

Kit let his valet brush down his coat and wished this evening well and truly over. No matter how many times he told himself a nobleman's saloon was a very different locale from a variety theatre pit, he still did not want the entire house party to see Susanna in breeches for an hour or more. He came out of his room in a thoroughly bad temper at the same moment that Susanna emerged from hers. For an instant he stood rooted to the spot, his mouth hanging open like a veritable gapseed. 'My pardon,' he said, collecting himself. 'You look — wonderful.'

Susanna groaned. 'The costume is too fine. I knew it.'

'No.' Kit put his hand on her arm quickly. He felt the little jump she gave at the contact. 'It is perfect and you are beautiful and if your maid and my valet were not watching us I would prove it.'

'Kit!' she said, blushing a delicious pink.

He drew her hand within his arm and walked her towards the staircase. 'Every man at Cheveley tonight will take one look at you and think I am the luckiest dog alive.'

'Whereas all the ladies will take one look at *you* and be ready to claw my eyes out. Kit, are you really and truly convinced you wish to throw yourself away on a nobody like me?'

'Utterly. I am depending on you to be my first line of defence from now on. And who knows? Once you and your father meet, you might *not* be a nobody.'

He wasn't prepared for her gasp or the way she pulled away from him. 'Kit! You wouldn't!' She plunged down the stairs so that he had to race to catch up. 'Is *that* what you were planning to do yesterday?' she said over her shoulder. 'Tell him I was not stillborn as he has always thought?'

'Well, yes.' Kit was at a loss. 'Susanna, I don't understand.'

She marched into the saloon, which fortunately was empty. 'Without informing me? Without doing me the courtesy of finding out how I might feel about such a disclosure? Without even telling me that he was still alive?'

'I . . . ' Kit stopped. He had never seen her so angry. 'Deuce take it, Susanna, you kept trying to run away. I thought if you knew you *did* have a place in the world, something that didn't depend on me, that you might not — '

'Vastly kind of you! Kit, whatever Major Fortune once felt for my mother, he has been a professional solder for most of his life and is a confirmed bachelor to boot. How is he likely to react to the news that his natural daughter has recently been reduced to exhibiting very near every inch of her legs to the hoi polloi of the pit in order to keep body and soul together? What do you imagine his feelings might be on learning that his one-time love died in pain and poverty? That if he had been stronger or less credulous in his youth, he might have prevented it? I keep telling you the past is dead and done with. I do not want to rake it up.'

She was trembling, her eyes pearly with unshed tears. Kit crossed the room and took her in his arms, thoroughly shaken. 'I didn't think. I'm sorry, sweetheart. I just couldn't bear you to leave me for the wrong reasons.'

She was tense, unyielding. Kit cursed under his breath as he heard his great-aunt descending the stairs. There was no time to mend matters now. He dropped a light kiss on her hair. 'I promise I won't say a word. I was a boorish clod even to think of doing so without consulting you first. Would you like my handkerchief?'

That produced a wavering smile. 'Thank you. I think I must be feeling a little overwrought with all the — '

As he had done once before, Kit placed a kiss on his own finger and transferred it to her lips. 'Hush. You have nothing to apologize for. The fault is mine alone. Shall we join the others?'

★ ★ ★

The tree-lined avenue leading to the Duke of Rutland's Cheveley residence was longer even than the sweep to Kydd Court. By the time they alighted at the house, Susanna was quaking, but Lady Penfold sailed inside as if she was in the habit of visiting the higher aristocracy every day of her life.

Susanna could hardly believe the size of the table at which they were bidden to eat. From her place next to Colonel MacGregor it stretched so far in both directions that she could barely make out her host and hostess. She was glad to see the Colonel, for Kit had been placed further up and Caroline was hidden by an enormous epergne across the table. The strain of maintaining her pretence with *two* unknown neighbours would have been immense.

'Well,' said Colonel MacGregor jovially,

'what do you think of this then?' He tapped one of the dishes in front of them. 'Kakeimon! One of the first sets to be brought into the country!'

'It is very fine,' said Susanna. She felt a prickling sensation in the back of her neck as if someone was watching her. The fault of this wretched outfit. She sat a little straighter. 'Do you know all of these people? Who is the gentleman in the startling yellow waistcoat?'

'Where? Oh, that's one of Rutland's tenants. Got a neat little manor I wouldn't say no to myself. Strange he's placed up there. I thought from something the Duchess said that he was going to be nearer me.'

'He was,' murmured a voice in Susanna's ear. 'Until I took the liberty of exchanging the cards. You look very fine tonight, my dear. I begin to see the attraction of your country squire if this is the sort of 'tick' he can command.'

Rafe Warwick! Taking the chair on her other side as easily as if he owned it! Susanna stiffened with paralysed disbelief.

'Surprised?' he continued in a sardonic undertone. 'I did warn you that you couldn't hide. This seating arrangement is but a small sample of how close an eye I shall be keeping on you from now on. I have to thank you, my dear. My ennui has all but disappeared.'

Colonel MacGregor was still talking. Susanna forced herself to respond, pretending an interest in the personages he was pointing out. 'That's Lady Ranleigh sitting by young Kit. Saucy little baggage. Not that you need fret, eh? He's fair besotted with you, so Emma tells me.'

Susanna felt Warwick's interest sharpen. 'And Lord Ranleigh?' she said quickly. 'Which is he? Does he not object to his wife bestowing her smiles on other gentlemen?'

Colonel MacGregor chuckled and continued to discourse on the table until politeness required him to turn to his right-hand neighbour.

'Besotted?' murmured Rafe Warwick. 'This gets ever more interesting.'

'Of course not,' said Susanna. She paused to let the footman remove her soup plate. 'He acts the part in front of his aunt. It would be suspicious indeed were he not to admire me when we are together.'

'He is not alone. I assume you have noticed the quizzing glasses raised in your direction?'

'Gently bred ladies are above such impertinences.'

'But you are not gently bred and I believe you are well aware of the effect you have on the male sex. Perhaps you seek to change your protector for one who is rather more

306

powerful? There are a number of influential men here.'

At least he was keeping his poisonous words low. Susanna let a careful pause ensue before saying, 'I am content with my current position, thank you.' She reached for a portion of fish.

Rafe Warwick's fork came down over hers, trapping it. 'As I am not,' he hissed. 'It was a mistake to dress so desirably this evening. I am minded to put an end to this little comedy after all.'

A stab of fear went through her. 'I beg your pardon,' she said aloud, trying to disengage her cutlery without drawing attention to herself. Out of the corner of her eye she saw Kit's face turn her way, his expression suddenly murderous as he recognized her dinner companion.

A malicious smile curved Mr Warwick's lips. 'Besotted was the word, I see. How very amusing. It will make my revenge far more satisfactory, knowing the humiliation I am inflicting on your puppy every time you are seen on my arm in public. Not to mention the torment he will suffer when he dwells on what I might be doing to you in private. Dear me, you are looking quite peaky. Let me help you to a morsel of this excellent cod.'

Susanna ate without any of the curiosity

which the delicate, unfamiliar sauce might otherwise have raised. Two matters occupied her mind to the exclusion of all else. How to prevent Rafe Warwick making known to the entire party what she really was, and how to escape his notice long enough to play Viola. That she would be safe once away from Newmarket and on Kit's acres at Kydd, she doubted no more than she had ever done. She risked a glance up the table to where Kit was seemingly engrossed by the animated Lady Ranleigh and felt a slow warmth fill her. His earlier interference regarding her father was forgiven. He was gentry. He was used to making decisions without reference to those concerned. She had been foolish not to tell him of Warwick's presence at the church, foolish not to warn him what she had allowed Warwick to think. She would have to trust to his wits should the Dishonourable Rafe refer to 'business engagements' once the ladies withdrew from the table.

Ah! *That* was how she would manage the acting! Susanna let the Colonel engage her surface attention again, thinking the plan through in her mind. She and Caroline would leave the room before the gentlemen joined them. Caro could then slip in and settle herself next to Lady Penfold just as the play was due to start. And at the end, Lady

Penfold would feel faint as they had already agreed, necessitating a breath of fresh air and giving Susanna and Caroline the chance to switch back.

She and Colonel MacGregor had exhausted all the patterns of crockery in their immediate vicinity before she was obliged to return to Rafe Warwick.

'I am impressed,' he drawled, twirling the stem of his wineglass. 'You are quite an expert.'

She shrugged. 'Kydd Court has a fine collection of porcelain. Lady Penfold would expect a future chatelaine to take an interest in it.'

'More and more I see that you were wasted at the Sans Pareil. Such attention to your role would hardly be out of place at Drury Lane.'

Susanna didn't think this was the moment to tell him that the reason she was not at Drury Lane was less to do with her acting ability than her lack of willingness to comply with the sleeping arrangements she had been offered. Such prudishness hardly went with the persona she was trying to project. 'This is a very handsome room,' she said instead, changing the subject. 'Are the rest of the principal apartments as splendid?'

Rafe Warwick's lip curled. 'Would that I could enlighten you. Alas, his Grace is not so enamoured of my company that I am an intimate here. Indeed, if it were not for the fact that he is unwilling to offend my host, who is a neighbour of his, I doubt I would be tolerated at the ducal board.'

Fortunately, the Duchess chose this moment to signal to the ladies to rise. Susanna thought she had never left a room quicker.

'Who was that next to you?' said Caroline once they were in the drawing room. 'He was watching you all the way to the door.'

Susanna shuddered. 'Rafe Warwick. A very, very dangerous man. And not a pleasant one either.'

'His eyes reminded me of a groom Papa dismissed for cruelty. Aren't there a lot of people here? I couldn't see Uncle Crispin at all. He must have been further up the table.'

Susanna felt as if she had suddenly plunged breast deep into an icy lake.

Caroline cocked her head. 'Now what have I said?'

'Oh dear, there is no easy way to tell you this. That long-ago disagreement you mentioned? It rather looks as though Major Fortune is my . . . that is, there is a distinct possibility that I am your lost, and not entirely lily-white, cousin.'

'You are Uncle Crispin's skeleton! Famous! *That* explains why I have sometimes fancied a resemblance between you and Harry. Oh, Mama is going to be so *mortified*!'

'Caroline! Your mama is not to hear a word about it! There is no sense dragging a years-old scandal into the light. The liaison was unlawful. Your uncle neither knows of my existence nor is he going to.'

'But if he *did* know of it, he'd surely want to meet you.'

'You have been reading too many romances. I wonder your mama lets them in the house.'

'She doesn't. The maids smuggle them in and I read them aloud in the laundry room. We get through a fearful amount of washing.'

She was incorrigible. Susanna chuckled in spite of her anxiety. 'How soon can we change? It will be best if you are already seated in the saloon with Lady Penfold when the gentlemen arrive. Did Kit request a special seat by one of the long windows for her?'

'He did. Lady Penfold is to give me a signal when she judges it is time to — Oh, she is nodding at us now.' She raised her voice. 'How tiresome! I have torn a flounce. Will you come with me to pin it up?'

'Certainly,' said Susanna in the same, clear tone. 'There is bound to be a retiring room, is there not?'

'In a house the size of this, I should think

there are several,' said Caroline irrepressibly.

They edged past the groups of genteelly gossiping ladies as they spoke and were soon in the hallway. 'This way,' said Susanna, recalling Kit's rough sketch of the principal rooms.

In the saloon where the play was to be staged, Adam greeted them with a heartfelt, 'Thank God, I thought you were never coming', and hustled them behind the velvet curtains to where Mary, pale but already looking better, was sitting to one side with Viola's costume. Susanna didn't waste time retreating behind the backcloth, but removed her dress where she stood. Caroline blinked a little at the rest of the company busy checking furniture and props, then resolutely began to wriggle free of her own befrilled sprig muslin, her colour only a fraction higher than usual.

'Good girl,' Susanna heard Mary say, but she was too intent on fastening her shirt, climbing into the breeches and listening to the arrival of the chattering audience to add her own praise.

'Will? Lottie? Peep between the curtains and tell us when you see Mr Kydd. He is wearing a pale blue waistcoat and a dark blue coat.'

'There's a lady in a gold dress. That's the Duchess,' whispered Lottie. 'And a lady in pink sitting down next to her. And one in blue with flowers in her hair. And — '

'I see him,' interrupted Will, on whom Kit and his horses had made a strong impression. 'He's with a stout gentleman and — ' He broke off and let out a reverent oath which he almost certainly hadn't learnt from his father. 'Is *that* Lady Penfold?'

Mary anchored the silver net to Caroline's ginger hairpiece and tweaked the folds of spangled gauze straight. 'Tell us when she is near her seat, then Miss Caroline can go out by this window and in at that one with no one the wiser.'

'Nearly there,' reported Will.

Susanna jammed a final hairpin into the black wig which Mary had tied into a queue, and gave her head an experimental shake. 'Good luck, Caro. Ready, Lottie?'

The little girl clutched the nosegay her mother had prepared, her eyes bright. Will took her hand and the two of them went between the curtains into the saloon. Peeping through the gap herself, Susanna saw them walk up to the Duchess and heard Lottie say in a clear, confident treble, 'Please, ma'am, these are all flowers out of Shakespeare for you. Thank you very much for inviting us to act in your lovely house and we hope you enjoy the play.'

There was a ripple of kindly laughter, under cover of which Caroline slipped through the long unlatched window and into a chair next to Lady Penfold. Kit moved closer on her other side. Will bowed, Lottie curtseyed and then the pair of them came back through the curtains.

'Beautifully done,' said Susanna. 'A perfect distraction.'

Adam had been at the door to the passage. Now he gave a nod to someone outside and hurried over. 'They are ready for us to begin. Places everyone.'

Susanna retreated to the side. From this edge of the curtain she could just see Rafe Warwick, seated inside the door. As she watched, he glanced across the width of the room to where Lady Penfold's party sat. She saw a satisfied smile cross his face. Triumph flickered inside her. He had been fooled and although he would recognize her the moment she came on, he would be powerless to do anything without drawing attention to himself. And hopefully by the time the interval occurred, he would have worked out that there was little point exposing her, since the threat of it was his means of blackmailing her into becoming his mistress. He might even reflect that it gave him *more* of a hold.

Adam was speaking, his rich voice filling

the grand saloon. 'Your Graces, my Lords and Ladies, ladies and gentlemen. My daughter has forestalled me in her wishes for your enjoyment, so I will say only that you are about to be transported to Illyria where the Duke Orsino — myself — pines for the love of the fair Olivia. Little do either of them know that a shipwreck is to bring two very interesting parties to their shores . . . The Chartwell Players present to you *Twelfth Night!*'

★   ★   ★

It was a good audience. As Adam spoke the opening line: '*If music be the food of love, play on . . . .*', there was none of the public-theatre chatter to obscure his voice, just the whisper of silk as the ladies made themselves comfortable. People were, Susanna realized with gratified pleasure, actually attending to the play.

The first scene was over in a matter of minutes. Orsino's couch was replaced by a battered sea-chest. Susanna took a deep breath, concentrated on visualizing the wind-torn shores of Illyria in her mind's eye, and went onstage.

Afterwards she remembered very little of the performance, yet at the time she lived

315

every word, breathed every breath and felt every one of Viola's conflicting emotions. Perhaps being in love herself had attuned her more fully than ever before to the role. Certainly at the end, when the curtains swung across, leaving Mr Furnell alone in front of them to sing the closing song, it took her a full second to come to herself.

'Hurry,' hissed Caroline, already in her own clothes and pulling her to the side of the stage. 'Lady Penfold says it's too cold to stay overlong outside. How ever many pins did you put in this odious wig?'

Susanna scrambled out of her shirt and breeches, suddenly galvanized. She flung the costume to Mary and put on her white and silver dress.

'And the hat,' said Caro, 'and here are your slippers.'

Susanna thrust her feet in them and smoothed her dress. 'I am ready. Good luck, Mary.' She followed Caroline out to the stone terrace, sped past the drawn curtains, then slipped her hand solicitously under Lady Penfold's elbow and ushered her back indoors.

Mr Furnell was just finishing his song. Under cover of the enthusiastic applause, Kit bent his head to Susanna's ear. 'You were wonderful.'

'Thank you.' Susanna flushed with pleasure. She too clapped as the curtains swung open and the Chartwell Players stepped forward to accept the house party's accolade. Mary, in the black wig, shirt and breeches, held her husband's hand and smiled, then swayed.

'Thank you,' said Adam over the ovation. 'I beg you will excuse my wife. She has risen from her sickbed to play for you today and I am under orders from the good doctor in this town not to let her tire herself a minute longer than necessary.'

There was a fresh burst of applause. Mary smiled and waved and moved backwards out of sight.

'Warwick knows,' said Kit under his breath, 'but I don't believe anyone else has the slightest suspicion.'

His Grace was speaking now, telling of his very great pleasure in the play and giving his assurance that the Chartwell Players would have his patronage whenever they were in Newmarket. If Mr Prettyman would see his steward, he would be reimbursed for his costs, and meanwhile the Duke had taken the liberty of bespeaking supper for the company which would be brought in shortly and which he hoped would find as much favour with them as their playing had with him.

Susanna let out a soundless breath of relief. 'He *did* enjoy it. Let us hope for Adam's sake that the purse is a fat one.' She took Kit's arm to join the general exodus towards the other rooms where card tables had been set up and wine was circulating.

'Yes,' agreed Kit in heartfelt tones. 'So fat, in fact, that the Chartwell Players never feel the need to call upon you again. Much as I admire you on stage, my love, just at this moment I have never wanted to see you adorn one less!'

'Which is where we differ,' said a smooth voice behind them. 'My pardon, did I startle you? Perhaps we should step out of the way of the door. I am sure you would not want any inadvertent witnesses to this little discussion . . . '

15

Kit's eyes hardened to twin chips of sapphire. 'I do not believe I have anything to say to you, Mr Warwick.'

Rafe Warwick rested his hand carelessly on his cane. 'No? That will certainly make the conversation shorter. I have a great deal to say to you, Mr Kydd, but if you do not wish to hear it, I can always talk to Lady Penfold instead. She is not so very far behind us.'

Susanna spoke rapidly. 'Kit, there is an anteroom just down the hallway. I saw it when we passed this way earlier.' Across the room, unnoticed by either of the gentlemen, she saw Caroline's eyes flicker from herself to Mr Warwick.

'If we must,' said Kit.

Warwick's lips curved. 'I thought you would see it my way. Lead on, my dear.'

Kit's muscles bunched at the familiar address; Susanna squeezed his forearm to enjoin silence. When they reached the anteroom she said bluntly, 'You wish me to come with you or you will tell all, is that it?'

Rafe Warwick strolled further into the

room, examining the paintings and ornaments. 'Let us not be precipitous. I have not yet congratulated you. I have rarely seen Viola so well acted. It was quite a revelation despite your Rosalind the other day. You bribed your maid to wear your clothes during the performance, I suppose? And took care to keep her out of the rich aunt's direct sight?'

'You can suppose what you like,' said Kit. 'Miss Fair is not coming with you.'

'Dear me, you have got it badly. I wonder if I was ever that innocent? She is not worth it, you know. Trollops of this class never are. Why, if a comely young baronet with a few thousand a year were to offer to set her up in a discreet little house in Curzon Street, she'd be off there tomorrow.'

'Miss Fair has done me the honour of consenting to become my wife,' said Kit stiffly.

Mr Warwick put down a filigree bowl and cast a look of cynical appraisal at Susanna. 'So *that* is why you refused me! Marriage! What a clever puss you are, to be sure.' He returned his attention to Kit. His voice grew cold. 'It will not do. I desire her. I find I have a great fancy to be known as the gentleman who owns Drury Lane's newest attraction.'

Susanna drew a silent breath. Kit was

playing the pugnacious greenhorn to perfection. It was time she took a turn. She gave a light laugh. 'Very flattering, but I went to Drury Lane when I first came to London and — '

'And they would not employ a nobody from the provinces,' said Warwick impatiently. 'I assure you, once they know you are under *my* protection, they will change their tune.'

'It was not that,' said Susanna with a very slightly petulant expression. 'It was the size of the theatre.'

'Nonsense! You may have deceived the rich aunt into thinking you modest and unassuming, but you will not hoodwink *me* into believing you do not want to play in front of three thousand people!'

'Naturally I would have liked it,' said Susanna, a touch of peevishness now creeping into her tone. 'They said my voice was too thin. Since Drury Lane was rebuilt, the theatre is so large that even my best speeches did not carry beyond halfway. Covent Garden was the same. Why else do you suppose I was at the Sans Pareil? Mr Scott promised me speaking parts next season and there I *can* be heard.'

Rafe Warwick's eyes narrowed. His hand slid down his cane. Did he believe her or not? 'No matter,' he said after a moment, 'I daresay I can hit on some other way of making you notorious. I shall install you as the hostess of a gambling hell I have an interest in whilst I ponder the matter. You can sing for us during supper.'

Kit took a step forward, his fists balling. 'I don't believe you heard. Miss Fair is going to marry me!'

Rafe Warwick's voice grew colder and more deadly still. 'If she does any such thing, I shall explode your little myth before you are an hour older. Your entire acquaintance will hear how you are passing off your gutter-born mistress as a lady. You will be shunned, your family will be disgraced and your great-aunt made out to be a fool. I doubt very much that she will leave you her money after that.'

'Tosh! Today's scandal is tomorrow's ancient history.'

'But mud always sticks. And unless you see fit to hand your little nobody over to me, I intend to make sure that the pair of you get a veritable avalanche of it!'

He was concentrating so hard on them that he had not noticed the door swing open. He did not see the lean, soldierly gentleman, red hair tinged with silver at the temples, tread noiselessly into the room. He had no idea, in fact, that his vitriolic words were heard by anybody except themselves until a clipped, cool voice spoke behind him.

'A nobody, sir? And just how can *my daughter* be counted as a nobody?'

Just seeing his face, age-marks and reality etched on the miniature in Mama's writing desk, Susanna's reason had told her his identity. Her hand flew to her breast and the room blurred around her.

Caroline Fortune appeared by his side. 'So this is where you are, Susanna,' she said merrily. 'See who I have found! Just fancy, Uncle Crispin had no idea you were Lady Penfold's guest.'

The anteroom continued to sway. Susanna was conscious only of Kit's arm about her waist, of a pair of grey eyes the image of her own fixed with painful intensity on her face. 'Papa?' she whispered.

'Very pretty,' sneered Rafe Warwick. 'But you had best play another scene. The likeness is clever, but it won't wash with one who has seen the wench dance at the Sans Pareil these last two months and who watched her perform the part of Viola with his very own eyes tonight!'

Major Crispin Fortune raised his quizzing glass. 'Do I know you, sir? It seems my friend Rutland is becoming a trifle lax in his perusal of the invitation cards. This is most definitely my daughter.'

'And I suppose you are about to present her to our illustrious host, are you?'

'To my host and long-time friend, and also to the Duchess, yes.' He extended his hand. 'If you are ready, Susanna. And you, Mr Kydd.'

Kit's arm fell away. Hardly aware of what she did, Susanna moved towards the door.

'You have not heard the last of this,' said Warwick, cold malignity in his eyes. 'Enjoy your reprieve, little linnet. It is like to be your final one.'

'Terrible. This is terrible,' said Susanna in a hysterical whisper as they threaded their way through the grand saloon. 'You must not think I am not glad to know you, sir, and I thank you for your intervention, but he will ruin us, I know he will. All the scandal will be raked up. All the gossip. Oh, why did I not simply throw myself into the Thames as soon as his eye lit upon me?'

'Courage, daughter,' said Crispin Fortune, still in that clipped tone. 'Lady Penfold has told me everything. I intend to recognize you before the whole of Society. I may have come late to my parental duty, due to my mother's despicable machinations, but that does not mean I shall be tardy in carrying it out.'

'You should not have had to come to it at all,' said Susanna. 'I had no intention of bringing myself to your attention. Caroline, how could you?'

'Lady Penfold thought I should,' said that damsel blithely. 'And I did not promise *not* to, you know.'

'It will be all right, my love,' said Kit, keeping pace with them. 'We will contrive a way out of this mess.'

'And will you also contrive to avoid a ball in your back the next time you go shooting?' said Susanna. 'Or find a way to deal with the footpads and cut-throats who are likely to set upon you every time you put your nose outside your own front door? Kit, I do not *trust* him!'

He gave a shout of laughter and turned loving blue eyes upon her. 'Today's great thought, my darling?'

Susanna moved distractedly around a small group that had turned to see who was in such good spirits. 'Simply being presented to the Duke of Rutland as his friend's long-lost daughter is not going to make me respectable enough for *you* to withstand all the scandal Warwick will churn up!'

Crispin cut in. 'Gentlemen like the Dishonourable Rafe are more wary of antagonizing the nobility than they care to admit. He will not do anything here at Cheveley.'

'So we have until supper is over and the carriages are ordered to work out a strategy,' said Kit buoyantly. 'Plenty of time.'

'Will you be serious?' She turned to the grave, upright man on her other side. 'Pray do not think I am ungrateful, sir, but — '

'Susanna.' Kit's now steady voice halted her. What she saw in his eyes made her heart turn over. 'When it comes to your safety, I *am* serious. I will stop Warwick threatening you if it is the last thing I do.'

She let out a faint moan. 'That is precisely what I am afraid of!'

They had reached a knot of people by this time, amongst whom were their host and hostess. Major Fortune stepped forward to claim the Duke of Rutland's attention.

Out of the corner of her eye, Susanna saw Rafe Warwick. He had followed them in and was leaning against the wall, watching intently. 'This is not going to work,' she said to Kit under her breath.

'No, but it has given me an idea. Stick to your papa like the bailiff's man, my love. I need to act quickly.'

'What? Where are you — ?' But he had melted away and she was being drawn forward to be presented to the Duchess. 'Your Grace,' she said, dropping a low curtsey. 'It is an honour to meet you.'

The Duchess of Rutland surveyed her with kindly eyes. 'And you, my dear. This is something of a fairy tale, is it not? To suddenly find that your father is not dead after all?'

Susanna realized she should have been listening to the Major's introduction rather than arguing with Kit. '*Exactly* like, ma'am,' she said with feeling.

The Duchess smiled. 'Ah well, no doubt by the time the attorneys have tied everything up to their satisfaction, they will have contrived to make it fusty and dusty. I never knew such a profession for reducing the miraculous to the everyday.'

Susanna smiled and inclined her head and moved on to receive his Grace's congratulations also. Attorneys? Tie everything up? What did the Duchess mean?

' . . . when I look forward to entertaining you again,' said the Duke, evidently finishing a small speech.

'Thank you, you are very good,' said Susanna, hoping this would cover whatever else he had said. I haven't any proof, she thought in panic. No record of my birth or to whom or anything! I will be labelled an adventuress for sure! She looked frantically around the room, but none of her friends were near. The only eyes which never left her were Rafe Warwick's. She could do nothing except stay by — she still had a struggle with the concept — her father's side.

'Well now,' said Crispin Fortune, extricating himself from the Duke's circle of friends and signalling to a footman. 'I rather think champagne is called for. I certainly need some and if your feelings are anything like as turbulent as mine, you will be glad of a glass too.'

'Thank you,' said Susanna, 'although I would as lief have tea.'

He gave the first laugh she had yet heard from him. 'Tea? Ha! You are indeed Fanny's daughter.'

Susanna's worries overflowed. 'Please, you are making it worse by talking thus. I should tell you that I have no proof of who I am. All I can offer are the memories of what Mama told me of her history, your miniature and an old wax impression of the Fortune seal. I did not even know her true family name until Lady Penfold supplied it.'

Major Fortune motioned her towards a couple of spindly chairs. 'There will still be the marriage entry, even if it was later struck out, and your own baptism record.'

'But nothing to show that the Widow Fair who was my mother was also the Miss Haven who was briefly your wife.'

'I will put my solicitor to work on it. That you are *my* daughter must be obvious to anyone with unimpaired vision and *I* know you are Fanny's also, for I see her in your every turn of countenance. Fanny was the most precious person in my life. I will not be denied you, Susanna. You are too new to me and I have too long thought you dead.'

Susanna attempted to smile. 'As we did you. I still cannot believe you are not.'

'So Lady Penfold informs me. She has offered me the hospitality of her house that you and I might become better acquainted.'

Susanna looked at him in consternation. 'But we go to Kydd Court the day after tomorrow. We are to be married as soon as may be.'

And thankfully, blessedly, Kit's hand was on her shoulder. 'You are very welcome to travel with us, sir. I regret the haste, but as I am unacquainted with any bishops and do not wish to add a flight to Gretna to our list of gossip-fodder, I must needs be back in my own parish without delay.' His gaze drifted in the direction of Rafe Warwick, who leaned now against a pillar but was watching them as unblinkingly as ever. 'I would also have Susanna safe within my own walls.'

Crispin Fortune's eyes narrowed. 'You do not trust me to protect my daughter?'

Kit inclined his head civilly. 'I intend no slur. Officers of His Majesty's army certainly should be able to keep their families safe. It is rather that I know *I* can.'

The older man gave a faint smile. 'You are determined to take her from me, I see. What if I should refuse my consent? I have heard your estate is encumbered.'

Susanna choked on a mouthful of champagne at the injustice of this. 'Sir! That is hardly fair, to discover your daughter one minute and be dictating to her the next. I have the evidence of my own eyes that Kit will work alongside his men to make Kydd Court profitable again. For myself, I am used to running a household on very little money. Mr Masterson was a shocking miser.'

The next moment she wished she had not added that last sentence because of the grey look that passed across her father's face. 'Your pardon,' he said. 'I was thinking you might rather live with me in London and enjoy the advantages that have been denied you before.'

And undergo evenings like this all the time? Susanna shuddered. 'I could not. Not now. And truly, sir, I have had more than enough of moving in Society for the while.'

A rueful smile tugged at his lips. 'So I am to lose you just as I have found you. Is life with this young man truly what you want?'

Susanna looked at Kit. 'Yes.' And into that one word, she put all her desire for him as well as her longing to be safe and quiet and *home*. Kit's eyes met hers — and she knew the feelings were recognized and reciprocated.

'Then I shall not interfere.' Crispin signalled to the footman again. 'Though I should certainly like to accompany you to Northamptonshire.'

Kit bowed. 'You will be very welcome.'

The conversation was now painful and exquisitely happy by turns. Susanna told her father of her early life and of how Mama had never wavered in her loyalty to his memory. He told *her* how his desperate loss had gained him an undeserved reputation for bravery under fire. Not, he said wryly, a method of advancement to be recommended.

Supper was announced. The Duke and Duchess of Rutland led the exodus from the room. Caroline, evidently considering that she had been quite forbearing enough, tripped across to remind her uncle that he had promised to take her in.

'Oh yes. Something to discuss, wasn't it? And if it isn't largely to do with that spendthrift rascal of a brother of yours, I miss my guess!'

Caroline beamed up at him. 'Well, it is a *little* about Harry . . . ' She tucked her arm in his and bore him away, talking earnestly.

Kit stood up and gave Susanna his hand. 'Mr Warwick is still watching us,' she said under her breath. 'I do not believe he has taken his eyes off me this past hour.'

'I know,' murmured Kit. 'And I intend making use of it. How brave do you feel, sweetheart?'

Susanna's nerves gave a convulsive jerk. 'Kit? What are you planning?'

'Nothing very dreadful, but in a few moments I am going to be hailed from the terrace. As soon as I step outside, I expect the Dishonourable Rafe to accost you. Will you trust me and keep him within earshot of everything which passes? You need not fear an abduction. Great-aunt Emma's Thomas is just over there.'

Susanna swallowed. 'I would trust you with my life.'

He quirked an eyebrow at her. 'I do not think it will come to *that*, love.'

One of the long windows had been set ajar to cool the room. They were passing it now. On cue came a voice from the terrace. 'Kydd! A word if you please!'

Kit produced a convincing start. 'I will join you in a moment,' he said aloud to Susanna then hurried outside. 'Your Grace!' she heard him say in surprised accents.

'No need to announce it to the world,' came the amused reply.

Susanna hovered, as if torn between good manners and the natural desire to eavesdrop.

'My trick, I believe,' said Warwick, his hand closing over her upper arm. 'What a sorry guard, to be distracted by the lure of nobility. However, his carelessness is my gain. Time to leave, my dear.'

Susanna stood her ground. 'Take one more step and I shall scream.'

His grip tightened. 'Please do. It adds to the enjoyment. Indeed, I may insist on it later. But not here, I think, unless you want your lover's conduct exposed to all these influential people.'

The Duke's voice came again from outside. 'Fortune told me about your betrothed. How she's been earning a living as an actress and about you rescuing her from that damned scoundrel Warwick.'

Susanna gasped. Rafe Warwick stilled, his attention focused on the shadowy terrace.

'The man's an affront to society,' continued the voice. 'Had to resign from White's, you know. Cut up rough over some bet he lost. Damn bad form. That's why he's marking time here. Waiting for the dust to settle. Sorry you had to meet him in my house. Came as the guest of a neighbour.'

'Pray do not apologize, your Grace.' Susanna heard the embarrassment in Kit's tone. 'It is very good of you to take an interest in us. I am persuaded we do not warrant such attention.'

'Nothing in that — known the girl's father a long time. Did me a service once. Besides, fine little actress. Fortune tipped me the wink over that too — realize now why Mrs Prettyman hurried away. Won't say anything. I just wanted you to know that I know. I respect loyalty, Kydd, especially loyalty under adversity. I'll send her a bride gift, if I may. And you must come and dine during the July Meeting.'

'You are very good, your Grace. Thank you.'

'Well, well. Supper calls, eh?'

'Yes, sir. Thank you again.'

Susanna jumped as Kit reappeared through the window. He looked dazed and gratified. His eyes fastened on her and he hurried across, not seeming to notice her grim shadow. 'Susanna, I — '

'So,' drawled Warwick, looking at Kit with dislike. 'Your infernal luck holds. Everybody knows your sordid secret and nobody minds. How unspeakably tedious.' He let go of

334

Susanna's arm. 'It seems I have no choice but to concede defeat since I prefer *not* to cross swords with the most powerful man in the county. But I really would not risk going into Society just yet if I were you. Oh, and stay well clear of the London road tomorrow. The temptation to smash your coach to flinders would almost certainly overcome me were I to encounter it in my path. Adieu. I wish you all the ill luck in the world.'

Susanna rubbed her arm numbly as they watched Warwick stride from the room. 'I can hardly believe it. A man like that to be in awe of the nobility?'

'His sort of gentleman is dependent on Society,' said Kit. 'Excesses are only tolerated so far. I daresay being thrown out of White's showed him how close to the wind he is sailing.'

Susanna's brow creased. 'But when could my father have told the Duke about me? He was not even aware of my existence until Caroline . . . ' She faltered, looking at Kit. 'And how did you know he was going to be on the terrace . . . ?'

Kit's eyes danced. 'Light of my life. Have you truly not realized? When it was you yourself who mentioned that Adam Pretty-man had only to hear a voice once before he could mimic it perfectly?'

Shock rooted her to the spot. 'Kit! You mean it was all a hum? That was *Adam*? Our position here is still as precarious as ever?'

'Compared to the threat to your safety, nothing is precarious.'

'But suppose Rafe Warwick finds out that he has been tricked?'

'From whom? In case you had not noticed, he is barely on nodding terms with his Grace.' He drew her arm through his. 'Come, are you not hungry?'

'I doubt I shall ever eat again,' said Susanna, and indeed the jumble of conflicting feelings inside her made the consumption of more than a few mouthfuls of the delicacies spread upon the table impossible.

Lady Penfold, sitting opposite with the Colonel, bemoaned her loss of appetite. 'You will be going back to Northamptonshire thinner than when you arrived! A fine state for my great-nephew's bride!'

'Dear ma'am,' said Kit, 'you will own that Susanna has had a few things to try her fortitude today.'

'All the more reason to eat.' Lady Penfold took another two crab patties.

Susanna was visited by a horrific thought. 'Penfold Lodge is secure is it not? Mr Warwick cannot gain access to it?'

'Hrmph! I should hope not!'

'Not at this hour, sweetheart. Indeed, not at any hour with Hibbert and Thomas in attendance.'

Susanna subsided. 'I am sorry. It is simply that he has been a threat for so long. And I cannot help remembering what he did at my lodgings . . . '

Kit took her hand comfortingly in his own. 'You are no longer unprotected. Nothing of the sort will happen here.' And at a beetling look from his great-aunt he explained, 'Once before Warwick took out his ire on Susanna's possessions.'

Major Fortune looked up, distracted from Caroline's earnest conversation. 'Blackguard,' he muttered.

The Colonel growled something about men being horse-whipped for less.

'It was all replaceable,' said Susanna, touched by their concern. 'Mostly clothes and books. Now if he had found Mama's writing desk I should have been devastated indeed, but he did not.'

'Writing desk?' said her father, his interest caught. 'Of oak? About so big?' He measured a space with his hands. 'With a walnut inlay?'

'Yes, do you remember it? It is all I have left of hers. She testified such concern when I wanted to sell it to pay the doctor's bill that I was obliged to desist. I am glad I did not now.'

'I gave that desk to Fanny for a wedding gift,' said Crispin gruffly. 'If we find no other records, that alone would be proof of our connection.' His eyes unfocused. 'I wonder . . . Might I look at it when I come tomorrow?'

Susanna smiled. 'Yes, of course.'

*　*　*

Penfold Lodge was reassuringly peaceful when they arrived back.

'One more day,' said Kit, looking up at the stars as he handed Susanna out of the carriage, 'and we shall be on our way home.'

Home. The word beat a light tattoo in Susanna's consciousness. Her cheeks grew warm and her pulse beat faster. She did not think that once under his own roof, Kit would be prepared to wait overly long for the rector to pronounce them man and wife.

'What shall we sell first to pay for the spring seed?' he said. 'The Meissen or one of the Sèvres sets?'

'Ha! As if you will need to sell either!' said Lady Penfold, overhearing. 'As soon as the bank learns that your bride's father is in the Duke of Rutland's set, they will be falling over themselves to extend your loan.'

Kit laughed. 'You mean I might even be able to set Johnny to finding replacement heavy horses for the farm?'

Susanna smiled with the others, but a cold chill had struck her. She had not considered before that her father being a wealthy man must redound to *her* credit. She did not doubt Kit loved her, but he was so accomplished an actor that if she asked him now whether Crispin Fortune's standing in society had had any bearing on his offer of marriage, she would never be able to tell his protestations of innocence from the real thing.

'You are looking pensive, love. Shall I bespeak tea or are you going to bed?'

'Bed,' she said, needing to be alone. 'I will see you in the morning.'

16

'Here it is.' Susanna put the writing desk on Lady Penfold's piecrust table. 'Your miniature is in the top left compartment. I am afraid the locket is gone.'

'Handsome piece,' said Lady Penfold. 'Where did you get it? London?'

'Oxford,' said Major Crispin Fortune absently. He picked the desk up and felt around the inlaid sides. Then he opened the writing slope, took the sheets of paper out of the recess and peered inside it.

Susanna glanced at Kit but he shrugged and spread his palms.

'Do you have a pen?' said Crispin.

'There is one in the drawer underneath,' said Susanna, her curiosity now strongly aroused. 'But the nib needs mending.'

'Oh, I do not want to write anything,' he replied mystifyingly.

He inserted the pen delicately into the recess, probing the inner lining. There was a soft click. Crispin smiled and folded the slope back into place. Clearly visible, a narrow section of decorated inlay just above the drawer was now standing proud.

'Ha! That's a pretty trick,' said Lady Penfold. 'Secret drawer, eh?'

'Yes.' He teased the delicate fillet of wood out.

'I never knew it existed,' said Susanna in wonder. 'But it is so shallow. What use could it be?'

Her father was smiling with quiet triumph. 'For preserving very special documents.' He unfolded two pieces of paper. 'Marriage lines, for example. And certificates of birth.'

Susanna's hand sought blindly for Kit's.

'Not that *I* needed the proof,' continued Crispin, 'but my solicitor will undoubtedly be the happier for it.' He looked up. 'May I tell him to wait upon your man, Kydd? They could perhaps travel up to Northamptonshire together.'

For a moment, Kit was completely still. Then, 'Yes,' he said. 'Yes, of course. I will give you Tweedie's direction.'

Barely had the Major left when Caroline arrived, bemoaning that she had missed him. It appeared she had satisfied her mama so well with descriptions of the notables at Cheveley together with what they were wearing, that Mrs Fortune had gone out post-haste with Honoria to pass on the details to her bosom bows, leaving Caroline to Harry's careless chaperonage. They had immediately come over to claim cousinship.

Susanna was astounded. She hadn't thought Mrs Fortune would allow her daughter anywhere near her after the revelations of last night. 'And she did not mention me at all?' she said incredulously. 'She had nothing to say about my parentage? Nothing about the scandal?'

Caroline looked innocent. 'There now, I *knew* there was something I had forgotten to tell her. I don't suppose you would like a bride-attendant would you? I shouldn't in the least mind coming to Kydd Court instead of doing the Season in London. I could mention Harry to Uncle Crispin some more. For some reason I do not think his attention was wholly mine yesterday.'

'I cannot imagine why. But surely Harry already assists your father and elder brother with the Fortune string?'

'Mmm. Only they do not entirely get on, you see, on account of Papa considering Harry an idle wastrel and John's tedious habit of being always in the right. Neither of them will listen to my — I mean, Harry's suggestions.'

Susanna grinned. 'Perhaps you should rather apply to Lady Penfold. She would certainly listen to you and nothing I have seen in the last fortnight indicates that *she* might have an aversion to an engaging young rake about the place.'

Caroline's eyes grew round with shock. 'Goodness, why did I not think of that for myself? It would be the very thing. And if she does leave Penfold Lodge to Kit, he will want to keep a manager here, will he not?'

Susanna laughed. 'That I cannot say. But it can do no harm to ask.'

The rest of the day passed in a hurry of packing, eating and writing farewell notes. After dinner, Susanna once again sang Bertrand's favourite airs.

'Thank you, my dear. It does not surprise me at all that you were such a success on the stage.' Lady Penfold blew her nose thoroughly and nodded to Hibbert to remove the tea tray. 'I declare, it will be very flat tomorrow. You're more like your grandfather than I expected, Kit.'

'Thank you.' Kit dropped a daring kiss on his great-aunt's cheek. 'I am sure I do not need to tell you that if you ever wish to visit Kydd Court, you will be very welcome.'

'Ha! I might surprise you yet.'

★ ★ ★

They were as expedient as possible on the road, but the slow pace of the post-horses seemed to irk Kit considerably. He was in a fret to be home, yet refused to let the carriage out of sight of his curricle even though both Colonel MacGregor and Major Fortune were travelling with them.

'Too many lonely roads,' was the only answer he vouchsafed when Susanna tentatively suggested towards the end of the journey that he might now ride ahead.

She saw his reasoning, but how long would Rafe Warwick's shade continue to dog them? Kit had been less at ease with her during this trip than at any time since their acquaintance began. 'Perhaps I should dress as your groom and sit beside you in the curricle,' she said, only half-joking, as they made another stop to change the horses. 'We could then be home in no time.'

'I hardly think your father would approve,' replied Kit.

They reached the Court too late to do anything but receive the congratulations of the staff on their betrothal, sit down to a belated dinner and then retire to bed.

There was a note in her room for Susanna from Nell, left with Lizzie Olivant.

Dearest Susanna, if you are reading this, then what Hugo and I hoped would come to pass has indeed done so. It gives me so much pleasure to address you truly as 'sister'. However — do not let Kit rush you into marriage before you have made over the master bedroom. It was decorated to Mama's taste and I cannot help but feel that your red hair amongst her pink hangings is not the most felicitous of combinations with which to embark on married life . . .

Susanna had a swift, appalling vision of this and thoroughly agreed.

. . . although if Kit is anything like Hugo, feasting his eyes on the walls will be the last thing on his mind for the first week or so! Hugo is arranging for something more suitable in blue to be delivered.

Susanna read this in considerable apprehension. Kit loved his mother dearly. How would he feel about a redesign of her room? For that matter, how would he feel about taking her, Susanna, to his parents' bed? Or any bed, come to that. She hoped desperately that he would come to her tonight so they could banish this odd coolness between them.

He didn't. After sending the maid away early, dressing herself in the gauze peignoir, reducing the candles in the room to two and waiting in increasing disquiet for his knock at the door, Susanna fell into a troubled sleep from which she awoke quite alone and not much refreshed. Outside her window, the landscape was grey with drizzle. She knew how it felt.

Colonel MacGregor greeted her at the breakfast table with the suggestion that they might stroll around the porcelain collection during the morning. 'Years since I saw it last,' he boomed happily.

'That sounds most agreeable,' said Susanna. She flicked a worried glance at Tom Olivant who was pouring out coffee.

'Mr Kit ate early and has gone over to the Home Farm,' he said, guessing at her unspoken question.

'Oh.' Susanna supposed it was only to be expected, but still Kit's defection caused her a stab of unease. She stiffened her spine and turned to her father with a fair degree of composure. 'Do you care to see the china as well, sir? It is well known in its way. Kit's grandmother purchased most of the collection and I own I would be glad to have Colonel MacGregor's views on it so I can henceforth pass off his opinions as a product of my own learning.'

Major Fortune smiled. 'I am entirely at your service, daughter. I must say I shall not be sorry to spend the morning indoors. Twenty years campaigning has not imbued in me a love of this weather. I wish Kydd joy of it.'

Kit did not return all day. A message arrived via a virtuously scrubbed young maiden to say that the master was a-helping Pa and Granfer to dig out a collapsed ditch and very dirty they were all a-getting too.

'That's what I like to hear,' said Major Fortune. 'A man who don't stand on ceremony with his tenants.'

Susanna smiled but remained uneasy. She knew her memory of the evening at Cheveley was not as clear as it could be, but rack her brain as she might she could not remember anything she'd done which might have given Kit a disgust of her. Unless it was still that she had acted at all? But he had congratulated her on that. She twisted the sapphire ring in agitation. Why would Kit not *talk* to her?

Later, Lizzie Olivant bore her off to the master apartments, leaving the guests to amuse themselves in the billiard room. 'And then there's the linen room and the laundry and the still room and the dairy. But we can leave them for another day if you like.'

Susanna's heart gave an unpleasant jolt. 'Are not these your areas?'

'Bless you, miss. You'll need to know about them. There's a powerful lot of putting right still to do yet.'

And mistress and maids would do it together, just as Kit and his men were doing outside. The thought of every person on the estate working as a team on the Court's revival brought a glimmer of reassurance to Susanna's heart. She began to make lists in earnest and jested later to Kit that she was inclined to think it a very good thing she had been brought up in Mr Masterson's make-do-and-mend household.

But Kit did not smile back, and Crispin Fortune looked more thoughtful than ever.

Colonel MacGregor left them next day for his own home. 'I'll be back for the wedding,' he said. 'Promised Emma I'd be groomsman. Need to anyway, to get away from my niece's sulks that you aren't taking her featherheaded daughter.'

'In truth, there was never any danger of that,' said Kit.

Susanna met his eyes, very blue and very intense. Her heart lifted. She was almost sure that had they been alone he would have said something more, but her father was pulling on his gloves and adjusting his hat ready to be shown the estate and so the moment passed.

The maids looked at her a little strangely

when she declared a wish to count sheets, but it did give her enormous satisfaction to witness Kit choking on his wine when her father inquired over dinner as to how she had spent her day.

He still didn't come to her room though.

★　★　★

The following day brought the solicitors to Kydd Court. Susanna despaired at how distant Kit was over breakfast. Had he changed his mind? Did he not want to marry her now?

She was crossing the hall from the kitchen, where she had been helping the cook with bread and a large batch of pastry for the company, when Kit flung out of the library. He had a face like thunder and he strode outside yelling for Johnny to saddle up Valiant without even seeing her. Susanna had a brief glimpse of Mr Tweedie and Major Fortune still at the table before the door shut again.

'Something's put his back up,' observed Tom Olivant. He smiled reassuringly at her. 'Never fret, miss, he's been like that since we were boys. A good, hard ride and he'll be right as a trivet by dinner.'

If not exactly right as a trivet, Kit was at least punctiliously polite the next time he was seen indoors and made no demur about returning to the library with the other men during the evening. Nevertheless, Susanna began to wonder whether she would ever be able to broach the subject of the hangings in the master bedroom.

In the morning he was again absent from the breakfast table.

'Lending a hand with the spring sowing,' said Tom as he pulled out a chair for Susanna. 'It's late all over the estate what with the lack of men and all.'

'Has he finished with the solicitors then?' she said.

The friend of Kit's youth shrugged. 'Seems so,' and then fell into a correct silence as Mr Tweedie and Crispin Fortune's lawyer entered the room.

Susanna was not unduly perturbed when her father requested her presence during the morning. He handed her the marriage lines and the registration of her birth which he had taken from the writing desk.

'To put back in safe keeping,' he said with a smile. 'We have made copies and witnessed where they were found.' He then gave her another official-looking piece of paper, heavy with an impressed wax seal. 'And this is your copy of the document which certifies you as my legal daughter.'

'Oh,' said Susanna blankly. 'Thank you.' A possible explanation of Kit's bad temper occurred to her. 'It does not mean that I cannot marry Kit, does it?'

He and the two solicitors smirked indulgently. 'No indeed, but the situation is in part why the business has taken us so long,' said Crispin. 'No, don't get up, my dear, there is more on this head which you need to be aware of.'

His next words sent Susanna flying out of the room — first for her cloak and boots, and then to the stables to demand that John Farley saddle up and take her instantly to wherever his miserable, cowardly, misbegotten master might be concealing himself!

Far from concealing himself, Kit was discovered perched on a stile with a group of farm-hands, all of them sharing a pie and a jug of ale and laughing at something one of them had said. Like them he was wearing a leather jerkin over an open-necked shirt with a Belcher handkerchief knotted carelessly around his throat. Like them, he shaded his eyes to see who was riding at such a furious pace down the lane. Discerning Susanna, he hurriedly set his tankard down and came forward to catch her as she slid from her precarious position in front of Johnny. The touch of his hands on her waist after so many

351

days abstinence added fuel to her fire.

'Will I wait, miss?' asked Johnny.

'No,' said Susanna. 'For I am going to stay here until I get a sensible answer from Mr Kit if it takes me all night!'

The groom transferred his carefully expressionless gaze to Kit. 'Will I fetch the curricle then?'

Kit threw a wary glance at Susanna. 'If that hack of yours can bear a double weight, I am sure Valiant will not find it too much of a strain.'

John Farley nodded and walked his mount back the way he'd come. The farm-hands exchanged looks, wiped their mouths and returned to the field. Kit followed them with his eyes as if wishing he had the same option.

Susanna stood with her hands on her hips and glared at her betrothed. 'Fifteen thousand pounds,' she said without preamble. 'He is settling *fifteen thousand pounds* on me!'

Kit winced. 'Yes, I know.'

'*Fifteen thousand pounds!* Without so much as a by-your-leave or anything! Why did you not stop him?'

'How? Susanna, the man is your father!'

'Yes, but fifteen thousand,' she wailed. 'How am I to know what to do with even half such a sum?'

'Ah,' said Kit, looking uncomfortable.

'They did not tell you the whole, then?'

Susanna scuffed a boot along the ground. 'I was so appalled I ran out and came straight down here to find you,' she confessed. 'What do I not know?'

Kit hunched his back and leant on the stile, staring at the field, his neck reddening. 'The money comes *with* you, but it is not all *for* you. Ten thousand is for me on our marriage to 'raise Kydd Court to a suitable standard for Major Crispin Fortune's daughter to live in'.'

'Oh,' said Susanna, digesting this. 'Oh, well that is all right then.'

'It is not all right!' yelled Kit, his eyes blazing. 'As soon as the *ton* gets to hear of it, I will be slated as a damned fortune hunter!'

Enlightenment dazzled Susanna. Relief flooded her. Was this the reason his behaviour had been so odd? 'I don't believe it!' she cried. 'You are worried about that when you discounted *my* fears of being thought one as so much moonshine?'

'I didn't say I was proud of myself,' muttered Kit.

She mastered a desire to shake him. Instead she let a doubtful note creep into her voice. 'I suppose, if it would make you more comfortable, I could refuse the settlement.'

'All that money? Have you no idea what we

could do with it?' Kit swung her to face him, then met her eyes ruefully. 'Oh, sweetheart, I am sorry. I have the devil's own temper when my pride has been stung. You are right. It does not matter what the world thinks of either of us. Forgive me?'

'I do forgive you, but please, Kit, don't ever shut me out like that again. I thought . . . I thought you had taken me in dislike . . . '

The rest of her sentence was lost as Kit demonstrated very thoroughly the absurdity of such a fancy. Hairpins pattered past her shoulders. Pressed against the safe, strong warmth of his body, her hand creeping inside the tantalizing opening of his shirt and her mouth locked to his, she felt herself melt with desire.

He pulled her closer still. 'Susanna, I love you so much. It is killing me, this waiting until we are man and wife.'

'I love you too,' she whispered. She took a shaky breath and addressed his shirt. 'We . . . we do not have to wait. I have been hoping every night since we arrived here that you would come to me.'

'I couldn't. Not before you knew about the money. It had not occurred to me until your father mentioned solicitors that he might want to settle something on you. It would have been dishonest to make you mine before

354

you knew your potential wealth. You could have changed your mind about marrying such a penniless prospect.'

She laid her cheek against his chest. 'Never,' she whispered.

She stood there, wrapped in his embrace, feeling his love envelop her. Then he stepped back, lifted her hand and removed the sapphire ring. Susanna knew a moment of truly dreadful panic until he said, 'I did not do this properly before.' He kissed the ring, slid it back on her finger, and then kissed it on her finger to seal it. There was a cheer from the men in the field. Kit ignored them. 'Yours. This and my heart both. Welcome to the family. May you never leave it.'

Susanna was so overcome she could barely stand. She stared down at the ring, then flung her arms around Kit's neck and kissed him with a passion that surprised both of them. Kit's breathing grew ragged.

'Sweetheart,' he said, his voice hoarse, 'I am going to have to take you back to the Court right now, or I will lose what little control I still possess.'

Susanna glanced across to where Valiant was cropping the new grass. Her gaze fell on his saddle. She swallowed as she remembered their previous ride. 'I think I had best walk,' she said. 'By the time I reach the house, I may have cooled enough to appear respectable.'

'Coward,' he said with a laugh. 'But we can walk if you prefer it.'

'Kit, if you walk with me it will likely take us the whole afternoon and I shall assuredly *not* arrive looking respectable. I will go alone. It is not so far.'

'But you do not yet know your way about the estate.'

She rose on tiptoe to kiss him. 'Up the rise, around the bend at the edge of the wood, then keep the hedge on my left until the stables are in sight. And if I *do* go wrong and find the road instead, I have only to follow it and I will come to the main gate.'

Still he looked dubious. 'What if you turn an ankle on the ruts?'

'Kit, this is absurd. I will be perfectly all right and I will see you at dinner.'

He touched his lips to hers. 'Until later, then.'

It was odd how the sky was bluer now, the hedgerows greener and the sun warmer. Susanna sang as she near danced up the rise. At the top she looked down and saw Kit working in the field with his men. As if he sensed her, the pale oval of his face tipped upwards and he lifted his hand. Joy and love suffused her all over again. What had she ever done to deserve such good fortune? She walked on, hugging herself with happiness.

And then Rafe Warwick stepped leisurely out of the wood — a pistol trained on her heart.

Susanna stopped dead. Just for a moment she was too stunned to be afraid, then all the fear she had ever felt in his presence slammed into her tenfold. 'How . . . how did you get onto Kydd land?'

Warwick strolled forward. 'Always so welcoming.'

Susanna stepped back. 'How?' she repeated.

'Your country squire really should do something about the shocking disrepair of his boundary wall.'

It was on Kit's list of things to fix. But even if the wall had been unassailable, Warwick would have effected entrance to the estate somehow. He would never give up. She had known his capitulation was too easy at Cheveley. He had simply moved the battle to a place more to his liking.

A place without witnesses.

The wood was on her right, thick with trees and brambles. Susanna stepped back again, off the path, edging towards the cover it might provide. 'What are you here for?' she asked.

He laughed. It was not a pleasant sound. 'You,' he said.

He was still advancing. She had to keep him talking. 'You could not have known I would come along this path,' she said, backing away.

'No indeed. Your appearance is most providential. I was waiting here to — '

Susanna screamed with every ounce of breath in her lungs and leapt to put herself behind the trunk of a tree where his aim couldn't find her. She crouched down, masked by oak and brambles, and prayed for deliverance as fervently as she knew how.

' — to kill your misguided suitor,' continued Warwick. 'A poacher's bullet gone astray. So very sad. You would naturally come down here making a pretty show of weeping and wailing with the rest of the household, and I could pick you off too. As it is, I perceive you have called your dupe for me. How fortunate that I have two of these pistols. One for you, the moment you step out from behind that tree, and one for the puppy as he rounds the bend to save you. I assure you I can shoot left-handed as well as right.'

'You're insane,' said Susanna, forcing the words through a jagged wall of terror. How could she have been so *stupid*, calling Kit to his death? Too late by far to retract her scream. Already she could feel Valiant's hoofbeats reverberating through the ground. And due to her cleverness in putting the brambles between herself and Warwick, she couldn't even rush at him to spoil his aim.

'Do you think so?' said Warwick. 'I suppose it does seem a waste to kill you without enjoying your pleasures first. Perhaps I should merely break an arm to begin with, to keep you quiet.'

Susanna shut out his foul words, trying to think as she peered around the bole of the oak. The thundering hooves were getting closer. She couldn't simply hide here like a frightened rabbit while the man she loved was shot. She must distract Warwick at the crucial moment. She tensed, watching the man, not the lane, ready to sprint across his field of vision to the next tree the moment he raised his arm. The ground was shaking now. Kit was nearly . . .

Susanna saw her enemy's eyes widen. 'What the — ?' and then Valiant burst past them, riderless.

And Kit threw himself at Rafe Warwick's back, the bullet from one firearm jerking into the path and the other pistol flying from Warwick's hand to skid along the woodland floor.

How had he done that? He must have

jumped off Valiant before the bend, but how had he dodged from tree to tree so quietly? There was no time for Susanna to speculate. The pair of them were a tangle of ripping cloth, flying fists — and bone crunching against flesh.

Susanna scrambled into the open. She smothered a cry at the blood on Kit's face. Warwick's rings must have cut into him during a punch. Kit hardly seemed to notice, delivering hit after punishing hit. He was forcing Warwick to give way at every blow.

No! Rafe Warwick *wasn't* giving way. He was retreating for a purpose, as Susanna herself had done earlier. Not towards the trees, though. Towards his undischarged pistol.

Susanna lunged for it fractionally before he did and balled herself over her prize. Her fingers curled around the barrel just as Rafe Warwick's hand came down hard on hers. His free hand grabbed painfully at her hair to tear her away.

'Desist, Kydd,' he rasped, the silk gone from his voice. 'Walk away, or I'll kill her.'

He would kill her anyway. The knowledge cleared Susanna's mind like a shock of cold water. He would kill her, kill Kit, and then escape to continue his vices elsewhere. He would never stop. Susanna could hear voices and running feet, whether the farm-hands from the field, or people from the house she could no longer tell. But she did know she had to finish this now. Finish it for ever.

She let the hand under his go slack. Triumphant, he pulled the pistol towards him. And Susanna's other hand clenched on the trigger.

★ ★ ★

Susanna came round to discover Kit slapping her face. 'Wake up. Wake up, dammit. I swear if you ever, ever, do something that stupid again I'll damn well throttle you myself.'

Her ears were still filled with the sound of an explosion. Her ribs felt as if she'd been trampled by a horse. 'I hurt,' she said, and opened her eyes to the sight of her gown covered in blood. She hastily averted her gaze to see Rafe Warwick lying nearby, a coat thrown over him, only his legs visible. 'What . . . what happened?' she said dazedly, putting out a hand to Kit to help her up. 'You and Warwick were fighting and I tried to get the gun out of the way and — '

'It went off,' said her father's voice gently. 'We all witnessed it. That demon had you on the ground, was threatening you. Kydd leapt for him completely unarmed. In fumbling for the gun, Warwick shot himself.'

'I thought it was you,' said Kit, gathering her close. 'I thought you were dead. I was going to tear his throat out with my bare hands.'

They believed Warwick had been responsible for the accident. As he had, in a way, because if he hadn't hauled on the barrel of the pistol, her finger wouldn't have tightened on the trigger. 'Is he . . . is he — ?'

'Dead,' said her father. 'Saved the hangman a job.'

Kit hoisted her in his arms. 'You'll be bruised from the recoil,' he said. 'I'm carrying you back, so don't argue. I may never let go of you again.'

Susanna had no intention of arguing. She felt weaker than a child's rag doll. Warwick was dead. He would terrorize no more women, cause no more suffering. It was worth it. She began to shake.

Kit let the others draw ahead. 'I pulled the gun from your hand when I landed on him,' he murmured for her ears alone. 'No one saw me. No one will ever know. Did you know, Susanna? Did you mean it?'

It didn't occur to her to deny it. Kit was her life, her soul, her other half. 'Oh yes,' she said.

He shifted his grip, making her more

comfortable. 'I love you.'

'I love you too.' She nestled into his chest, her tremors subsiding.

'I would have killed him for you.'

'I know. But now you don't need to.'

Crispin Fortune looked back to check on them, then returned to the earnest conversation of the solicitors.

'Did they tell you Tweedie brought a special licence with him?' asked Kit. 'Your father thinks ordinary banns are unsuited to our consequence.'

Susanna's heart thumped. She lifted her head. 'How soon can we be married, then?'

He chuckled, dropping a kiss on her hair. 'As soon as we like. Which means you'd best make haste and get the rest of those sheets counted.'

'Why?' she asked in mystification.

Kit grinned broadly. 'Because Lord only knows when you'll see the inside of the linen room again after the wedding.'

Other titles published by
The House of Ulverscroft:

A BITTERSWEET PROPOSAL

Wendy Soliman

When Marcus Rothwell, Earl of Broadstairs, is forced to spend the night alone with Harriet Aston he willingly does the honourable thing. In this marriage of convenience, Harriet determines to engage Marc's affections. However, she is brutally attacked, and whilst suspicion falls upon the dowager countess, who disapproves of Harriet, there's the village beadle's unaccountable behaviour to be considered, as well as Marc's Machiavellian steward. Wanting to protect Harriet, Marc delves into the mystery surrounding her attack. Now he must examine his feelings for the woman he married on a whim. But he too is in mortal danger . . .

JILTED

Ann Barker

When Eustacia Hope is jilted at the altar, her parents send her to stay with her godmother Lady Agatha Rayner, a clergyman's widow. Her mother warns her to shun Lady Agatha's brother, the notorious Lord Ashbourne and his son Lord Ilam. And she soon discovers that her godmother isn't all she seems either. Then Eustacia meets Lord Ilam and the two are attracted to one another. But it is only after the arrival of Eustacia's estranged fiance and the unexpected appearance of Lord Ashbourne that matters can be resolved in a way that is satisfactory to all parties.

A DISGRACEFUL AFFAIR

Marina Oliver

Sylvie Delamare's great-uncle Sir George sends her a mere £20 — claiming it to be a whole half of her inheritance — and she's infuriated. Her parents had been wealthy, so she wants to go and confront him in Norfolk. Meanwhile, she is invited to visit Lady Carstairs, her friend's aunt in London, to be presented. However, Sir Randal is suspicious of Sylvie, after seeing her with Monsieur Dupont, who he suspects is one of Napoleon's spies. Then when Sir Randal follows Dupont, he meets Sylvie in Norwich on her way to see Sir George. And when he offers her a lift — he becomes embroiled in her affairs . . .

A DANGEROUS CHARADE

Anne Barbour

Prim and proper Alison Fox was a lady's companion. However, she had once been Lissa Reynard, successful gambler and adventuress. And now the man she feared the most, the Earl of Marchford, nephew of Alison's employer, had shown up on his aunt's doorstep. The iron-willed Lord Marchford was suspicious of the woman who had gained the affection of his aunt. Could Alison prevent the discovery of her previous identity? And what was she to do about the attraction that had sprung between herself and the earl? An attraction that soon turned to passion, wild as a wind-blown fire.